THE RESURRECTION OF
THE
KING

by

Bruce Lawrence Kearns

Published by Forum Communications Group, Ltd.
Wayne, PA 19087

Copyright 2005
Bruce Lawrence Kearns

ISBN 1-4196-7222-3

Second Printing
July 2007

www.theresurrectionoftheking.com
www.elvisdeadoralive.com

FORWARD

Although this is a novel, many of the events portrayed here are factual, including those surrounding Elvis' reported death at Graceland on the afternoon of August 16, 1977.

In Chapter 17 you will read a fictionalized conclusion to the mysteries of the event. On the day of Elvis' reported death, Vernon Presley (Elvis' father) was visited by Shelby County medical investigator Dan Warlick, police lieutenant Sam McCachern and Assistant District Attorney Jerry Stauffer. According to media reports, when Warlick, McCachern and Stauffer entered the dining room at Graceland, Vernon was on the telephone talking in what was described as "an upbeat mood." But as at the sight of the trio of officials, it is said his mood tumbled into despair. What caused this 180-degree shift in Vernon's mood?

It was the perfect opportunity for me to inject a fictionalized interpretation into the reported scene which explains the reason for Vernon's change of heart. Moreover, it launches a series of fictional situations, also based on facts, concerning the life and death of the King of Rock and Roll and those close to him.

In addition to all of the actual people appearing in this novel, you will meet a number of fictional characters who support the *resurrection* in action and theme, thus providing the novel with a strong basis of reality. When actual people engage in conversation with fictional characters, however, dialogue has been, understandably, created or rather, invented. Still, the characters, real and invented, remain loyal to their public personas, in truth and in fiction.

On occasion, I have included actual as well as summaries of reported quotes. If I have misquoted anyone, living or dead, or inadvertently altered the context, I apologize. However, I have done it for the sake of the story and its wide intentions to be portrayed as a possible set of events. And, of course, I offer the caveat that any similarities of fictional characters to any persons living or dead, is purely coincidental.

I sincerely hope you enjoy *The Resurrection of the King* and find it believable as well as entertaining. It is not meant to incite any notions that Elvis is alive; rather, it is a dramatic blend of fact and fiction that combines pure speculation with a smattering of wishful thinking.

Bruce Lawrence Kearns
July 13, 2006

ACKNOWLEDGMENTS

First, I would like to thank Peter Guralnick, who wrote the definitive biography of Elvis Presley's life from 1950 to 1977, in his two-volume best sellers, *Last Train to Memphis* and *Careless Love,* both of which served as a source for many of the factual portions of *The Resurrection of the King.*

Special thanks must also go to Charles C. Thompson II and James P. Cole for their tirelessly researched book, *The Death of Elvis - - What Really Happened?* Were it not for these two dedicated journalists, I probably would have completed my novel at least one year sooner. Indeed, Thompson and Cole provided so *much* detailed information about the days leading up to Elvis Presley's reported death, that I had to rethink the entire premise that served as the basis for *The Resurrection of the King.*

Last but not least, I would like to thank my wife Donna for her insightful criticism and limitless patience. She hasn't been able to use her kitchen counter where we normally eat, as well as the dining room table, for more than three years. *BLK*

Dedicated to Dr. Robert A. Ersek, my lifelong friend, whose own true story serves as an inspiration to anyone who *believes* they can do it.

TABLE OF CONTENTS

FORWARD		*i*
ACKNOWLEDGMENTS		*iii*
TABLE OF CONTENTS		*iv*
One	San Francisco: Late October 1989	1

PART ONE: SEPTEMBER 1976 - JUNE 1989

Two	Memphis: Late September 1976	12
Three	Memphis: April 1977	24
Four	Italy: December 1977 to February 1989	29
Five	Return to America: March 1989	45
Six	Las Vegas: Early June 1989	50
Seven	Las Vegas: June 24, 1989, 10:08 PM, PDT	67
Eight	Austin: June 25, 1989, 12:40 AM. CDT	74

PART TWO: JUNE 1977 - AUGUST 1977

Nine	Memphis: Early May 1977	81
Ten	Austin: Mid May 1977	86
Eleven	Graceland: Early July 1977	95
Twelve	Memphis: August 16, 1977, 6:15 AM, CDT	112
Thirteen	Memphis: August 16, 1977, 7:30 AM, CDT	119
Fourteen	Austin: August 16, 1977, 1:05 PM, CDT	133
Fifteen	Graceland: August 16, 1977, 1:35 PM, CDT	140
Sixteen	Austin: August 16, 1977, 2:45 PM, CDT	142
Seventeen	Graceland: August 16, 1977, 2:50 PM, CDT	150
Eighteen	Austin: August 18, 1977, 7:00 AM, CDT	159

PART THREE: JUNE 1989

Nineteen	Austin: June 25, 1989, 2:00 AM, CDT	173

PART FOUR: FOR YOUR INFORMATION

Twenty	Off the Record	185
REFERENCES		201
ABOUT THE AUTHOR		Back Cover

San Francisco: Late October 1989

CHAPTER ONE
San Francisco: Late October 1989

Friday, October 27th was like many Fall days in San Francisco: sunny and breezy, with temperatures hovering in the mid sixties. Although the Oakland A's had recently swept the Giants in the World Series, there was still a feeling of apprehension in the air from the omnipresent effects of a devastating earthquake. In spite of those headline-grabbing events, what might be remembered even more about October 1989, were the implications behind the testimony heard in Federal Court, implications that would challenge the beliefs of the entire world and yes, implications that would give added credibility to the lingering suspicions of millions of Americans.

"Please rise and come to order," announced the bailiff. "Court is now in session, with the Honorable Anthony Blackwell presiding."

Tony Blackwell at age 49, stood just over six feet tall in his stocking feet. A Yale Law School grad, Blackwell served two tours of duty in the Marines during the Viet Nam War era, not in the Judge Advocate General Corps, but as a Battalion Commander in a battle-hardened combat unit. A no-nonsense judge, Blackwell possessed that rare combination of judicial temperament, fairness, and extraordinary legal skills. Just last month, he received the highest accolades ever bestowed upon a Federal judge by the California *Trial Lawyers Association*.

Prior to his 1983 nomination to the Federal bench by President Reagan, Blackwell, a Californian by birth, had distinguished himself as a prosecutor in San Diego, as a law professor at UCLA, and prior to his most recent appointment, as a judge on the California Superior Court. When compared with most of the other members on the bench in the Ninth Circuit, Judge Blackwell was indeed a rarity. In addition to being a Conservative, none of his rulings and opinions had ever been overturned by the sometimes even *more* liberal Appellate courts.

"Please be seated," announced Judge Blackwell as he approached the bench. "Bailiff, would you please recall Glen Watson?"

"Would Mr. Glen Watson please come to the witness stand?" replied the bailiff.

Watson, 44, was the Chief Investigator for Sierra Life Assurance, Ltd., a Nevada insurance company that provided financial services for many of the Las Vegas and Hollywood megastars. Although he received his law degree from Stanford at the age of 24, his true passions lay with the investigative process. Shortly after being hired by Sierra Life, he was assigned to the company's Las Vegas headquarters. Five years later, he had been promoted to the Fraud Division's top leadership post.

Watson had developed quite a reputation for solving sophisticated crimes involving fraud and other irregularities. Some would say his success was due to his street-smart intelligence, uncanny intuition, and dogged determination. Others would say that it was because of his nondescript physical appearance and laid-back demeanor. At 5 feet 10 and 175 pounds, Glen Watson was so average looking that he almost defied description. In fact, he would probably be overlooked in a crowd of two. But this worked to his advantage. Most prospective witnesses felt quite at ease when they first met Watson, knowing full well that they were about to be interviewed.

Desmond Howard, the lead counsel representing Sierra Life, had more than twenty-five years experience litigating fraudulent insurance claims. Compared with Watson, Howard came across like a bull in a china shop. Of greater importance, particularly to Sierra Life, Howard had won more than ninety percent of his cases while recovering tens of millions of dollars for his numerous clients.

San Francisco: Late October 1989

In the courtroom, Howard employed a unique style when questioning his *own* witnesses. What was particularly unorthodox, perhaps even risky about Howard's approach, was the way he examined them under direct. He was relentless and overbearing, frequently asking questions that should have been left to the opposing counsel. But his methods worked well because testimony from Howard's witnesses had an unmistakable ring of the truth.

"Ladies and gentlemen," began Howard as he approached the jury, "to refresh your memory, I obtained a transcript of yesterday's proceedings. Just before we adjourned, I asked Mr. Watson the following question:"

MR. HOWARD: Mr. Watson, once a person has been declared legally dead and the entire proceeds of his life insurance policy were paid to the policy's only beneficiary, his father, can those proceeds be recovered by the insuring company if it can be proven twelve years later, that the insured never died?

MR. WATSON: Yes Mr. Howard, if the beneficiary can be located and has the financial resources to repay the face value of the policy, plus any accumulated interest. And that's a big if!

"I then asked Mr. Watson this followup question."

MR. HOWARD: What if the beneficiary transferred the proceeds of that policy to a trust administered by a Swiss bank? The trust was accessible only through a numbered account that was opened by the insured, prior to his reported death. The only two people who knew the bank's name and account number, were the insured and the insured's father. The father, who was also the executor of the will, died in 1979. From whom do we then seek relief?

MR. WATSON: Either from the insured, if in fact he is still alive and can be located, or from the insured's estate, if he has an estate.

The Resurrection of The King

Turning to Watson, Howard assumed his favorite position, slightly to the right of and in front of the witness stand. "Mr. Watson, when did you first hear about the death of Elvis Aaron Presley?"

"I don't recall the exact date, but I think it was sometime in August 1977, on the *NBC Evening News.* David Brinkley made the announcement about Presley's death at the opening of his broadcast."

"And when you saw and heard that broadcast," continued Howard, "did you believe David Brinkley?"

"Of course I believed him! I doubt if he would joke about someone's death, especially someone as famous as Elvis Presley."

"And during that same broadcast, Mr. Watson, do you recall if any of Elvis' film clips or concerts were shown?"

"I don't believe that I saw any of his concerts or film clips on that *NBC Evening News* program," Mr. Howard, "but I do recall seeing some of them on a TV special shown later that evening."

"Prior to that *NBC Evening News* broadcast, and it was on August 16, 1977, had you ever met or seen Elvis Presley in person, *prior* to his reported death, Mr. Watson?"

"No, Mr. Howard."

"Other than the video tapes and film clips you saw on a TV special later that evening, Mr. Watson, had you ever seen any of Elvis' *live* concerts, either in Las Vegas, while he was on tour, or on TV?"

"No, and to be honest, Mr. Howard, I wasn't much of an Elvis fan."

"Did you see any of Elvis' movies on that special?" Mr. Watson.

San Francisco: Late October 1989

"Only excerpts Mr. Howard, the ones from some of his more popular films."

"Did you ever see Elvis Presley on TV *before* August 16, 1977?"

"Yes, many years ago on *The Ed Sullivan Show*. We were celebrating my twelfth birthday, so it must have been on Sunday, January 6, 1957. My mother and sister kept reminding me all day long that we had to finish our ice cream and cake before 8 o'clock because they didn't want to miss Elvis Presley on *The Ed Sullivan Show*. Being curious, I wondered what it was that they didn't want to miss, so I watched the show with them. At the time, as I recall, I thought Elvis looked kind of goofy!"

The court room chuckled, but Howard continued. "Based on your recollection of Elvis Presley from that 1957 *Ed Sullivan Show,* were you able to recognize him from any of his movies or concerts shown on the TV special . . on the *evening* of August 16, 1977?"

"Yes, Mr. Howard, but only from those movies and concerts when he was much younger . . the ones he made in the fifties and sixties."

"On that same TV special, in one of his last 1977 concerts, the one in Rapid City, South Dakota, he played the piano. Were you able to recognize Elvis in the concert where he played the piano?"

"Not at first, and certainly not based on my recollection of the Elvis I saw on *The Ed Sullivan Show*. First of all, he was considerably older and much heavier. His face was bloated, and his hair and sideburns were also much longer than they were in 1957. As for his voice, it seemed strained, especially when he sang *Unchained Melody* while he was playing the piano. If the announcer hadn't mentioned Elvis by name, I would never have known that it was Elvis Presley. Until that evening, I wasn't aware that Elvis even played the piano."

"Mr. Watson, did you see Elvis' body, either at the viewing on August

The Resurrection of The King

17th or at his funeral on August 18, 1977?"

"No, I didn't go to Memphis until the following week, after it was discovered that Elvis was one of our policy holders."

Just then, Hillary Caruthers, counsel for Elvis' estate, interrupted. "Objection! Where is this leading to, Your Honor? What is the relevance of *Mr. Watson* ever seeing Elvis Presley, either live or on television, or before or after he died?"

"What do you have to say, Mr. Howard?" replied Judge Blackwell.

"Your Honor, it's been widely reported that Elvis Presley gained nearly forty pounds during the last year of his life. If the last time someone saw Elvis was *before* he gained all of that weight, it's quite possible that when they saw him *after* he died, they could have mistaken him for someone who strongly *resembled* Elvis Presley, especially if they saw the body several hours *after* death had occurred. Many people who recently died aren't even recognized by their *loved* ones a few hours after their death. Elvis, according to the coroner, had been dead for approximately four hours before Ginger Alden found him on the bathroom floor."

"That's all well and good, Mr. Howard," replied Judge Blackwell, "but you should be making that point through the testimony of the individuals who actually *saw* Elvis' body. Objection sustained!"

"Yes, of course Your Honor." Once again, Howard turned towards Watson. "Mr. Watson, when did you first learn that Elvis Presley had a life insurance policy with Sierra Life Assurance, Ltd.?"

"It wasn't until a week after his death, Mr. Howard. The Claims Supervisor in our Las Vegas headquarters had just come back from vacation. Being an Elvis fan herself and on a hunch, she checked our corporate records. Sure enough, in July 1977, Elvis had submitted an application at our Los Angeles office, along with a check for $200,000, for a prepaid $1,000,000 whole-life policy. The policy was approved and was in force

San Francisco: Late October 1989

when Elvis' reportedly died. On August 30, 1977, we settled on the policy with a check for $1,000,000, payable to Vernon Presley."

"According to the records of Memphis Fire House 29, Mr. Watson, the body of Elvis Presley was removed from Graceland shortly after 2:30 PM on August 16, 1977. It was then transported by ambulance to Baptist Memorial Hospital on Madison Avenue in Memphis, where it arrived at about 2:50 PM. Who was inside the ambulance with Elvis' body during the trip to the hospital?"

"Dr. George Nichopoulos, Elvis' personal physician; Joe Esposito, his tour manager; Charlie Hodge, a longtime friend and member of Elvis' staff; and one of the EMTs who arrived in the ambulance when it came to Graceland," replied Watson.

"And did you interview each of those individuals?"

"Yes. I interviewed all of them within two weeks after Elvis' reported death and again last month to corroborate their initial recollections."

"Did you interview them together, or separately, Mr. Watson?"

"Separately. I interviewed Hodge first, Esposito next, and then Dr. Nichopoulos, or Dr. Nick as he was called . . last."

"And did each of *those* individuals believe it was Elvis Presley's body they took to Baptist Memorial Hospital on August 16, 1977?"

"Yes they did, Mr. Howard, but they indicated that they were much more preoccupied with trying to restore Elvis' vital signs, particularly Dr. Nick. He was applying CPR to Elvis in the ambulance, on the way over to the hospital. Although Hodge, Esposito, and Dr. Nick didn't *seem* to have any doubts about the *identity* of the body in the ambulance, both Esposito and Dr. Nick hesitated when they were asked one particular question."

The Resurrection of The King

"And what was that question, Mr. Watson?"

"Were you absolutely certain that the body you accompanied in the ambulance to Baptist Memorial Hospital on the afternoon of August 16, 1977, was the body of Elvis Aaron Presley?"

"And what were their answers, Mr. Watson?"

"At first, neither of them answered my question directly. In fact, they both seemed visibly annoyed after I asked the question. I was beginning to think there was some sort of collusion going on, but upon further questioning, both Dr. Nick and Esposito convinced me that they really *did* believe it was Elvis Presley's body they accompanied to the hospital."

"What about the two EMTs, Mr. Watson, the ones who initially responded to the call from Graceland? Did they believe that it was Elvis Presley's body?"

"I'm not sure, Mr. Howard. Both of the EMTs described the body as *almost unrecognizable!* Of course, that doesn't necessarily mean that they didn't believe it was Elvis Presley's body."

"Mr. Watson, did you interview anyone else who saw the body on the bathroom floor at Graceland, on the afternoon of August 16, 1977?"

"Yes! I interviewed everyone who came into the bathroom except Lisa Marie Presley, Elvis' daughter. I didn't want to upset her since she was only nine at the time. Everyone else I interviewed and who saw the body, believed it was Elvis Presley's body."

"In your 1977 report, Mr. Watson, Ginger Alden, who was living with Elvis at the time, stated that she had discovered Elvis' body on the bathroom floor shortly after she had awakened at 1:30 PM. Did Ms. Alden have anything else to add when you interviewed her?"

San Francisco: Late October 1989

"Yes she did, Mr. Howard. After she finished dressing, she knocked on Elvis' bathroom door, but there wasn't any answer. Upon opening the door, she saw Elvis lying face down on the floor, in front of the toilet. Terrified, she shouted his name, but there was no response. She then called downstairs on the intercom and Al Strada heard her voice. Al immediately came up to the bathroom. As soon as he arrived, he tried to turn the body over, but couldn't. Just then, Joe Esposito arrived, and together they turned the body over."

"Were Alden, Strada, and Esposito able to identify the body?"

"Not at first. When I interviewed Ginger Alden and Al Strada separately, both of them stated that Elvis was lying on the bathroom floor, face down. When Esposito arrived in the bathroom, he helped Strada turn the body over, and all three of them could see Elvis' face clearly. Both Strada and Alden certainly believed that it was Elvis. Ms. Alden also recognized the gold pajamas that Elvis was wearing when he got out of bed to go to the bathroom earlier in the morning."

"What were Joe Esposito's recollections, Mr. Watson?"

"When Esposito arrived in the bathroom, he and Strada turned the body over and checked for a pulse. There was none. The body felt cold, and it appeared that rigor mortis had begun to set in. Esposito had a clear view of Elvis' face, which by now had turned dark blue. He thought Elvis had probably been gone for some time."

"In your deposition, Mr. Watson, you stated that Vernon and Patsey Presley, Elvis' father and cousin, came into the bathroom together. Did Vernon or Patsey have any doubts about whether it was Elvis' body?"

"Patsey didn't, but I can't be sure about Vernon. I had mixed feelings about *his* answers. I got the impression that he really did believe that it was Elvis' body, yet on the other hand, there was something about the *manner* in which he answered that bothered me."

"And what was it about his manner that bothered you, Mr. Watson?"

"Whenever I asked Vernon a question, any question, he seemed very defensive. In a second interview, he told me that Elvis had been receiving death threats, and he went so far as to suggest that Elvis may have been murdered. Unfortunately, Vernon died in 1979, so I couldn't interview him again prior to *this* hearing."

"Referring again to Baptist Memorial Hospital, Mr. Watson, did you interview everyone who was present in the emergency room when Elvis' body was first brought in?"

"Not everyone, Mr. Howard. I only interviewed those in the E. R. who either knew Elvis or could make a positive I. D., including the nurses and Cardiologists on the Harvey Team who tried to revive him."

"Among those you interviewed, had any of them ever met Elvis in person, *prior* to August 16, 1977?"

"Yes, two! Dr. Nick, who accompanied the body in the ambulance, and Dr. Lawrence Kaye, who was called in for backup after the EMTs had advised the E. R. that they were bringing a cardiac arrest patient in from Graceland. Dr. Kaye had arrived just a few minutes before Elvis' body was brought in."

"Was Dr. Kaye able to identify Elvis' body?"

"No, he never saw the body because he was examining another patient. Everyone else in the E. R. who saw Elvis' body and *could* make a positive I. D., believed it was Elvis Presley."

"Mr. Watson, did you interview everyone in the Pathology Department who participated in the autopsy?"

San Francisco: Late October 1989

"Yes I did, Mr. Howard, and that included the county coroner who was called in for the autopsy."

"Did *anyone* you interviewed at the hospital and who saw Elvis' body, believe that it *wasn't* Elvis Presley's body?"

"No, not a single person, Mr. Howard. Not one!"

"You stated earlier that Dr. Kaye had met Elvis *prior* to August 16, 1977. Where and when did Dr. Kaye meet Elvis?"

"Mr. Howard," interrupted Judge Blackwell, "I'm getting the distinct feeling that your examination of Mr. Watson is going to take us well past the lunch hour. Let's take a break now and we'll continue with his testimony at 1:30 this afternoon. Court's adjourned."

* * * * * * *

The Resurrection of The King

CHAPTER TWO
Memphis: Late September 1976

It was an unusually cool Saturday afternoon in late September 1976 when Eduardo Alberto Pirelli arrived in Memphis . . a few high clouds partially obscuring the sun, a slight breeze out of the northwest, and temperatures hovering in the low seventies. All in all, it was one of those ideal Fall days for watching football, jogging, or playing a round of golf.

Eduardo, nearing his 40th birthday, was beginning to develop the usual signs of approaching middle age. At just over six feet tall, he tipped the scales at 220 pounds, perhaps more a testimonial to his own cooking while working in his father's South Philadelphia restaurant.

Prior to coming to Memphis, Eduardo had managed to save a substantial sum of money. For in addition to managing his father's restaurant for the past ten years, *Alberto's Ristorante and Pizzeria,* he'd also been living at home virtually rent free.

Shortly after arriving in Memphis, Eduardo found a furnished, one bedroom apartment, one of those garden-style units with parking only a short walk to the front door. "Just perfect." he thought, "I won't have to buy any furniture or fight the neighbors for a parking space like I did on my street in South Philly."

* * * * * * *

In early October, after Eduardo was comfortably settled in his new apartment, he began exploring some of the main streets of Memphis. But it wasn't just a sightseeing tour Eduardo was taking. He was looking for a location to open his new restaurant, preferably one near a hospital.

After parking his car across the street from a nearby park, Eduardo began walking down Madison Avenue while keeping a watchful eye open for

Memphis: Late September 1976

possible restaurant locations. Seeing nothing for sale on Madison, he found an empty building one block north of Memphis Baptist Memorial Hospital with a FOR SALE sign in the window. Hanging above the entrance was a faded sign reading *Bradley's Pub*. The location was perfect, just a short walk from the hospital. More importantly, the property had a parking lot . . . a parking lot with spaces for nearly 100 cars.

Spotting a pay phone, Eduardo contacted the real estate agent listed on the sign. As it turned out, the previous owner had recently passed away, and his only living relative, a married daughter residing in St. Louis, wasn't particularly interested in running a restaurant, nor did she want to move to Memphis. Eduardo had lucked out. It was a classic example of a motivated buyer crossing paths with a more highly motivated seller.

Upon coming to an agreement on the selling price, Eduardo made arrangements to purchase the property. A quick settlement followed and soon *Bradley's Pub* had been transformed from an Irish bar and grill into an Italian restaurant, renamed *Eduardo's Ristorante and Night Club*. Not only would Pirelli be able to show Memphis how Italian food *should* be prepared, but he now had the perfect venue for his Elvis impersonations. After spending more than twenty-five years working under the watchful eye of his father, Eduardo Pirelli was now on his own.

By late February, *Eduardo's Ristorante and Night Club* had become one of the Memphis areas' most popular restaurants and night spots. In fact, it would become so crowded at lunch time that many of the patrons had to wait outside for a table. To handle the overflow, Eduardo added some awnings that stretched out over the sidewalk, plus a half dozen tables with chairs. This permitted the overflow of patrons to eat outdoors on those warm winter days when the temperatures reached into the sixties. To avoid the lunchtime bottleneck, many simply phoned in their orders, preferring to pick them up at the takeout counter. By now, *EDUARDO'S* was attracting a broad mix of patrons that ranged from office workers to medical professionals, many of whom were employed by, or had offices

The Resurrection of The King

in, Baptist Memorial Hospital. Among the more frequent patrons was Dr. Lawrence Kaye, an emergency room physician.

Although Larry Kaye had recently celebrated his forty-first birthday, he seemed to be blessed with a pool of genes that made him appear much younger. Moreover, he was in superb physical condition, due largely to his love affair with marathon running. Seemingly always in training, Dr. Kaye would run ten miles each day just to maintain the minimum level of conditioning required for the two or three marathons he entered yearly. It was no wonder then, that at five foot nine inches tall, Larry weighed only 148 pounds, a weight he had maintained for the past five years.

Dr. Kaye loved Eduardo's cooking so much that whenever he was on the afternoon shift, he would usually have dinner at his restaurant. Eating too much pasta was not a particular problem for Dr. Kaye. Due to his rigorous training schedule, he needed to consume more than 3,000 calories each day just to *maintain* his weight.

Eduardo and Dr. Kaye soon became fast friends and enjoyed having lengthy, sometimes heated discussions about sports. Larry was from the Philadelphia area too, so there was much to talk about, particularly the plight of two of the City of Brotherly Love's most popular sports teams. As it turned out, both were diehard *Eagles* and *Phillies* fans but neither of them followed the *Flyers* or *Seventy-Sixers*. In spite of their lack of a sports background, they were both convinced they could do a better job running the Phillies and Eagles than the present head coach and manager. Based on those two teams' records during the early and mid seventies, they probably could have.

On his most recent visit to Eduardo's restaurant in early April, Dr. Kaye diverted their usual conversation about sports to Eduardo's health. "When did have your last physical, Ed?"

"I haven't had one for a long time, Larry, probably not since the Army.

Memphis: Late September 1976

You know how it is when you're busy. You don't have time for those things."

"I hear that excuse all the time, Ed. If I thought that way myself, I'd never find time to do my daily 10-mile run. It's simply a matter of priorities. If you'd like, I can arrange a convenient appointment time with an internist friend of mine, Dr. Harvey Franklin. His office is also located at Baptist Memorial Hospital, on the second floor in the adjoining office building. How about if I give him a call?"

"What's involved with the physical, Larry? I don't have a lot of time."

"Franklin will probably want to do an EKG, check your blood pressure, sugar, cholesterol, you know, the usual tests. He may even want you to take a stress test, although that would be scheduled for a later date. Remember, on the evening before your physical, you can't eat anything for twelve hours prior to your appointment. It would probably mess up your blood sugar readings. I'll call Dr. Franklin tomorrow and set something up. When's a good time for you?"

"I guess the mornings are best, before the lunch crowd arrives."

"Okay, I'll see if I can get something around nine. By the way, Ed, and I know this is a sore subject with you, it looks like you've put on some more weight over the past month. How are you feeling these days?"

"To be honest, Larry, a little tired. I have to come to the restaurant between 6 and 7 in the morning to check on the incoming food deliveries. I don't stop serving until just before midnight to accommodate the second shift at the hospital. Two or three nights a week I perform for an hour or so after that. Some nights, I have to stay even later to close the restaurant and count the day's receipts. I'm lucky to get out of here before one or two in the morning. And your right, I have gained some weight. It seems like I'm always hungry."

The Resurrection of The King

"God, Eduardo, you're burning the candle at both ends. When do you sleep? How do you make it through the day?"

"It's tough, Larry. But I'm getting used to it."

"Other than your tiredness, how are your feeling otherwise, Ed?"

"Not bad. Maybe a little constipated once in awhile."

By now, Dr. Kaye was starting to become a little suspicious. Years of experience and too many drug ODs coming into the E. R. gave him more than a little insight. "Eduardo Pirelli," thought Larry, "was keeping a hectic schedule and getting very little sleep or any significant exercise. Moreover, he was gaining weight as fast as a newborn calf. He had to be taking something just to stay awake at the restaurant, and probably something else to fall asleep when he went to bed. And now the constipation. If I were a betting man, I'd wager that Eduardo was experiencing the side effects of too many contraindicating drugs, prescription or otherwise."

Resuming his questioning, Larry gently pressed for some more substantive answers, "What are you taking for your constipation?"

"It's really not that much of a problem, Larry. Honest."

"How about bowel movements . . how often do you have them?"

"Once or twice a week, and that's when I take a laxative. Christ, Larry. I feel like I'm on trial here."

Not wanting to unduly alarm Eduardo, nor reveal his *true* suspicions, Dr. Kaye quickly apologized. "I'm sorry Ed, I didn't mean to sound that way."

Eduardo relaxed a little. "I know you have my best interests at heart, Lar-

Memphis: Late September 1976

ry, but I'm managing. I just happen to be under a lot of stress, lately."
"You may have to slow down a little, Ed. You're not getting any younger. Besides, you're starting to remind me of Elvis. He tells me the same things, too."

"I remind you of Elvis?" replied Eduardo with surprise. "Elvis *Presley?* Do you know Elvis Presley, Larry?"

"As a matter of fact I do, Ed. I have for quite awhile. And I keep pleading with him to slow down, but he refuses to. His stock answer is always the same. 'Everything's under control.' "

"Where did you meet Elvis, Larry? I mean, you seem to spend most your time at the hospital . . or eating here."

"It may appear that way, Ed, but I have a pretty active life. I go camping with my wife and two kids about once a month, except when I'm running marathons. I only eat dinner here when I'm on the 3 to 11 shift, and that's only every three weeks. When I'm on the day shift, I eat my lunch here, so I guess it seems like I'm always here. But to answer your question, I first met Elvis back in the late fifties when we served in Germany. I was drafted just like Elvis, but I was a medic at the Army's 97th General Hospital in Frankfurt. Elvis was admitted as a patient, suffering from tonsillitis and a throat infection. When word got around that he was staying there, half the teenage girls in Frankfurt wanted to visit him. I made it my job to keep them away. Elvis was so appreciative that he offered me a job at Graceland when I got out of the Army."

"I guess you didn't accept his offer, now that you're a doctor."

"No, I didn't, but I was certainly flattered. I told him I was planning to go to medical school when I got out of the army. He seemed to understand, but he always left the door open if things didn't work out."

The Resurrection of The King

"Were any of those rumors about Elvis true? I mean, did he get special treatment while he was in the Army?" asked Eduardo.

"Nothing could have been further from the truth. Elvis was a damn good soldier, or he would never have been promoted to a Sergeant E-5, a rank few 2-year draftees ever achieve. Although Elvis and his father lived off post in Bad Nauheim, it never seemed to interfere with his Army duties. In fact, many of the soldiers in his outfit were invited over to play touch football or attend his parties."

"Ah ha! I always thought you were a party animal, Larry. So how come you still see him?"

"That's a long story, Ed. At one of his parties, Elvis asked me again if there was something he could do for me. This time, I asked him if he could come to the hospital and entertain some of the more seriously ill and injured patients. So many of them were just lying around in bed, staring at the walls. When I assured Elvis that there wouldn't be any photographers or publicity people, he warmed up to the idea. He finally agreed, and quite frankly, I was somewhat surprised. Remember, while he was in Germany, Colonel Parker didn't want Elvis to perform, even for his fellow soldiers, unless he was paid. Parker was so mercenary that he wouldn't dream of losing *his* slice of the action. Although offered the opportunity, Elvis didn't want to be assigned to Special Services. His greatest fear was that if he were, he would become an Army poster boy, so to speak. He'd then be at the mercy of the photographers and reporters who would be hounding him at every performance. Besides, he didn't want his fans to think he was getting special treatment."

"It sounds to me like Elvis just wanted to be a regular guy, Larry."

"Well, as regular as the most popular recording star on the planet could be. But he positively didn't want any special treatment. In any event, about once a month during his off-duty hours, Elvis would come to visit

Memphis: Late September 1976

the patients on my floor. He'd talk to them personally, even putting on some impromptu performances. You can't begin to imagine how that boosted their morale," continued Dr. Kaye. "To be perfectly honest, I think Elvis had a more beneficial influence on their collective psyches than all of the psychiatrists assigned to the 97th."

"I wasn't aware of that, Larry . . I mean . . that he entertained all of those troops when he was off duty."

"That was by design, Ed. The press never found out about Elvis' hospital visits, simply because he didn't want to capitalize on the publicity he undoubtedly would have received. To this day, Elvis Presley is still one of the most charitable human beings on the planet. Were it not for him, the monument for the *USS Arizona* at Pearl Harbor may never have been erected. Elvis raised a huge amount of the money for that monument from his concerts in Hawaii. And when Elvis did a charity concert, Ed, he donated the *entire* proceeds . . not just a small percentage of the profits like some celebrities do."

"Jesus, you learn something every day," replied Eduardo. "I never heard that about Elvis and the *Arizona* Memorial."

"It wasn't widely known outside of Hawaii. Shortly after I got out of the Army, I entered Medical School at Vanderbilt University. I always liked the varied patient load that went on in a hospital emergency room, so after completing my internship, I did my specialty work in emergency medicine at Temple University Hospital in North Philadelphia. Needless to say, I got lots of hands on experience in Temple's emergency room."

"I can just imagine." replied Eduardo. "Venture too far east or west from Broad Street, and you'd better have the armored cavalry with you."

"It wasn't quite that bad, Ed. Any way, in 1970, I was offered a position in the Emergency room at Baptist Memorial Hospital here in Memphis.

The Resurrection of The King

Shortly after I arrived, I called up Elvis at Graceland. After finally convincing the switchboard operator that I was a doctor and knew Elvis from Germany, I was put through to his father. While in Germany, I got to know Vernon pretty well, having met him on a number of occasions at Elvis' parties. Well, after Vernon and I chatted for several minutes, rehashing old times so to speak, he put me through to Elvis."

"Did Elvis remember you?" asked Eduardo.

"Elvis remembered me instantly, and frankly, I was somewhat surprised since it had been nearly twelve years since I'd last seen him. Being the prankster he is, he asked me if I still needed a job. I said something like no, not now, but keep me in mind. One never knows how things are going to work out at Baptist Memorial Hospital."

"Elvis laughed," continued Dr. Kaye. "He wanted to know what I was doing at the hospital. When I told him I was an emergency room physician, he was pretty excited. 'You really did it. You always said you wanted to become a doctor when I was at the hospital in Frankfurt.' Elvis and I continued to talk on the phone for almost two hours. He seemed very anxious to renew our friendship, and he invited me over to Graceland that same evening. We must have talked for another two or three hours after I got there."

"I didn't realize Elvis was such a conversationalist. I mean, he always impressed me as a man of few words."

"Elvis can talk a blue streak when he wants to, Ed. Of course, he has to trust you and have confidence that you're not going to blab the details of those conversations to the media. Elvis hates to be used. Well, for the most part, we talked about our former Army days. During the course of the evening, he mentioned that after he sold his ranch in Mississippi, he moved his horses up to Graceland. Elvis and I would go horseback riding once or twice a week whenever he was back in Memphis. Those horses

Memphis: Late September 1976

truly relaxed Elvis. I used to kid him by suggesting that since he loved those creatures so much, he ought to cut back on his tour schedule, and buy some race horses. 'You could become a trainer.' I told him."

"What did he have to say about that, Larry?"

"Elvis laughed, but to my surprise, he said that maybe some day he would . . after his concert days were over," continued Dr. Kaye. "I went on to tell him that before I was drafted, I used to go with my friends to Brandywine Raceway, in Delaware . . not to see the thoroughbreds, or *runners* that raced at Delaware Park, but the horses that pulled those little carts . . sulkies they call them. Why, if he owned some of those trotters like they race at Brandywine, he could drive them himself . . like Pat Boone did in the movie, *April Love."*

"Pat Boone!" replied Eduardo. "Boy, that must have struck a nerve!"

"Well . . it certainly got his attention. Both Elvis and Pat were very popular back in the fifties. In a way, they were both competing for the same audience, largely teenagers who bought records. Elvis had that rebellious image parent's loathed while Pat projected a more respectable, clean-cut image. This used to bother Elvis a lot, because he really was a decent guy. Even Ed Sullivan said as much."

"I still don't get the connection, Larry. I mean, what does Pat Boone have to do with Elvis training race horses?"

"In the movie, *April Love,* Pat actually drove a trotter. He didn't use a double for some of the racing scenes, and there was a distinct element of danger. Some of those drivers have accidents during races, and they can be injured or even worse. Elvis admired Pat for taking those risks, and being so competitive, he wanted to see if *he* could drive one."

"One weekend, we flew up to Wilmington on the *Lisa Marie* to visit this trainer I knew at Brandywine. I once told him about Elvis and his interest in horses during a phone conversation. Mack Leeds, that was the trainer's name, well he was sort of anxious to meet Elvis. After we arrived at Brandywine, Leeds took Elvis out to the track on one of his *experienced* trotters, a 12-year-old named *Limitation*. Mack had hooked the horse up to a jog cart because they were much easier to sit in than racing sulkies."

"Now jog carts aren't really made for two people, but Mack kind of sat on the side of the seat, while Elvis took up most of the remainder. After a few laps around Brandywine's main track, Mack jumped off, and Elvis continued to drive by himself. Elvis was really hooked. 'Lordy, that was more fun than riding motorcycles,' he remarked. 'Now I know how Pat Boone must have felt.' Believe me, Ed, Elvis was like a little kid in a toy shop. I wouldn't be surprised if some day he would buy a trotter and becomes an amateur driver. Can you imagine how many fans would show up at a race track if Elvis were driving?"

"I'd hate to be caught in the traffic jam." replied Eduardo.

"In any event, as Elvis faced more and more pressures in his career and marriage, my visits to Graceland became much more frequent. As far as anyone at Graceland other than Vernon and his Aunt Delta knew, I was just another one of Elvis' parapsychology advisers who would show up from time to time. Only Vernon had remembered that I was one of Elvis' friends from the Army hospital. Even Joe Esposito didn't recognize me, although we met briefly on several occasions at some of Elvis' parties. Of course, I was much younger at the time, and I used to wear glasses, so Joe probably didn't recognize me with my contacts in. I still see Elvis once or twice a week, whenever he's back at Graceland. By the way, what did your father think about you moving to Memphis?"

"Well, at first he didn't like the idea," replied Eduardo. "After all, I managed his restaurant, and someone would have to replace me. And he wasn't too happy about my being an Elvis impersonator, either. Remem-

Memphis: Late September 1976

ber, Papa was an opera fan, especially Caruso's music, and he despised rock and roll. Saying that Papa didn't *like* Elvis Presley would be a gross understatement. He *loathed* him and everything he represented!"

"Yeah, fathers can be like that, Eduardo."

"But there's more, Larry. Papa always wanted me to be an opera singer, so I began taking voice lessons just to keep peace in the family. But I was literally consumed by Elvis' music. I could sing all of his hits from memory when I was twenty-one. By the time I was thirty, I'd developed quite a following as an Elvis impersonator at Papa's restaurant. I also made some money on the side doing Elvis gigs at wedding receptions."

"So you decided to give Memphis a try, and enter some of the local contests. Well . . at least you'll have your restaurant to fall back on if things don't work out. Any way, it's getting late, Ed. We'll have to continue this discussion at some other time. Elvis came back to Graceland this afternoon, and he asked me to come over later this evening, after my shift ends. I told him I'd be there at about 11:30, and I still have some paperwork to finish up before I go on duty."

"Okay, Larry. Next time you're here, we'll just pick up where you left off. And bring Elvis sometime. Just tell him that dinner's on the house."

"I'll mention it to him, Ed, but don't get your hopes too high. Elvis doesn't make many impromptu visits in Memphis any more, unless he's having a party and rents out the entire facility."

"Well, that could be arranged. Tell him how good the food is."

"I'll tell him that too, Ed."

* * * * * * *

The Resurrection of The King

CHAPTER THREE
Memphis: April 1977

The following Tuesday, Eduardo made it a point to arrive at Dr. Franklin's office 15 minutes early. After a 10-minute wait, the nurse called him into one of the examining rooms and told him to get on the scale so she could record his weight. "Hmmmm, 245," she remarked. After getting off the scale, Eduardo walked over to one of the chairs and sat down. The nurse left the room and a few minutes later, she returned and began taking his blood pressure. Just then, Dr. Franklin entered the room.

Harvey Franklin was a slightly balding man in his mid fifties who had a penchant for colorful bow ties and short crew cuts. Since he was on the slender side, he appeared to be taller than his 5-foot 9-inch frame would suggest.

"Did you fast for the past 12 hours?" asked Dr. Franklin.

"Actually, I haven't eaten since yesterday afternoon," replied Eduardo. "Too nervous, I guess."

"Most people are nervous the first time they visit a new doctor," replied Dr. Franklin. "You were telling Dr. Kaye last week that you moved to Memphis to compete in some of the Elvis impersonator contests, is that right, Eduardo?"

"Well, partially right, Dr. Franklin. I also opened my own restaurant and night club. Several times a week, I put on an Elvis show for the patrons, and they seem to enjoy it. You never know if Elvis himself might stop by some evening. As far as the Elvis impersonator contests go, there aren't that many in Memphis, but they do have them all over the south and midwest. So far, I haven't been having much luck in the contests I've entered around here. Competition is so much tougher than in Philadelphia. I

Memphis: April 1977

shudder to think what it must be like at the *big* one held in Nashville each year. It seems like all of the best Elvis impersonators in the country come to Memphis. I've never seen so many good ones concentrated in one area. Makes me wonder whether my dream of winning the Nashville contest was more wishful thinking than an honest appraisal of my abilities. It's so damn discouraging, Dr. Franklin. Before I moved to Memphis, I was considered one of the best Elvis impersonators in the Philadelphia area . . maybe even *the* best. In fact, I'd won a number of contests, including the last two Philadelphia Regionals. It's really hard for me to understand how I could be so successful in Philadelphia and be such a failure down here."

"I wouldn't get too discouraged, Eduardo. A lot of Elvis impersonators have been coming to Memphis for years, yet the vast majority never make it to Nashville. Most of them don't quit trying, and neither should you. Think of the valuable experience you'll gain. Besides, you have your restaurant. You can do your Elvis act whenever you want to."

"Performing in your own restaurant is not the same as competing in a contest, Dr. Franklin. You never know if the patrons are just being polite, giving me an *A* for effort, so to speak. Or maybe they just like my cooking and they're just showing their appreciation."

"Don't be so harsh on yourself, Eduardo. Give it some more time."

"I guess I'll have to, Dr. Franklin, but my lack of progress is really getting me down."

"I'd like to continue this discussion, Eduardo, but I have a couple of patients in my waiting room, and we still have to do your EKG. After that's completed, I want you to go up to Hematology to get your blood work done. It's on the third floor, just across from the elevator, Room 301. You can't miss it."

"Blood work, Dr. Franklin?"

"Yes, that's why you fasted, and they'll also want a urine sample, too. Relax, Eduardo. Those technicians in Hematology are so good, you won't even feel the needle going in. It won't hurt you a bit."

Dr. Franklin didn't want Eduardo to feel overly suspicious, so he didn't make a big issue about his sudden weight gain, his constipation, or the puffiness in his face . . at least he didn't make an issue about it to *Eduardo*. Nevertheless, he was determined to get to the bottom of Dr. Kaye's concerns . . concerns that he also shared. As soon as Eduardo left, he called Dr. John Brewster, head of the Hematology Department.

"John, it's Harvey Franklin. I just sent up Eduardo Pirelli to have some blood work done. Do me a favor, John. Have one of your technicians ask Eduardo to provide a urine sample, in addition to the blood work, on the pretext that they have to test for diabetes. I want you to send both the blood and urine out to that lab we use in Chicago. Both Larry Kaye and I suspect that Mr. Pirelli may be abusing drugs, prescription or otherwise. Larry thinks he's getting them from one of his doctor friends in Philadelphia, and we want a confirmation. And John, test for everything."

* * * * * * *

After leaving the Hematology Department, Eduardo walked down to the E. R. Upon arriving at the counter, he was greeted by the receptionist, an attractive blonde in her late thirties. "Can I help you?" she asked.

"I'm here to see Dr. Kaye. Could you tell him Eduardo Pirelli is here?"

"Is he expecting you?"

"Yes, he was in my restaurant last week, and he suggested I stop by and see him after my physical. I hope he's not too busy," replied Eduardo.

"Oh, you're the owner of the Italian restaurant that opened last year, the one who does the Elvis songs. Dr. Kaye did mention that you'd be stop-

Memphis: April 1977

ping by today. Actually, I just saw him go on a break a few minutes ago. I think he's down at the cafeteria. Do you know how to get there?"

Suddenly, Dr. Kaye appeared in the reception area. "How did the physical go, Ed? What did you think of Dr. Franklin?"

"Okay, I guess. He's pretty thorough. We still have to wait for the test results on the blood work and urinalysis," replied Eduardo. "That could take a week or two."

"Why don't we go back to my office? Fortunately, things are a little slow, now," replied Dr. Kaye as they began walking back through the Emergency Room.

After they entered Dr. Kaye's office, Eduardo resumed their conversation. "I'm pretty disappointed over last week's contest, Larry. Even though it was just a local event, I didn't even make the top ten. I honestly thought I gave one of my best performances ever. In Philly, I probably would have won hands down."

"Christ Ed, Rome wasn't built in a day. Don't get so discouraged. Anyone who ever succeeded in anything important, at least important to them, and no matter how difficult the challenge, met with at least *some* disappointment along the way. When I first saw you perform in your restaurant, you sounded more like Elvis than any impersonator I've heard down here. In fact, Ed, it would have been hard for a blind man to tell you two apart. But there's so much more to winning these contests than just *sounding* like Elvis. You have to have the looks and moves of Elvis. Stage presence and audience interaction count for much more than an Elvis-sounding voice. It wouldn't hurt if you had a choreographer, either."

"Larry, the results speak for themselves. Much as I hate to admit it, I'm just not cutting it. I may just have to accept the fact that my dream of winning the *big* contest in Nashville is not going to happen, at least in the foreseeable future. I probably should have followed Papa's advice and studied opera."

"Not so fast, Ed, there may be another option. I took my family to Italy last summer, and we saw an Elvis contest in Milan. It seemed to me that the Italian judges placed much more emphasis on *sounding* like Elvis than *looking* like Elvis. You could always go to Italy and enter the Elvis contests there. If you won the finals in Rome, you'd qualify for the big contest in Nashville. With your voice and the way the Italians judge contests, you'd have a very good chance of winning. Maybe it's something you should consider. Besides, you could probably use a vacation."

"Well, it's certainly something to think about, Larry. But I do have a business to run. I doubt if I'll be going to Italy very soon."

"I still say you need that vacation, Ed. From what I hear, most of those Elvis contests in Italy are held over a two-week period, and you could enter all of them. You can take a couple of weeks off, can't you?"

"You're making it sound very tempting, Larry, but as I said before, it's something to think about. I'm not ruling it in, and I'm not ruling it out. Let's just leave it at that, okay?"

"Of course, Eduardo, but I just hate to see you this disappointed."

"I appreciate your concern, Larry. I really do. Let me think about it."

* * * * * * *

Italy: December 1977 to February 1989

CHAPTER FOUR
Italy: December 1977 to February 1989

"Would you like something to drink Mr. Pirelli?" inquired the well-groomed, thirty-something flight attendant, speaking impeccable English. "We'll be making our landing approach soon."

"I'll just have a Coke, and some of those honey peanuts if you have any left. It seems like I've been flying forever. I left Chicago last night and flew from there to Amsterdam where I arrived this morning. I will say one thing. The weather sure has been nice . . . no turbulence whatsoever. I just hate turbulence. It makes me sick, and sometimes it can get downright scary. I've got to tell you Ma'am, flying is not one of my favorite activities."

"Well, it won't be much longer, and I doubt if we'll be experiencing any turbulence, Mr. Pirelli. We'll be landing in Florence in about twenty minutes. Perhaps you'll get a chance to see some of the art museums while you're there, especially the *Pitti* and *Uffizi* Palaces. Some of their paintings date back to the Middle Ages."

"I'm afraid I won't be seeing much of Florence today," replied Eduardo. "They're expecting me in Siena later this afternoon. I'll be joining the choir at Saint Antonio's Monastery."

"You'll be joining their choir, Mr. Pirelli? I thought only monks sang in the choir at Saint Antonio's."

"We'll Ma'am, it used to be that way. But now they have an exchange program where one of their choir members goes to the United States, and someone from America comes to Saint Antonio's. I'm the replacement from America."

"That sounds wonderful, Mr. Pirelli. I hope you enjoy your stay. Perhaps

The Resurrection of The King

when you return to Florence, you'll be able to visit the art museums."

At 10:20 AM, Italian time, KLM Flight 3134 from Amsterdam touched down in Florence. After breezing through customs, Eduardo had only a short walk to the awaiting Siena tour bus.

* * * * * * *

"The Abbey at Saint Antonio's is incredibly beautiful especially during the Christmas season." continued the tour guide. "It was built from travertine stone, an elegant type of rock formation found in the local quarries. The church seems to stand all alone, by itself, in the middle of a field that is surrounded by tree-covered hills. You'll also want to visit the City Hall. It's one of the tallest buildings in Italy."

The tour guide, a blonde-haired, blue-eyed young woman in her early twenties, spoke English with a slight Italian accent, repeating her well-rehearsed speech in both Italian and Dutch. Eduardo listened intently, dwelling on her every word, but somehow, something was lost in her translation to English. "I guess she still *thinks* in Italian," thought Eduardo.

Upon arriving in Siena, Eduardo got off the bus, retrieved his luggage, and immediately hailed a passing cab. After a twenty-minute drive, the taxi, a late model white Mercedes, pulled up to Saint Antonio's main entrance where Eduardo was met by a young man, perhaps twenty, dressed in a black business suit. His name tag identified him as Lorenzo. Eduardo introduced himself, and Lorenzo, speaking passable English, asked him to follow him to the gate house where there was a phone. After a brief conversation, Lorenzo picked up Eduardo's luggage and escorted him down the travertine stone walk, to the side entrance of the Abbey. Once inside, they turned right and walked another twenty feet to the Choir Director's office. Waiting at the door was Father Rocco Collivera, a stocky, slightly balding man, who appeared to be in his late forties.

"Grazie, Lorenzo. Welcome, Eduardo! I've been expecting you. I just

Italy: December 1977 to February 1989

spoke to Dr. Kaye, and he said you'd be arriving just about now. Let me show you to your quarters. You must be tired after such a long flight."

"Just a little tired, Father, but I did manage to get some sleep on the flight from Chicago. By the way, your Abbey is simply beautiful. And if you don't mind me saying so, it's a relief to hear someone speak such good English."

"I *should* speak good English, Eduardo. I'm from the Philadelphia area, just like Dr. Kaye. But how about you? I heard that you lived in South Philadelphia before moving to Memphis, but you don't sound like most South Philadelphians I know. I seem to detect a slight southern draw?"

"Father, when you live in Memphis, even for a short period of time, you start to sound like those people. But I was actually born in Naples. My family came to America when I was a young boy. Several years after we arrived, Papa opened a restaurant in South Philadelphia. I started working for him when I was about twelve. I'm afraid, however, that over the years my Italian has suffered. Papa insisted that we always speak in English, both at home as well as in the restaurant. Most of the time, I had to remind *him* to speak in English."

"Well, I have a feeling that your Italian will be improving much faster than you think, Eduardo. Everyone here at the Abbey speaks Italian, even our Irish tenor. Fortunately, we have a school right here in Siena that teaches Italian to foreigners. Maybe you should consider enrolling . . so you can brush up a little."

"That sounds like a good idea, Father. I think I will. Besides, I need something else to do besides singing in your choir."

"Oh, I'm sure there will be plenty of things to do here at the Abbey. You never know when we might need another cook. By the way, Eduardo, what made you decide to come to Italy?"

The Resurrection of The King

"After working in my father's restaurant for what seemed like most of my life, I moved to Memphis and opened my own restaurant. It was doing quite well, but I decided to sell it when someone made me an irresistible offer. I've always wanted to come back to Italy, but I was so busy that I could never find the time for a vacation. When Dr. Kaye told me about your exchange program, it seemed like a great opportunity. I certainly hope I live up to your expectations, Father."

"Oh, I'm sure you will, Eduardo. Dr. Kaye told me quite a bit about you, particularly your marvelous voice."

"Well, I hope he didn't tell you *too* much," replied Eduardo laughingly. "I'm not quite ready for confession yet. Incidentally, Dr. Kaye told me that Saint Antonio's has quite a reputation for its Gregorian Chanters."

"Yes, that's true, Eduardo, but we also have a more traditional choir as well. That's the one you'll be joining. Perhaps you'd like to hear them sing tonight. We're going to have a rehearsal later this evening, so try and get some rest first. Meet me back here at my office for dinner at about 7 o'clock."

"I'll be on time, Father Collivera. By the way, could I get something to eat before I take that nap? Other than the airline peanuts and a Coke, I haven't had anything else to eat since breakfast, and that was early this morning at the airport."

"Of course, Eduardo. I'll ask Brother Pietro to fix you something. What would you like?"

"I hope this doesn't sound too strange, Father, but could Brother Pietro make me a couple of turkey sandwiches on whole wheat toast, with a light coating of mustard? That should tide me over until dinner time."

"That doesn't sound strange at all, Eduardo. I rather like turkey sandwiches myself . . . but I prefer them on pumpernickel toast. Incidentally,

Italy: December 1977 to February 1989

what a shock it was to hear about Elvis Presley. I've been a big fan of his for years. I still can't believe that he's dead. He was so young . . what was he . . forty-two? And so talented. You know, Eduardo, I sometimes wonder if people actually realize how versatile a singer Elvis really was? He could sing in so many different styles . . rock, ballads, rhythm 'n blues, country, gospels, spirituals . . I don't think there will ever be another Elvis."

"Yes, his death was quite a shock to me, too, and he certainly will be missed. He had such a complicated life, poor guy. It seems like he was damned if he did or damned if he didn't. All he ever wanted to do was entertain his fans. I have a feeling his memory will live for a very long time. I for one will certainly miss him. By the way Father, if you have pumpernickel, I think I'd rather have that instead of whole wheat."

"Of course we do. Now you've talked *me* into an appetite, Eduardo. I'd better have Brother Pietro make an extra sandwich for me. In the meantime, let me show you to your room. After we drop off your luggage, we'll come back and get those sandwiches."

* * * * * * *

After finishing his lunch, Eduardo retired to his bedroom, set the alarm clock for 6:30, and lay down on his bed. For the first few minutes, he began reviewing in his mind, all of the events that led to his coming to Italy. Soon, he drifted off to sleep.

At precisely 6:30, Eduardo was rudely awakened by the penetrating sound of the alarm clock. "I can't believe I've been asleep for nearly five hours." thought Eduardo. Slowly, he climbed out of his bed, and after finding his luggage, he began searching for a pair of slacks and one of his favorite sport shirts. After finding two socks that matched, he placed his slacks, shirt, and shorts on top of the bed, and headed for the shower in the adjoining bathroom. "I've got to hand it to Dr. Kaye," thought Ed-

The Resurrection of The King

uardo as he stepped into the hot shower, "he certainly knows how to arrange things. Up until now, things couldn't have gone more smoothly."

After he got dressed, Eduardo headed down the hall towards the choir director's office. Father Collivera was waiting for him in front of the open door. "I hope you're feeling better after your nap, Eduardo. It's still going to take you a few days to adjust to the jet lag. Let's go and eat dinner. Everyone in the choir is anxious to meet you."

Upon entering the dining room, Eduardo was confronted by one of the strangest sights he'd ever seen. Sitting around the table were twelve monks, appearing very much like the painting he once saw of the Twelve Disciples attending the Last Supper. The mood seemed quite somber, almost surreal. However, as soon as Eduardo and Father Collivera entered, the monks' spirits picked up dramatically. Father Collivera was the first to speak. "Gentlemen. I'd like you to meet Brother Angelo's replacement, Eduardo Pirelli. He just arrived from America a few hours ago, and he wants to meet you. He's very anxious to join our choir, and he was hoping he could listen to our rehearsal. But first, let's have dinner. Who will be saying the blessing tonight?"

* * * * * * *

After the Monks finished rehearsing their program for Sunday's Mass, Eduardo could hardly contain his enthusiasm. "Father Collivera, that was simply beautiful. I find it hard to believe that twelve singers could produce such a beautiful sound. I'd swear I was listening to twice that many voices. I'm already beginning to feel like I made the right decision about coming to Saint Antonio's. I can hardly wait to join your choir, but I must warn you. It's going to take a little time before I get used to singing in Italian, so I hope you'll bear with me."

"I thought that might be a problem for you, Eduardo. One of our monks, Brother Antonio, has been translating our hymns' lyrics into phonetics. I think you'll do just fine, and within a couple of weeks at that. Mark my

Italy: December 1977 to February 1989

word, Eduardo, you'll be singing in Italian before you know it."

"I'll take your word for it, Father Collivera. I just wish I had as much confidence as you do."

"Oh, I'm sure you'll do just fine, Eduardo. Remember, you're at a monastery. If there's one thing we have an abundance of, it's time. By the way, Dr. Kaye told me that you were an Elvis impersonator in Memphis. In fact, he told me that he once heard you sing in one of the contests and that you sounded remarkably like Elvis."

"Yes, that's true, Father . . at least the part about me being an Elvis impersonator. Actually, I used to do an Elvis show in my own restaurant, too. But I don't know about my voice sounding like Elvis'. We always sound different to ourselves than we do to others. The fact is, I didn't do very well in the Elvis contests in Memphis. That's why Dr. Kaye suggested I come to Italy to enter the contests here. He told me that the Italian judges place much more emphasis on sounding like Elvis than looking like Elvis, just the opposite of what they judge you on in Memphis. Even though I was was considered a pretty good Elvis impersonator in Philadelphia, it seemed like I was just another face in a very large crowd in Memphis. I couldn't even place in the top ten in any of the contests I entered. It was so disappointing . . . kind of depressing."

"I'm sorry to hear that, Eduardo. But I would still love to hear you sing some of your Elvis numbers. And I'm certain the rest of the choir would, too. Let's consider it part of your audition. When would you like to sing for us?"

"Well . . . how about right now, Father, while the choir members are still here? I know a few hymns and spirituals that Elvis recorded, even some of his Christmas songs."

Father Collivera then turned to his choir, by now engaged in a very heated discussion about Italy's prospects in next years' World Cup. Tapping his baton to get their attention, he addressed them in Italian. "Gentlemen, Signore Pirelli would like to audition for our choir . . now. I told him that when Brother Angelo left for America, we lost our best baritone. That means he better come up to speed pretty quickly, or he'll be going back to America as soon as we can raise enough money for his return flight."

With that last remark, the entire choir burst out laughing. Father Collivera, of course, was just kidding, but Eduardo didn't realize this since he didn't understand Italian. When he saw a big smile emerge on the choir director's face, he suspected that he'd been the object of a prearranged prank, so he too joined in with the laughter.

"Okay, Eduardo, you're on." commanded Father Collivera.

Suddenly, a hush came over the the choir, as the focus of attention shifted to Eduardo.

"I'd like to start out with one of my favorites, *The Battle Hymn of the Republic,* began Eduardo somewhat nervously. I think most of you are familiar with that song, at least I hope you gentlemen from America are. Does your piano player know that one, Father?"

"I'm sure Brother Francis does, Eduardo. He's from Gettysburg and a Civil War buff at that."

Eduardo glanced over at Brother Francis, nodding at him to begin. After he completed the introduction, Eduardo joined in.

"Mine eyes have seen the coming of the glory of the Lord . . . ."

After Eduardo finished the last verse, it was so quiet you would have thought the Pope had walked in. And then suddenly, as if on cue, the choir broke into a spontaneous outburst. *"Bravo! Bravo! Encore! Encore"* they all shouted in unison, while applauding rhythmically, a prac-

Italy: December 1977 to February 1989

tice that was so typical among Europeans.

Eduardo was taken aback. After all, it was merely his first song, and he hadn't really warmed up yet. Nevertheless, the choir loved his performance, and they insisted that he sing another song.

Just then, Father Collivera interrupted. "Gentlemen, Eduardo tells me he was an Elvis Presley impersonator in America. Perhaps he'd like to sing one of his favorite Elvis numbers. How about it, Eduardo, would you sing an Elvis song for us?"

"Well, since you insist." Eduardo took a deep breath, pausing briefly, and then continued. "This is a song that was recorded by Elvis at a time when the Cha Cha was very popular. Brother Francis, do you know *It's Now or Never?*"

Brother Francis nodded his head in the affirmative, as he started playing the first few bars. "Is this the right key for you, Eduardo?"

"That will be just fine, thank you," replied Eduardo.

"It's Now or Never . . . come hold me tight . . kiss me my darling . . be mine tonight . . . . It's now or never, my love won't wait."

Once again, the monks responded with thunderous applause, but this time with even more enthusiasm. Just then, Brother Francis motioned Father Collivera over to the piano. "Father Collivera," exclaimed Brother Francis excitedly, "did you hear how easily Eduardo reached those high notes in the last stanza? What an incredible range he has. I don't think we'll have to worry about losing Brother Angelo."

"I have to to agree with you, Brother Francis." replied Father Collivera. "My friend in America, Dr. Kaye, never mentioned that Eduardo had *this* good a voice. And just in time for the Christmas tourist season, too."

The Resurrection of The King

Walking back to Eduardo, Father Collivera had a big smile on his face. "Well, I guess you know what that means, Eduardo. I don't think it will be necessary for you to continue your audition. By the sound of that enthusiastic reaction from the choir, it's safe to say that you've passed with flying colors."

"I appreciate your vote of confidence, Father Collivera, and more than you can imagine." replied Eduardo, genuinely flattered. "I think I'll quit while I'm ahead."

Suddenly, all of the monks began approaching Eduardo, each one reaching out to shake his hand. One by one they began introducing themselves. After singing a mere two songs, Eduardo had gained the respect of his peers and he was ebullient. "It's much more important," he thought, "to be respected by the choir members, all of whom have excellent voices, than by some judge who probably never sang a note in public, or for that matter, never sang a note in his life other than in a hot shower."

* * * * * * *

Several weeks had passed, and Eduardo was feeling more and more comfortable with his new role in the choir. One evening, Father Collivera approached him in the dining room shortly after dinner. "You know, Eduardo, when I first heard you sing *It's Now or Never,* it occurred to me what a truly magnificent voice you have, and with such an incredible range, no less. Hearing you sing those solos in the choir for the past several weeks, especially the higher notes you seemed to reach so easily during some of the Christmas carols . . well . . it made me even more convinced of what I'm about to ask you." Pausing briefly, Father Collivera attempted to collect his thoughts while searching for just the right words. "Eduardo, have you ever considered . . . studying opera?"

Flattered by the implications of Father Collivera's suggestion, Eduardo replied with genuine humility. "Father, I've been listening to opera ever since I was a child. Papa always had Caruso music playing in his ristor-

Italy: December 1977 to February 1989

ante. Actually, he hoped I would study opera. I think he wanted me to be another Mario Lanza, but I was much more interested in rock and roll, especially the music of Elvis Presley. Besides, I don't think I have the right voice for opera."

"But Eduardo, you sing with such passion. With the proper voice training, I think you *could* sing opera. And another thing, Eduardo. There's something about how you captivate our congregation whenever you sing a solo. You have this charisma about you. I've been hearing many flattering compliments, especially from the tourists visiting the Abbey. Even our own parishioners talk about you. They're always asking me who that new singer is in the choir, the tall one standing in the back, the one with the dark hair and *la voce bella.*"

"La voce bella?" inquired Eduardo.

"That's Italian for *beautiful voice."* replied Father Collivera.

"Did they really say that? What a nice compliment. As far as *me* singing opera, Father, I've always loved performing in front of an audience, but I don't know if I could sing opera. Aren't they sung in Italian?"

"Actually Eduardo, operas are sung in languages other than Italian, especially German. Even Elvis recorded a song in German, *Wooden Heart*, I think. But yes, most operas are sung in Italian. Many opera singers who never spoke a word of Italian, managed to sing in Italian, and they became very big stars, just like you're singing in Italian here at the abbey. Opera singers come from many countries besides Italy . . Sweden, Spain, Mexico, Japan, and of course, the United States. Robert Merrill was born in New York and Beverly Sills is from Brooklyn. Neither of them spoke Italian until they studied opera."

"Okay, Father, you've convinced me. I'll give it a try."

The Resurrection of The King

* * * * * * *

With Father Collivera's endorsement, Eduardo was accepted at the Saena Iulia School in Siena, while he continued performing each weekend with the choir at Saint Antonio's. Among the courses he took were Italian, Introduction to Opera, and Basic Cinema, with the latter two being part of the school's Cultural Seminar Program.

While attending his classes at Saena Iulia, Eduardo became good friends with Antonio Franchetti, one of his voice instructors. Franchetti, who spoke English better than many Americans, assumed the role of Eduardo's mentor. More importantly, he was convinced that Eduardo had enough talent to apply for additional voice training at the Benedetto Marcello Conservatory in Venice. If he were accepted and continued to show progress, he might be considered for advanced *master* training at La Scala Opera School in Milan.

* * * * * * *

After completing his course work at Saena Iulia, Eduardo could now speak Italian with sufficient fluency that he could carry on a limited conversation without resorting to his phrase book. Following Franchetti's advice, he applied to and was accepted at the Benedetto Marcello Conservatory. This, of course, meant leaving Saint Antonio's and moving to Venice. How would he break the news to Father Collivera and the other monks? After all, he had made a commitment when he replaced Brother Angelo.

The next day, Eduardo knocked on the door at Father Collivera's office.

"Entrato. Il portello è sbloccato." replied Father Collivera.

Eduardo opened the door haltingly and meekly entered the office.

"Come in, come in, Eduardo. What can I do for you? And how are your studies going? We haven't spent much time having our lively discussions

Italy: December 1977 to February 1989

since you started attending Saena Iulia."

"They are going very well, Father, and that's why I'm here . . to get your permission."

"To get my permission? Permission for what, Eduardo?"

"Father, I've been accepted at the Benedetto Marcello Conservatory in Venice for additional voice training. I know it sounds selfish, but I'd like to pursue this opportunity. Unfortunately, in order to do that, I'll have to leave Saint Antonio's and move to . . ."

Interrupting before Eduardo could complete his sentence, Father Collivera quickly replied, "Of course you have my permission to leave Saint Antonio's, Eduardo. After all, it was my suggestion in the first place that you study opera. I knew full well that you would have to have additional training . . . training that would require you to leave us. Go with my blessings. And keep in touch. Just write me on occasion and let me know how you're doing."

"Thank you Father, and I will. You have my word."

* * * * * * *

Venice was everything every tourist guide said about it. Canals were everywhere, replacing just about every major thoroughfare that you'd expect to find in a city of that size. And those water taxi drivers . . . it seemed like they were just as adept at maneuvering in the canals of Venice as New York cabbies were in dodging pedestrians in the narrow streets of Manhattan. "If I don't succeed at Benedetto Marcello, I could always become a water taxi pilot." thought Eduardo laughing to himself.

After his first year of study at Benedetto Marcello, the headmaster, Vincenzo Castellani, had openly expressed how pleased he was with Eduardo's progress. By now, he had increased the upper range of his voice by nearly half an octave. It certainly appeared that he had the potential for meeting the *vocal* challenges of an operatic tenor, well beyond what even *he* thought was possible. But could he master the necessary nuances and subtleties of opera, especially when he had to sing in Italian, a language he was just beginning to learn? Apparently he could . . and did.

Castellani was so impressed with Eduardo's progress that he personally recommended him to the Head of Admissions at the prestigious La Scala Opera School in Milan. The following September, Eduardo enrolled in La Scala's "masters" program.

* * * * * * *

By May 1980, Eduardo had completed his training at La Scala, having received the top award for novices. When Castellani suggested he enter some of Italy's opera contests, Eduardo chose the three most prestigious: Lonigo, Peschierta del Garda, and Parma. To no one's surprise, especially Vincenzo Castellani's, he won all three of them.

Shortly after leaving Parma, Eduardo returned to Saint Antonio's where he was warmly greeted by Father Collivera. That evening he returned to choir practice for the first time in nearly three years. "Gentlemen, announced Father Collivera, "I have some very good news to report. Eduardo was too modest to tell you, so I guess I'll have to be the one. Signore Pirelli has just won the three most prestigious opera contests in Italy, and he has been invited to join the chorus at La Scala's main opera company this fall. He'll be staying with us again at Saint Antonio's, but just for a few months, so make sure he doesn't get *too* swelled a head."

"There's little chance of that happening, Father Collivera," remarked Brother Pietro. "I'll keep him busy in the kitchen. Maybe he'll teach me how to make some of those Philadelphia cheese steaks I've heard so much about."

"I'll vote for that, too." replied Father Collivera. "I haven't had a cheese

Italy: December 1977 to February 1989

steak in years."

"But fellas . . . I haven't done any cooking for the past three years. Are you sure you want to take such a risk?" replied Eduardo with a broad smile on his face.

"We'll take the risk, Eduardo. After all, you'll be eating the same food, too." replied Brother Francis.

With that remark, everyone broke out into laughter.

* * * * * * *

The following August, Eduardo returned to Milan to receive his orien-tation prior to joining the main opera company at La Scala. Although he would be starting in the chorus, Eduardo was already beginning to have more ambitious goals, and it wasn't long before he was singing some of the smaller solo parts.

For the next five years, Eduardo progressed through increasingly more lengthy and challenging roles at La Scala, and by 1986, he was the principal tenor's understudy. Moreover, that tenor's contract would terminate at the end of the season. Rumor had it that he would be going to the opera house in Sidney, Australia. Pirelli would take over as principal tenor at La Scala, and he would open the following season in the role of *Alfredo Germont* in Giuseppe Verdi's *La Traviatta*.

The 1987 Fall season at La Scala seemed like it would never arrive. Eduardo was finally getting the opportunity to show the opera critics in Milan just how talented he really was. For his debut, he invited two guests from America, as well as Vincenzo Castellani, the headmaster at Benedetto Marcello. He also invited his mentor and favorite voice teacher at Saena Iulia, Antonio Franchetti, and of course Father Collivera and the choir at Saint Antonio's. Drawing upon his status as principal tenor, Eduardo was able to obtain orchestra seats for all of them.

The Resurrection of The King

Finally, on September 8th, opening night arrived. Eduardo was suffering from his usual stage jitters, something he always experienced just before appearing in front of an audience. By the time the curtain opened, however, his nervousness had greatly subsided.

After completing his near-flawless opening night performance, Eduardo literally brought the house down, having been summoned back to *stage front* for three additional curtain calls. By his third performance, he was receiving accolades from some of the world's most discriminating opera critics. More importantly, Pirelli had managed to garner the respect of his peers, not only in Italy, but throughout the rest of the operatic world.

Eduardo remained at La Scala through February 1989. He was now considered one of the premier operatic tenors in the world, with serious offers coming in from companies in New York, London, Paris, and Sidney. But Eduardo wasn't interested in performing in just one city or for just one opera company. Instead, he decided to go on tour in the United States and Canada, with appearances scheduled for more than a dozen cities. Beginning in early March, he would appear in New York at the *Met,* where he would reprise his role of *Alfredo Germont* in *La Traviatta.* This would be followed by his next two appearances in Boston and Toronto, and concluded with a two-week engagement in Las Vegas.

****

Return to America: March 1989

CHAPTER FIVE
Return to America: March 1989

When Eduardo arrived in New York in early March, he was accompanied by his interpreter, Bella Fontana, one of his instructors at *Saena Iulia*. In an effort to distance himself from the Eduardo Pirelli of Philadelphia and Memphis, whenever he was interviewed by the print media, he would speak in broken English with his well-rehearsed Italian accent. If he was interviewed on the radio or television, he would speak in Italian, with Bella translating.

During the eleven and a half years he spent in Italy, Eduardo had shed nearly forty pounds. To maintain his lower weight, he maintained a strict diet while working out four to five times a week. His efforts certainly paid off, for by the time he returned to America, he weighed a trim 180 pounds. Although now 54, he looked even younger. It's doubtful that anyone from Philadelphia or Memphis would have recognized him.

New York proved to be a stunning success for Eduardo, as all of his performances at the Met were sellouts. Feature stories were appearing on a daily basis in virtually all of the national media. In fact, there hadn't been an Italian tenor who received this much attention since Luciano Pavarotti.

Eduardo's last tour stop before Las Vegas was in Austin, Texas for a one-night engagement. Usually when performers of Pirelli's stature appear in Texas, they prefer to play the much larger cities like Dallas and Houston. Due to his unscheduled stop in Austin, however, Eduardo was booked into the 3,000-seat *Bass Concert Hall*, located in the *Performing Arts Center* at the University of Texas. To no one's surprise, Pirelli's engagement was a sellout within hours after it was first announced that he would be appearing. Unless one had University of Texas connections, however, getting one of those tickets was virtually impossible. Performing in Austin would also give Eduardo an opportunity to meet with Al and Terry Kesre, friends he hadn't seen since before he left for Italy.

Back at the Kesre residence in Austin, Terry and her two daughters were sitting in the family room watching television. Lori and Becky were chatting about their boy friends when suddenly the phone rang. Becky, who was expecting a call, answered after the third ring so as not to appear too anxious. "Hello?"

"Is this a the Kesre residence?" asked Eduardo with uncertainty, as if he weren't sure he had dialed the right number.

"Yes it is." replied Becky.

"This is Eduardo Pirelli. Is a your mama or a papa there?"

"Yes, my mother is right here. Would you like to speak with her?"

"Si . . grazie," replied Eduardo.

Holding her hand over the receiver, Becky glanced over towards her mother with a puzzled look on her face. "Mom, there's a man on the phone and he's asking for you. He's talks with an accent, I think Italian. He says he's Eduardo Pirelli. Do you know an Eduardo Pirelli, Mom?"

"Eduardo Pirelli? Oh indeed I do!" exclaimed Terry. "Let me have the phone."

Terry was so excited that she nearly tripped when she got out of her chair. "Eduardo, this is Terry. How are you? How's the concert tour going?"

"Just great, Terry," he replied having dropped his Italian accent. "How are you and Al? It's been months since I last talked to you."

"We're both doing fine, Eduardo. Where are you calling from?"

"Salt Lake City . . at the airport. I just finished a concert with the Mor-

Return to America: March 1989

mon Tabernacle Choir. What an unbelievable experience! I've never performed with such a large group of singers, Terry. When I spoke with you last Christmas, it occurred to me that I hadn't actually seen you and Al in a number of years. I can hardly believe how fast the time has passed. After I arrived in New York, I decided to add Austin to my tour schedule so I could get to see you folks again. I know this is very short notice, Terry, and I do apologize, but my Austin concert is scheduled for 8 o'clock tomorrow night at the *Performing Arts Center*. I've arranged for you to pick up four, front-row tickets at the box office. I hope you can make it, 'cause I'm anxious to see you and Al . . and meet your daughters, too."

"Yes, I'm sure we can come," answered Terry. "We'll be so thrilled to see you again and of course, to hear you sing. Becky, our younger daughter . . the one you just spoke to? She's studying opera at the University, and I'm sure *she* would love to hear you sing, especially from front-row orchestra seats. Would you like to speak with Al?"

"I would Terry, but I don't have time right now. They're telling me I have to board my flight, and they mean NOW! Give Al my best, and be sure to thank him for everything. And that goes for you too, Terry. If it wasn't for the both of you, I don't think I'd be making this call."

"I'm not so sure about that, Eduardo. Let's just say it was destiny and leave it at that." continued Terry.

"They're calling me again, Terry. Listen, I'd like you all to meet me back stage after the concert tomorrow night. Perhaps we can go out for some coffee and I'll bring you up to date on things. It's been so long since we've seen one another and there's so much to talk about. Remember when we got together before I left? I had very mixed feelings about going to Italy in the first place."

"Yes, I remember, Eduardo" replied Terry. "I'll tell Al and the girls about tomorrow's concert. They'll be so thrilled. You'd better get on that plane, now, or *you'll* miss the concert. We'll see you tomorrow night. And have a safe flight, too, Eduardo. Goodbye, now."

Terry gently hung up the phone, just as Dr. Kesre was returning from the kitchen. "Who was that, Honey?"

"You'll never guess in a thousand years, Al. It was Eduardo Pirelli . . you remember . . the Eduardo Pirelli who was here just before he left for Italy. He's giving a concert tomorrow night at the *Performing Arts Center,* and we're all invited. He's leaving us tickets for front-row orchestra seats at the box office. Oh Al, isn't this exciting?"

Before Dr. Kesre could answer, Becky chimed in. "Who is this Eduardo Pirelli, Mom?"

He's that opera star from Italy who is touring the country," replied Terry with an affected hint of nonchalance in her voice.

"But Mom, why would he be calling *you?"* persisted Becky.

"Yeah, Mom, why *would* he be calling you? Since when did *you* become friends with an opera star, and from Italy no less?" chimed in Lori.

"It's a very long story, girls," replied Terry. Al . . you can make it tomorrow night, can't you? Eduardo can't wait to you again. And he wants to meet Lori and Becky, too . . backstage after the performance."

"Of course I can, Terry. Nothing in the world would stop me from seeing Eduardo sing . . *opera* . . at least nothing short of a hurricane, and you know how often we get hurricanes in Austin."

"What are you two talking about?" asked Becky in her usual inquisitive manner. "Do you know this Eduardo Pirelli, too Dad?"

Dr. Kesre, acting equally nonplussed, replied, "Of course I know him,

Return to America: March 1989

Becky. I'm getting the feeling that you two think your mother and I don't have any friends outside of Texas."

"Try outside of Austin, Dad . . just kidding," added Becky.

"You're forgiven, Becky," replied Dr. Kesre.

* * * * * * *

The Resurrection of The King

CHAPTER SIX
Las Vegas: Early June 1989

The last stop on Eduardo's tour was in Las Vegas where he was booked for a two-week engagement. All of his performances were sold out within twenty-four hours after his schedule was announced in New York. In his previous tour stops, Eduardo sang many of the more recognizable *tenor* arias from the operas he had performed in Italy. Las Vegas, however, would be different.

Pirelli was gifted with a voice that had one of the broadest ranges ever heard among operatic tenors, a range that spanned well over three octaves. While performing at La Scala, he would often display this unusual talent by singing both tenor as well as baritone roles, in the same opera, and after a quick costume change, on the same evening. Many in attendance did not realize that Eduardo was playing an additional role during the same performance. Unlike his previous tour stops in the United States where he sang only as a tenor, in Las Vegas Eduardo would sing some of the more prominent arias performed by baritones, much to the surprise and delight of his many fans.

* * * * * * *

After his final performance, Eduardo noticed a sign in the lobby promoting *The Great Elvis Impersonator Contest,* an event that was going to be held at the same hotel on the following weekend. The opportunity was entirely too tempting. "I wonder," thought Eduardo. "Should I do it? Would anyone believe that an opera singer from Italy would compete in an Elvis contest in Las Vegas? What the hell," he thought, "nothing ventured, nothing gained, as he approached the Entertainment Manager's office."

A few minutes later, Eduardo was ushered into see Joe Carrazini. "Eduardo, how good to see you again." greeted Carrazini with genuine affection. "You were truly magnificent. I never dreamed that an opera sing-

Las Vegas: Early June 1989

er could bring such crowds into a hotel-casino. I wish you could have stayed for another two weeks."

"Thank a you for your very kind a words, Signore," replied Eduardo. "Maybe you have a me come back again, no?"

"Just let me know when, Eduardo. You're always welcome."

"Signore, I have a favor to ask a you. I see a the sign in the lobby about your Elvis a contest next a weekend. Would you be a so kind as a to permit a me . . to enter the Elvis a contest?"

Carrazini, a short, stout, middle-aged man with a shaved head and handlebar mustache, was stunned by the unusual request. "Eduardo, why would a world-famous opera star lower himself by singing in an Elvis contest? These aren't just *any* Elvis impersonators. These are the four best in the country, each having won their regional finals. Audiences can be brutal, Eduardo. If you weren't up to this level of competition, trying to do an imitation of Elvis Presley might lower your fans' opinion of you as an opera singer. I don't think either of us wants you to make a fool of yourself. Personally, I don't think it's a very good idea, and there's always the possibility that you could fall flat on your face."

But Eduardo was very persistent. "At first, I have a the same thoughts as a you, signore. But I have a done it before . . in Italia. We have a the Elvis a contests a there, too. While I was a studying the opera at Benedetto Marcello Conservatory in a Venezia, I had a to pay for my voice a lessons. To make enough a money, I had a to perform with a rock and a roll a band in a singles a bars. I was a big a fan of Elvis since a the mid a fifties when I learn a to play the guitar. I know most of his hit a songs, a too. I did a my own Elvis a shows in a Venezia e Milano . . excusa me, in Venice and a Milan," replied Eduardo with a touch of humility, attempting to appeal to Carrazini's sense of fairness. "Please a let a me try, Signore. I won't a let a you down, I promise a you."

The Resurrection of The King

Carrazini was so taken back by Eduardo's sincerity that he began having second thoughts, and another idea. "Eduardo, I don't want to insult you, but I insist on hearing you sing a few Elvis numbers first. If I think you're up to this level of competition, then you can perform with the contestants that same evening. Fair enough?"

"Oh grazie, grazie, grazie, signore." exclaimed Eduardo with relief. "What would a you like a me to sing? I can do it right a here."

"Without a band?" asked Carrazini somewhat surprised.

"That won't a be necessary, signore. If I can just a use a your piano here, that should a be good enough. What would a you like a me to sing?"

"Okay, okay, Eduardo." replied Carrazini with some apprehension. "I did give you my word. How about singing . . let me see . . here's one that only the best of the best Elvis impersonators even try. Can you sing *Unchained Melody?*"

Eduardo sat down at the piano, played a few introductory chords, and then began singing:

"Oh my love . . my darling . . I hunger for your touch . ."

After finishing, Eduardo quickly spun around on the piano stool to gauge Carrazini's reaction. Before he could say a word, the manager blurted out, "That's incredible, simply incredible, Eduardo! That's my favorite Elvis song. If I didn't know better, I'd swear I was listening to Elvis himself. You're unbelievable!"

"Oh signore, I'm a so happy you like a my singing. Does this a mean I can appear in your Elvis a show?" asked Eduardo with the anticipation of a young boy about to see his first major league baseball game.

"Well . . yes and no, Eduardo. No, I can't let you enter the actual contest.

Las Vegas: Early June 1989

The four Elvis impersonators appearing that night are competing for the national championship. But yes, I can let you perform in . . let's call it Eduardo Pirelli's *Tribute to Elvis.* And Eduardo. If I were you, I don't think I'd check out of the hotel . . just yet."

"Thank a you, Signore. Thank a you so very much!"

* * * * * * *

Eduardo, still excited about the prospects of doing his Elvis impersonations, immediately went up to his penthouse suite. According to the contest rules, each of the finalists would be singing six Elvis numbers. As a concession to Pirelli's popularity as an opera star, and since he wasn't actually a contestant, Carrazini would allow Eduardo to sing up to *twelve* Elvis songs. In addition, he would provide a band for Eduardo's rehearsal sessions. Shortly after he arrived back at his suite, Eduardo reviewed in his mind, some of his favorite Elvis recordings.

* * * * * * *

Saturday evening, June 24th, was hot and windless, typical of Las Vegas in the early summer. The big event along the strip that night was the Elvis contest, and it was just about ready to get under way. As the usual background music began playing over the speakers, there was a noticeable buzz of anticipation in the air. When it was announced that Eduardo Pirelli would be appearing as an Elvis impersonator, many who saw his opera concerts extended their vacations just to see the show. The event was a sellout with standing room only, as literally hundreds of fans had to be turned away.

After the four contest finalists had completed their performances, it was time for Eduardo to make *his* appearance. The orchestra, prior to Eduardo's entrance, began playing the familiar introduction to the theme from *2001: A Space Odyssey,* the usual prelude to most of Elvis' concerts back in the seventies. None of the other contestants were shown this courtesy.

The Resurrection of The King

Perhaps this was due to Eduardo's popularity as an opera singer, but if the truth be told, Carrazini wanted to give Pirelli all of the help he could offer, fearing that his audition may have been a one-time fluke. He also provided some male and female background singers, who at the very least, could help drown out Eduardo's voice if the situation called for it.

As Eduardo hurried out towards the front of the stage, the audience literally erupted into applause. It was obvious that many in attendance that night were his opera fans who had been to one of his recent concerts. Nevertheless, many others came to see if he could really pull it off. The prospects of a world-renowned opera star impersonating *The King of Rock and Roll* almost defied credulity.

Approaching the microphone, Eduardo looked out at the audience with apprehension. Many were staring back at him with a look of pity on their faces, like he was a lamb being led to slaughter, quite unlike when he performed his opera arias where he sensed overwhelming love, support, and adulation. There was a noticeable silence as he nervously picked up the microphone before beginning his well-rehearsed speech.

"Ladies and a gentlemen. Thank a you so much for coming a tonight. I hope I don't a disappoint a you. Many people have a been asking a me why I want a to appear in an Elvis a show. When I was a studying the opera in Italia, I didn't have a much money, and I had a to pay for my opera lessons. I'm a big a fan of Elvis since I was a young a man. I was a singing his songs even a before I begin a studying the opera. In a Venezia and a Milano while at the opera schools, I would a sing in the local, how you say, *singles* a bars? Well, I start a to sing a the Elvis a songs, and a the people, they want a me to sing even a more Elvis a songs. You might a say that Elvis a paid for my opera lessons, and a believe a me, I had a take a them for a long a, long a, time."

The audience lapped up Eduardo's monologue like it was melting ice cream dripping down a sugar cone, and they promptly broke into spon-

Las Vegas: Early June 1989

taneous applause. Eduardo Pirelli had won over the crowd before he sang a single note.

"But that was a many, many a years ago," continued Eduardo. "I hope a you like a my Elvis a songs, especially all a my opera fans. It's a been a so long since I do this, but I think a these are some of the songs . . Elvis would a sing if he was a here tonight. For my first a number, I would like a to do one of a my favorites, *Unchained a Melody*. I hope a you like it."

Eduardo sat down in front of the piano, played a few introductory chords, and then began singing as the orchestra joined in:

"Oh my love . . my darling . . I hunger for your touch . ."

It's been alleged that *Unchained Melody* was the first song Elvis sang to Priscilla Beaulieu in Germany, and the last song he sang in his concert on June 21, 1977 in Rapid City, South Dakota. In fact, in that concert, Elvis also played the piano while singing, as did Eduardo tonight, the only Elvis impersonator to play the piano during the entire evening. Moreover, Pirelli was the only one who even attempted to sing *Unchained Melody*, and later, *It's Now or Never*, perhaps due to the higher notes a singer had to reach. Very few Elvis impersonators could reach those high notes, and if they did, they couldn't sustain them. Eduardo could . . and with ease.

Needless to say, Eduardo Pirelli did not disappoint his many fans. In fact, he created quite an emotional outpouring in the audience, as *his* rendition of *Unchained Melody* literally brought tears to the eyes of many in the audience. Some of them actually attended Elvis' June 1977 concert in Rapid City, further contributing to their heartfelt response. After completing *Unchained Melody*, Eduardo stood up and took a polite bow. The audience responded with thunderous applause, demanding an encore. Once again, he sat down at the piano and repeated the last few stanzas:

"I need your love . . . I need your love . . God speed your love . . .

The Resurrection of The King

tooooooo . . . . meeeee"

Before Eduardo had finished the last line, the crowd was up on its feet in unison, giving him another, even more robust round of applause. It was obvious that this crowd thought Eduardo Pirelli was at the very least a legitimate Elvis impersonator, and certainly one worthy of being on the same stage with the four contest finalists.

"For my next a number, I'd like a to sing one of a my favorite rock and a roll songs . . . the Ray Charles a classic, *What'd I Say?*".

Eduardo picked up his guitar, and along with the orchestra, started playing the song's familiar intro. Suddenly, what appeared to be the *Sweet Inspirations* burst onto the stage. Eduardo was caught totally off guard, for he wasn't told they would be appearing with him. Little did he know that they were impersonators from another legends show that Carrazini had hired . . to give *Pirelli's* performance more of a Ray Charles sound.

It was fairly common knowledge that Elvis adored the *Sweet Inspirations*, and they him. In fact, they virtually worshiped him, and if it wasn't worship, they certainly thought of him as their hero. Back in the sixties, when they were scheduled to appear with him in Houston, he was informed by management that his three young black singers couldn't appear in the *Astrodome*. Elvis perceived this as unabashed racism, which it was, and he gave them an ultimatum: "If the *Sweet Inspirations* can't appear with me on stage, I won't do the concert." Management begrudgingly relented, and the *Sweet Inspirations* did indeed perform with Elvis at the *Astrodome*.

After recovering from the shock of seeing whom he believed were the *Sweet Inspirations*, Eduardo turned towards the audience and along with the orchestra, continued repeating the intro of *What'd I Say?*. For those who never heard it, Elvis' recorded version took nearly four and a half minutes. Eduardo's rendition took even longer, as he milked everything it

Las Vegas: Early June 1989

was worth out of that song. Even at the age of 54, Eduardo Pirelli was performing with the passion and enthusiasm of someone twenty years younger, and seemingly with boundless energy.

By now, the crowd was nearly uncontrollable, almost to the point of mass hysteria, and worked up to a fever pitch not seen since Elvis himself performed in concert back in the early seventies. Throughout the audience people were chanting ELVIS! ELVIS! ELVIS! Middle age women were dancing in the aisles with utter abandon.

Suddenly, hundreds of women started rushing toward the stage en mass, as if they were an advancing army of starving soldier ants. The security guards were getting nervous and called for backup, fearing they might have a riot on their hands. Those fears, however, turned out to be groundless, as Eduardo wisely calmed them down by responding with *Old Shep,* a sorrowful tune guaranteed to touch the hearts of all dog lovers. Based on the reaction of that audience, most of them must have owned dogs at one time or another, or at the very least, certainly liked dogs.

For his next two numbers, Eduardo sang *It's Now or Never,* followed by *It Hurts Me,* both of which few Elvis impersonators ever attempt, unless, of course, they sing them in a lower register. After completing *It Hurts Me,* the crowd resumed their mantra of *ELVIS! ELVIS! ELVIS!* This audience simply didn't want Eduardo Pirelli to stop singing and neither did Joe Carrazini, as he signaled him to continue. Eduardo was only too happy to oblige, and he did so by singing *Love Me* and *Such a Night.* He then followed those up with *Bridge Over Troubled Waters* and *American Trilogy.*

Once again, Eduardo approached the front of the stage with his microphone in hand. "Ladies and a gentlemen. Thank a you so very much. You such a nice a people. I can't a believe that so many of a my opera fans like Elvis a so much. Would you like a me sing a more Elvis a songs?"

The crowd erupted with a resounding, earsplitting, Y E S!

The Resurrection of The King

"Then for my next a number, I like a to sing one of a my favorite Elvis a gospels. It's a called a *So High,* and it goes a like this: *He made me so high . . . so wide . . . so low . . .*"

After completing *So High*, Eduardo quickly followed with *A Big Hunk o' Love, Suspicious Minds,* and *Love Me Tender.* By now, the air was so highly charged that it seemed like lightning was about to strike. Dozens of women had already made it past security, right up to the front of the stage, and more were following them. Eduardo wouldn't disappoint them either, and after placing his mike back on its stand and picking up a supply of scarves, he came down to greet them personally. Out of the corner of of his eye, he spotted a very young girl, perhaps ten, sitting in a wheelchair. He immediately walked over to her, placed a scarf around her neck, and then leaned down and kissed her. The little girl's eyes lit up like beacons, as a broad smile radiated across her face. The audience broke into applause, as Eduardo climbed back up onto the stage.

* * * * * * *

In the audience that evening were the former Gina Minelli and her sister Maria, both of whom were accompanied by their husbands. Paul Antonini, Gina's husband, was a serious opera fan. He frequently attended the *Met* in New York with Gina, who usually came to keep him company, but primarily to go shopping. Paul, of course, came to Las Vegas to see Eduardo Pirelli sing his opera arias, having missed him at the *Met* last March. Gina, Maria and her husband, Marty Santangelo, had come to Las Vegas for totally different reasons. They wanted to see the Elvis contest, having no idea whatsoever that Eduardo Pirelli would be performing as an Elvis impersonator, and on the same stage on the same evening.

By now, Gina and Maria had worked their way up to the front of the stage. It seemed like such a short time ago that both of them literally flirted their way into three of Elvis' concerts in Philadelphia some eighteen years earlier. What was so memorable about those performances was that the security guards at the *Spectrum* had allowed Gina and her sister to

Las Vegas: Early June 1989

remain near the front of the stage. In at least two of those concerts, both of the Minelli sisters had been recipients of Elvis' *scarf and kiss* routine. The experience of actually being kissed *twice* by Elvis Presley, was something that Gina and Maria would never forget.

After finishing *Love Me Tender,* Eduardo approached the front of the stage, but suddenly turned towards Gina, who by now had managed to work her way up to the edge of the stage. For a brief moment their eyes were riveted upon each other as if destiny were playing an unfinished melody from the distant past. Eduardo cautiously approached Gina and upon reaching her, he leaned down and nervously placed a scarf around her neck. He then gently kissed her on the lips.

As if in a delayed reaction, Gina nearly collapsed into Maria's arms. Eduardo, unaware of Gina's behavior, had turned towards some of his other fans, many of whom were now leaning over the stage, beckoning him to come a little closer. Suddenly, after taking just a few steps, Eduardo abruptly stopped, turned around, and headed back towards Gina. When he reached her again, he knelt down on one knee and spoke directly into her ear. In a voice that was audible only to Gina, he asked her a question that would haunt him forever: "Haven't I met you before . . many many years ago . . in Philadelphia?"

Gina nodded in the affirmative while attempting to speak. Although her lips were moving, the words simply wouldn't come out.

Before Gina could gather her wits, Eduardo kissed her again and headed off towards his other expectant fans. Suddenly, he paused again, as a look of utter self-deprecation spread over his face. For Eduardo realized he had done the unthinkable . . the one thing he swore he would never do again. He had spoken in his normal voice without his Italian accent, an accent he had perfected into a virtual art form over the past twelve years.

After Eduardo kissed her the second time, Gina nearly fainted, barely

The Resurrection of The King

getting a grip on the front of the stage in order to maintain her balance. Maria was so startled that she literally screamed at her sister: "Gina! What's wrong? Are you okay?"

Gina looked as if she were about to go into shock, as the blood began draining from her face. After a pause that seemed like an eternity, she struggled to blurt out her words: "Maria." Gina stammered, "that man . . up on the stage . . . Eduardo Pirelli. That's . . . that's Elvis! Elvis Presley! Eduardo Pirelli is Elvis Presley!"

Maria shrugged off Gina's remark, realizing how emotional her sister can get, particularly since she never believed that Elvis died on that memorable Tuesday afternoon in August 1977. "Elvis is dead, Gina. He's been dead for almost twelve years."

But Gina was adamant. "How can you be so sure, Maria? Elvis kissed you, too. I remember you saying that you'd *never* forget those kisses for the rest of your life. You said that nobody ever kissed you like Elvis Presley. Well, I didn't forget either, especially the second time he kissed me. And Maria, did you forget that after his last concert at the *Spectrum,* Elvis invited us back to his hotel suite, along with the rest of his Philadelphia fan club? Remember you couldn't come because you had a job interview?"

"Yes, I remember, Gina . . . all too well. Not only did I not get the job, but I missed the opportunity to meet Elvis in person. I was heart broken. But that still doesn't mean that Eduardo Pirelli is Elvis Presley. Besides, he doesn't look the least bit like Elvis."

"Maria, when Eduardo came back to me the second time, he leaned down and he actually spoke to me. He asked me if he had met me before . . in Philadelphia. I'm sure he remembered me from our meeting in his hotel suite after the *Spectrum* concerts. And his voice, Maria. It was Elvis Presley's voice . . without the Italian accent. How could *anyone* who met

Las Vegas: Early June 1989

him in person, face to face, and spoke with him for nearly an hour . . how could they ever forget what his voice sounded like? Eduardo Pirelli *is* Elvis Presley, and he remembered me, Maria. Elvis remembered ME! As God is my witness, Maria, Eduardo Pirelli *is* Elvis Presley!"

"Can we talk about this later, Gina?" still not taking her sister *completely* seriously. "Eduardo is getting ready to do his next song."

After Eduardo walked away from the Minelli sisters, he headed towards the center of the stage. The audience was still repeating their ELVIS mantra, begging him to do one more song. Glancing over to his left, he saw two familiar figures. Staring at Eduardo was a stunningly beautiful brunette who appeared to be about forty. Next to her was a much younger woman, perhaps in her late teens or early twenties, with somewhat lighter hair and decidedly sharper features.

Eduardo approached the two women haltingly. As soon as he reached them, he paused to remove one of his two remaining scarves. He then kneeled down and placed it around the younger woman's neck, draping it over the front of her shoulders. Suddenly, she reached up and hugged him, unwilling to let him go. "I've been waiting for this moment ever since we met you backstage at La Scala. I sensed even then that you wanted to do your old act again. Thank you so much for inviting us. We wouldn't have missed it for the world. By the way, you never sounded better. And based on the reaction of this crowd, they seem to agree with me, too. Just listen to them!"

Eduardo, turning his back to the audience and now on the verge of tears, replied so only she could hear him: "It's so wonderful to hear you say that, *Buttonhead*. And I love you more than you can imagine. But you knew I had to do this, honey . . at some point in time."

"Yes . . I know you did," she replied. "But now that you're back in the states, I hope we can spend some time together, and very soon."

"We will honey, just as soon as I take care of some unfinished business

The Resurrection of The King

in Texas. I promise you."

After gently pulling away, Eduardo shifted over towards the other woman. Leaning down, he placed his remaining scarf around her neck and gently kissed her on the lips.

She gave him a brief hug, but this time with a far different look on her face than on that memorable night in 1976 in Beverly Hills. This time, instead of pity on her face, she had that unmistakable look of adoration and respect, the look she had for him more than thirty years earlier when they first met. By now the crowd had grown very quiet, as Eduardo had summed up all of the courage he could muster to contain his emotions. Kneeling down on one knee, he whispered directly into her ear so only she could hear him, "You know I still love you, darlin' . . always have . . always will."

"I know . . I know. And by the way, you look wonderful. Has anyone told you that recently?"

"No one that really mattered," he replied.

Composing himself once again, Eduardo grabbed his microphone off its stand and again approached the front of the stage. "Ladies and a gentlemen! I'd like a to dedicate my next a number to you, the nicest a people in the world. It's a called, *My Way,* and it goes a like a this:

And now . . the end is near . . and so I face . . the final curtain . . My friend . . I'll say it clear . . I'll state my case . . of which I'm certain . .

Again, the audience erupted with applause, pleading for Eduardo to continue. But the band had rehearsed only one more song. Eduardo looked out towards the audience, pausing before he spoke. "For my last a number, I like a to sing this a song for all a my *opera* fans who came a to see me tonight. It's a called, *I'll Remember You,* and I hope a you like it.

Las Vegas: Early June 1989

"I'll remember you . . . long after this . . . and the summer . . . is gone . . . I'll be lonely . . . oh so lonely . . . living . . ."

* * * * * * *

Gina Minelli wasn't the only person in that Las Vegas audience who thought Eduardo Pirelli was Elvis Presley. The video taping and marketing of Elvis impersonation shows had become very big business. Steven Dunne, a former wedding photographer, was one of Las Vegas' most sought after video producers. Just last year, he had successfully negotiated exclusive rights to tape, record, and market all of the legend shows held in Las Vegas, including the hotel where Eduardo Pirelli performed his Elvis impersonation.

As soon as he arrived back at his studio, Dunne replayed his video tape of Eduardo's recent performance. "This is just just too incredible," he thought as he reviewed each one of Eduardo's songs. "Pirelli's voice, particularly his phraseology and enunciation, sounds exactly like Elvis' Presley's, and I taped dozens of Elvis' concerts back in the seventies."

After digging out some of his video tapes of Elvis from the early seventies, Dunne began his perfunctory, but unscientific audio test. Initially, he compared each one of Elvis' earlier video taped recordings with the identical number performed by Pirelli. To accomplish this, he first played a song that Pirelli had sung tonight, and then immediately compared it with the identical song Elvis did in concert back in the early seventies so it was still fresh in his mind. Next, he reversed the order. As a final test, he replayed each song from the Pirelli videotape while playing the identical number from one of Elvis' earlier concerts, but simultaneously. This enabled him to compare any variations in the pitch, tempo, and enunciation of their voices, as well as any differences in their choreography, timing, and overall showmanship. Dunne could detect none.

On a hunch, he decided to call his neighbor, Glen Watson, an insurance investigator. "Perhaps Glen knows a voice print expert. Christ, it's almost three in the morning. I'd better call him later," he thought.

That afternoon after Steve woke up, he reviewed the Pirelli and Elvis tapes once again. He was now even more convinced that Pirelli was Elvis Presley and immediately called Watson, uttering a silent prayer that he'd be in his office. As luck and divine intervention would have it, Glen answered on the first ring. "Watson."

"Glen? It's Steve Dunne."

"Long time no hear, old buddy. What have you been up to lately? And when are we going to get together for some golf?"

"Hopefully soon, Glen. All of these legend shows on the strip have been keeping me busier than hell. And that's why I'm calling you. I just taped another Elvis show last night, and you're not going to believe this, but I think one of the performers, Eduardo Pirelli, the Italian opera star . . . are you ready for this Glen? I'm convinced that Eduardo Pirelli . . is Elvis Presley!"

"You think Eduardo Pirelli is *Elvis Presley?* I saw Pirelli's concert last week, Steve. He has a great voice . . a great *opera* voice. Are you sure it's the same Eduardo Pirelli . . I mean . . why would an opera star of his stature perform in an Elvis show?"

"I have no idea, Glen, but I also saw Pirelli's *opera* concerts at the hotel. In fact, I videotaped two of them. It's the same guy . . trust me. Come on over and hear for yourself."

"But Steve, Elvis died nearly twelve years ago . . ."

Before Glen could complete his sentence, Steve interrupted. "I know, and that's why you have to hear these tapes yourself. This guy Pirelli

Las Vegas: Early June 1989

sounds more like Elvis Presley than any impersonator I've heard, and I've seen and heard the best of them. He has this incredible charisma and flair for showmanship, Glen. He even caused the same kind of frenzy that Elvis used to stir up back in the early seventies. But of course I can't be entirely sure just on the basis of comparing by ear, some of Elvis' old concert tapes with last night's taping of Eduardo Pirelli's impersonation act. Do you know anyone who does voice analyses . . you know . . voice printing?"

"As a matter of fact I do, Steve. His name is David Abbott, and he's with the FBI in Washington. Dave is regarded as one of the nation's leading authorities on voice printing. We've used him as an expert witness on some of our wire taps. Would you like me to give him a call?"

"Could you Glen . . . like yesterday?"

"I'll call him as soon as I hang up. What would you like me to ask him?"

"See if he can come out to Las Vegas and listen to my video tapes of Pirelli, and then he can compare them with Elvis' concert tapes where he sang the same songs. If he thinks that Pirelli and Presley sound the same to him, I'm sure he'd want to take the tapes back to D. C. and analyze them more thoroughly. I tell you, Glen, I can't tell the two apart."

"Let's not get too carried away, Steve . . at least until Dave analyzes the tapes. After all, this isn't the first time someone reported seeing Elvis Presley alive."

"Seeing isn't the same as hearing, and to be perfectly honest Glen, Pirelli doesn't look the least bit like Elvis, but he sure has the same mannerisms and stage moves that Elvis had during his concert days. He also sings some Elvis numbers that few impersonators, if any, even try in these contests and legend shows, either because the songs are too obscure or the notes are too high for most impersonators to reach. Anyway Glen, I certainly hope that Abbott will come to Las Vegas and look at these tapes."

"I hope he does, too, Steve, but I hope even more that you're not setting yourself up for a big disappointment. I'll let you know if Dave can come, but I have a feeling he probably will."

"Why's that, Glen?"

"Because he's a huge Elvis fan with one of the biggest memorabilia collections in the country . . at least outside of Graceland. Your observations about Pirelli's performance should, at the very least, arouse his curiosity."

* * * * * * *

As soon as Glen hung up, he immediately called Dave Abbott at his office in Washington. As luck would have it, he was sitting at his desk.

"Dave, it's Glen Watson. I hope you're sitting down, 'cause you're not going to believe this. I just received a phone call . . . ."

Glen proceeded to go over the details of the conversation he had with Steve Dunne. Dave quickly agreed to fly to Las Vegas the following day. Glen would meet him at the airport and drop him off at Steve's studio.

* * * * * * *

Las Vegas: June 24, 1989, 10:08 PM, PDT

CHAPTER SEVEN
Las Vegas: June 24, 1989, 10:08 PM, PDT

After completing *I'll Remember You*, Elvis quickly left the stage and was immediately escorted by a phalanx of security guards to his waiting limo in the hotel's underground garage. In spite of what certainly *appeared* to be a permanent departure, the audience, still at a fever pitch, was pleading for his return.

Suddenly, the MC appeared on stage and made with what he believed was tongue in cheek, that once-familiar announcement, *Elvis has left the building!* Little did he know that it really *was* Elvis who left the building. The collective moans of 3,000 people was indicative of their genuine disappointment. Once again, they resumed their familiar chant: ELVIS! ELVIS! ELVIS! But their pleas were in vain. Elvis was not returning.

* * * * * * *

As the limo sped away from the hotel on its way to the airport, Elvis was beside himself. Thinking over the events of the evening, his mind was moving at warp speed. "Did I blow my cover? I think that first lady I kissed recognized me. God knows, I certainly recognized her. I'm pretty sure I kissed her at one . . no . . it was at two of my concerts in Philadelphia . . and I'm almost certain she came back to my hotel suite with her fan club. Now it's coming back to me. I think I told her how much she looked like 'Cilla. Jesus . . after all these years . . taking such care to speak only Italian in Europe, and broken English or Italian in the states. When I arrived at the Memphis airport twelve years ago and thanked that young lady for holding open the door into the terminal, I swore I would never speak in my normal voice again, and tonight I blew it. All of those years of discipline and caution . . right down the drain."

Once his chartered jet was airborne, Elvis immediately got on the phone and dialed Dr. Kesre's number in Austin. Fortunately, Al was home in his study that evening, deeply engrossed in some medical journals. When the phone rang, it startled him since it was relatively late. "This is Dr. Kesre. . . . . I've got the call in here, Terry." After she hung up, Dr. Kesre repeated himself. "Dr. Kesre."

"Al, it's Elvis. Boy, am I glad you're still up."

"Yeah, I've been trying to catch up on some of my reading. Where the hell are you calling from?"

"I'm in a Lear Jet somewhere over Arizona. We just left Vegas."

"How did things go?"

"I depends on which *things* you're referring to, Al. I had two weeks of sellouts for the opera concerts, but I didn't tell you about the Elvis impersonation I did tonight."

"You impersonated *yourself?*" asked Dr. Kesre incredulously. "What ever possessed you to do something like that?"

"I've been asking myself the same question, Al. It's a long story that goes back many years. Let's just say I had something to prove."

"Well . . . did you prove what you had to prove?"

"Yes, I believe I did."

"And how did your Elvis impersonations go over with your opera fans in the audience?"

"In one word, *unbelievable!* You can't even *begin* to imagine how they reacted, Al. It was like the reception I received when I returned to Las Vegas back in the late sixties, only much more intense. It was almost

Las Vegas: June 24, 1989, 10:08 PM, PDT

like, well, like I'd never left in the first place."

"I can't say I'm surprised, Elvis. What did the contestants think about *you* appearing in what was really *their* show?"

"I think they liked the idea. They certainly had a bigger audience. In fact, it was standing room only. But I didn't really interfere with their contest, since I didn't come on stage until after it was over. One of the contestants was so nervous, he forgot some of the words to *Blue Suede Shoes*. The poor guy was so embarrassed that the hotel's entertainment manager had to actually beg him to finish his program. It kind of reminded me of when I first appeared in front of a big crowd as a teenager. But after each song *I* sang tonight, the crowd literally went crazy. They didn't want me to leave the stage."

"What did you expect, Elvis? I mean, who do you think you sounded like . . Bing Crosby? And did you go through your usual gyrations like you did back in the sixties, or were you more laid back like Perry Como? God Elvis, even if you looked like Eduardo Pirelli but sounded and performed like your old self, to the people in that audience, you *were* Elvis Presley! And of course, you really were. Remember, there are literally hundreds of thousands, maybe millions of your fans who don't believe you died. Or they don't *want* to believe it. You simply reminded them of the Elvis they all loved, even if you are fifty-four now. I'll bet that some of the people in that audience thought you even *looked* like the Elvis Presley they remembered, especially since you were probably wearing an Elvis outfit. After all, every fan attending tonight was at least twelve years younger when you last performed. The passage of time has a way of blurring memories."

"Al, fifty-four isn't *that* old. You must be around fifty, yourself, so give me a break. All kidding aside, I think there's going to be a problem. Do you remember what I used to do at my concerts when I sang those love songs? It became almost a ritual. One of the boys would hand me some

The Resurrection of The King

scarves, and I would make my way down to the front of the stage where dozens of screaming ladies were just begging to touch me or kiss me. After I put a scarf around their neck, I would usually kiss them . . especially the prettier gals. Some of those ladies were pretty aggressive. They would actually grab me 'round the neck and try to French kiss me. Now I'm not saying I didn't enjoy it . . *sometimes* . . 'cause I did . . *sometimes.* But during tonight's show, one lady . . I'd guess she was in her mid thirties . . well she looked familiar . . . like I'd met her before . . but in the past."

"Elvis, when you were on the opera tour, you must have met hundreds of women, many of them autograph seekers. Maybe you met her while you were in Austin, or even New York when you performed at the *Met.*"

"No, Al, it was much longer ago. Any way, after kissing this one lady, I headed back towards some of the others who were crowding up to the stage, and then it suddenly occurred to me where I remembered her from. I went back to her again, and this time, I was sure I recognized her. I leaned down until my mouth was virtually in her ear and then I asked her if we had ever met before . . in Philadelphia?"

"I *still* don't get it. So you asked her if you ever met her before in Philadelphia. Maybe she knew Eduardo Pirelli . . remember, you look just like him . . maybe a little older and certainly thinner . . . maybe she knew Eduardo from the old neighborhood in South Philly or from his father's restaurant. I think you may be overreacting to this, Elvis."

"But Al! I spoke to her in English *without* my Italian accent. When I left Memphis twelve years ago to see you the first time, I made a promise to myself never to speak to anyone in my normal voice. Even when I first arrived in Italy, I tried to disguise it so I'd sound like a damn yankee . . . like you talk, Al. But after I learned to speak Italian, I only spoke in Italian . . at least in Europe. Nobody ever recognized my voice when I spoke in Italian. But here in the states, when I first came back to New York to perform at the *Met,* I always had a translator with me. After I left New

Las Vegas: June 24, 1989, 10:08 PM, PDT

York, I had enough confidence to speak in English, but with my Italian accent . . just like I spoke to one of your daughters when she answered the phone last month . . when I called from the airport in Salt Lake City."

"That was Becky. But I still don't understand why this is such a problem for you, Elvis . . . oh oh . . . wait a *minute*. I think I'm getting the picture. The lady at the Elvis contest recognized your voice . . the Elvis voice the entire world knew."

"Al, I'm almost certain she did. I could tell by the look on her face. After I spoke to her and kissed her the second time, she almost fainted. And then it came back to me. I think I kissed her at one . . no, it was at *two* of my concerts in Philadelphia . . either in '71 or '74. In fact, I'm pretty sure she came back to my hotel suite after my last concert at the *Spectrum*. She was part of the Philadelphia Fan Club. To make matters worse, we talked for nearly an hour. I seem to recall telling her how much she looked like 'Cilla. Any way, she probably remembered our conversation. Now it's coming back to me. I think her name was Jean or Gina."

"Elvis?" asked Dr. Kesre, "Why do I get the feeling that I'll be going back to work . . and how shall I say . . make Eduardo look like somebody else . . perhaps the *Marlboro Man* this time?"

"That ain't funny, Al. You know I don't smoke," he replied in a deadpan manner, trying to keep things in a more humorous vein. Suddenly, his mood perked up. "Al, remember when you did the first operation? Terry was so disappointed that she couldn't tell your daughters about me being there in your home."

"Yes, I certainly do, Elvis."

"And remember when I said that some time in the future, but probably not for awhile . . I would tell them myself . . . in person? Since I'm going to have my appearance changed again, maybe tonight is a good time to tell them. As long as they don't know what I'll look like *after* you do another operation, what harm will it do? Besides, if they ever told anyone, who would believe them?"

"You might be right, Elvis, and they'll be absolutely shocked, particularly Becky. She was such a big fan of yours. When they announced your death, she took it pretty hard. And Terry will certainly be relieved that you're coming, too. By the way, since you've apparently made up your mind about coming to Austin, what time will you get here?"

"Let me check with the pilot. Remember, it's a chartered flight . . on a Lear Jet, but I'm the only passenger. I leased it for the entire weekend. Hold on a minute, Al."

A few minutes later, Elvis was back. "The pilot told me he'll have to submit a new flight plan, but we should arrive in Austin in about 2-1/2 hours. We have a pretty good tail wind, so we should be touching down around one in the morning. Is that too late for you folks, Al?"

"Elvis, what time is it where you are?"

"A little after 10:30."

"Well, it's a little after 12:30 in the morning here. There's a 2-hour time difference between Las Vegas and Austin, so you won't be arriving here much before three in the morning, our time. That's okay with us, Elvis, and I'm certain the girls will want to come along too and meet Eduardo Pirelli, especially after missing the chance to meet you in Austin. They'll be thrilled to death."

"That's great! I can't wait to see you all, especially Terry, Becky, and Lori. I'd better change my watch now before I forget. One last thing, Al. I was really disappointed when I couldn't get to meet you folks after the Austin concert. It took much longer than I thought it would, and I had to fly to Las Vegas that night. The charter service had another flight scheduled for my plane shortly after I was due to arrive, so I couldn't take the

Las Vegas: June 24, 1989, 10:08 PM, PDT

time to see you."

"Elvis, things like that happen. And thanks for sending the message over to let us know. It certainly helped ease our disappointment."

"It's the least I could do. Listen, Al. It's been a long day, and I'd like to get a little shuteye before I arrive in Austin. I'll see you in a couple of hours. Give my best to Terry."

"I'll do that Elvis. We'll be waiting for you."

Before dropping off to sleep, Elvis reviewed the incredible events of the past several hours. "I still can't believe how that audience reacted," he thought. "It was . . . . well like I'd never left Las Vegas in the first place. God, how I love performing my old routine in front of a live audience. To think that I actually spoke to that lady without my Italian accent. Maybe Al was right. Maybe I *am* overreacting."

* * * * * * *

The Resurrection of The King

CHAPTER EIGHT
Austin: June 25, 1989, 12:40 AM, CDT

As soon as he hung up, Dr. Kesre headed for the family room where Terry, Lori, and Becky were watching a movie on *HBO*. Living in the Austin area had more than it's share of benefits, including educational. For example, the University of Texas was located just a short drive away. Becky, taking more after her mother, was also blessed with Terry's musical talents, having inherited a truly magnificent voice. A senior at UT-Austin's School of Music, it's been Becky's fondest dream to become an operatic soprano, wanting to follow in the footsteps of Kiri Te Kanawe, ever since she heard at age twelve, Kanawe's recording of Puccini's *O Mio Bambino Caro*. Not surprisingly, Becky was particularly thrilled to see Eduardo Pirelli at the *Performing Arts Center* back in May.

Lori, the older of the Kesre daughters, took more after her father. She taught autistic children part time in a nearby private school while pursuing her PhD in Psychology at UT-Austin's Graduate School of Education.

Upon entering the family room, Al could hardly contain himself. "Terry, you won't believe who that was on the phone!"

"Who was it, Honey?" replied Terry with only token curiosity, still engrossed in the movie.

"Eduardo . . Eduardo Pirelli," replied Dr. Kesre.

"Eduardo Pirelli?" interrupted Lori. "Wasn't he the opera singer we saw at the *Performing Arts Center* last month, the one who was *supposed* to meet us for coffee? I hope he was calling to apologize."

Turning toward Lori, Al replied. "He's flying into Austin in a couple of hours, and he asked me if your mother and I could meet him at the airport. He'd like you girls to come, too, since he couldn't meet you at the

Austin: June 25, 1989, 12:40 AM, CDT

concert. Terry, remember when he was here in '77 for the surgery?"

"How could I ever forget?"

"And remember what he said when you told him how difficult it would be for you to keep such a secret?"

"Yes, Al, I remember, and it's been agonizing, too."

"Terry," continued Dr. Kesre, "I know you've . . we've . . been waiting for nearly twelve years, but . . . ."

"Suddenly, Becky interrupted. "Just what are you two talking about? And Dad, what did you mean when you asked, *how difficult it would be for you to keep such a secret?"*

"Lori and Becky," replied Terry, "please try and understand why we never told you about this, but you must trust me when I tell you that we simply couldn't . . at least not until now."

"Mom, you're talking in riddles. Both you and Dad aren't making any sense at all," replied Becky with more than a hint of frustration in her voice. "What have you been waiting for . . *for nearly twelve years?"*

"Girls, I want you to sit down, for what I'm about to tell you may be the most shocking story you've ever heard, but it's not a story. It's the unvarnished truth! It actually occurred right here in our home and in your father's clinic," replied Terry with a long-awaited sense of relief. "Becky, who is your favorite popular singer of all time?"

"You know who that is, Mom . . Elvis! Elvis Presley. And you both re-remember all too well how saddened Lori and I were when he died. I still haven't completely gotten over it, and I guess I never will. If you want to know the truth, Mom, I don't think Elvis really died." stated Becky with

The Resurrection of The King

the convictions of a true believer.

"I didn't know you felt that way, Becky," cut in Lori. "I feel the same way too. I don't think Elvis is dead, either. I just can't explain why, but it's just how I feel."

"I didn't know either of you girls felt that way." replied Terry.

"Why do you think I'm still such a big Elvis fan, Mom?" continued Becky. "When I discovered that they offered a course on *Elvis Music Appreciation* at UT-Austin, I was one of the first in my freshman class to sign up. Once I began studying his music seriously, I became aware of things I'd never noticed before. What a range he had! In one of our classes, we conducted some tests on his voice with some pretty sophisticated equipment, recording the amplitude of his highest and lowest notes on a sampling of his recordings. According to our test instruments, his range spanned well over three octaves. I often wondered if Elvis had received the proper voice training, could he have sung opera? Oh, what am I saying?" sobbed Becky. "I guess I just miss him."

"Girls." as Terry searched for the right words. "Becky and Lori . . I have something to tell you . . and I don't know quite how to say this."

"Terry." interrupted Dr. Kesre, "are you sure you want to do this . . I mean *now?*"

"Yes, Al. It's better to tell them now. They might not believe Eduardo if *he* told them. It would be quite a shocking revelation when almost everybody in the world believes you're dead."

"Tell us *what,* Mom?" chimed in Becky.

"Just what do you mean, *they might not believe Eduardo,* Mom?" asked Lori, equally puzzled. "And what's this stuff . . *when almost everybody in the world believes you're dead?* What's that all about?"

Austin: June 25, 1989, 12:40 AM, CDT

"Girls, take a deep breath, for you may not believe what I'm about to tell you, but it's true."

"What's true?" cried Lori, by now clearly agitated.

"Elvis . . Elvis Presley . . he isn't dead. He's still alive."

"What did . . what did you say, Mom?" stammered Lori with disbelief. "Did I hear you say that Elvis Presley is still . . *alive?"*

"Yes you did. That's exactly what I said," replied Terry.

"Mom, you don't really believe that do you?" interrupted Becky. "This isn't something one jokes about. I remember that day twelve years ago like it was yesterday. It was the saddest day of my life. Lori and I were back in Pennsylvania visiting Grandpa and Granny."

"Lori . . Becky . . have I ever lied to you?" asked Terry in a soft, reassuring voice so typical of mothers when they *really* want their daughters to take them seriously.

"Never, Mom," replied Becky, as Lori nodded in agreement.

Terry went on to explain about when Elvis came to visit. After she finished, Lori spoke first. "I *knew* he was alive! I just knew it! Mom, you actually *met* Elvis Presley? Elvis was right here . . in *our* home . . . right here . . in *our* family room . . sitting right here on the same couch where *we're* sitting?"

"Yes . . . right here . . . sitting on this very couch," replied Terry.

"Mom, why did you wait so long to tell us?" asked Becky with a puzzled, almost disappointed look on her face.

"Because I made a promise to Elvis," replied Terry, "and I just had to keep that promise."

The Resurrection of The King

"But why are you telling us now, Mom?" chimed in Lori.

"Becky," replied Terry, "you weren't too far from the truth when you wondered if Elvis could have sung opera. That man who just called your father . . . Eduardo Pirelli? Eduardo Pirelli, the opera star you saw last month at the *Performing Arts Center?* Eduardo Pirelli . . . Eduardo . . . *is* Elvis Presley. And we're meeting him at the airport in a couple of hours. Elvis wants you two to be there with us."

Both Becky and Lori had a look of shocked disbelief on their faces. In fact, they were *so* speechless that their jaws literally dropped in unison.

"When he was here back in 1977," continued Terry, "we told him what big fans of his you were. Realizing how hard it would be for me to keep such a secret, he promised me that sometime in the future, he wanted to tell you two in person. I thought it would be best if I told you before we meet him at the airport. I wasn't sure how you'd handle things if Eduardo . . I mean Elvis . . broke the news to you first. When we get to the airport, that is, if you want to come, we can't even hint that we know he's Elvis. Just call him Mr. Pirelli. You never know who might be at the airport when we meet him. As my mother used to say, little pitchers have big ears."

Both Becky and Lori then looked over towards their father as if they were seeking confirmation. Dr. Kesre shook his head in agreement. "It's true, girls, everything your mother said is true."

"Daddy," asked Becky, "why would Elvis come *here?*"

"He wanted to look like Eduardo Pirelli," replied Dr. Kesre.

"But why *here* and why did he want to look like Eduardo Pirelli?" continued Becky. "I mean, there are lots of reconstructive surgeons in Memphis, aren't there? And how did you keep such a secret for so long, Dad-

Austin: June 25, 1989, 12:40 AM, CDT

dy? It must have been agonizing."

"The pressures he was experiencing were becoming just too unbearable, and he wanted to get away from it all. He couldn't have the surgery done in Memphis because the press would have found out. Remember, Elvis was a *very* high-profile celebrity. Dr. Larry Kaye, an emergency room physician in Memphis and a lifelong friend of mine, recommended that *I* do the surgery. It was also Dr. Kaye who came up with the idea for Elvis having a double. The real Eduardo Pirelli, a Memphis restaurant owner and an Elvis impersonator, had a singing voice that was indistinguishable from Elvis'. Eduardo had reconstructive surgery here, too, but *before* Elvis had his. When we finished with Eduardo, he was a virtual dead ringer for Elvis. Several hours after Elvis and Eduardo had made the switch at Graceland, Eduardo died. Of course, the whole world believed that it was Elvis who died."

"That's simply incredible, Daddy." remarked Becky.

"But there's more. We discovered after doing some blood tests, that Eduardo was a prescription drug abuser, and it finally caught up with him. That's why he died. Although the medical term is *Polypharmy,* it doesn't account for the real cause of death which was an impacted colon."

"Did anyone else know that it was Eduardo, not Elvis, who died?" asked Becky.

"Yes. Elvis' father, Vernon and Dr. Kaye. According to the plan, Elvis would call Dr. Kaye when *he* decided to make the switch. Larry would then relay that decision to both Eduardo and Vernon. W*hen* to make the switch could only be determined by Elvis, and the timing had to be perfect. Elvis decided to make the switch at about six in the morning on August 16th. He then called Dr. Kaye to put everything into motion. From that point on, events had to go like clockwork in order for Eduardo to get *into* Graceland and Elvis to get out, without either of their identities being revealed. Since Larry had to take Elvis to the airport for his flight to

The Resurrection of The King

Austin, he didn't have time to call Vernon and tell him that the switch had already taken place. Poor Vernon. He actually *believed* that it was Elvis who died. Fortunately, Dr. Kaye was able to get in touch with Vernon later that afternoon. But after what happened tonight, Elvis wants to change his appearance again and that's why he's flying to Austin."

"What do you mean, Daddy, *after what happened tonight?*" chimed in Becky. "What happened tonight?"

"Elvis thinks someone recognized him tonight in Las Vegas. After his final opera performance last week, he decided to appear in an Elvis impersonator show, and it was tonight. He thinks someone from the audience recognized him. It's a complicated story Becky, so I'm going to save it for the ride to the airport, that is, if you want to come with us when we go to meet Elvis."

"Of course, we want to come with you, Daddy," replied Becky, "at least I do."

"And so do I," replied Lori.

"Well then . . don't you girls have to get ready? I mean, would you really want to meet Elvis wearing your pajamas?"

Before Dr. Kesre could get the words out of his mouth, the girls were sprinting off to their bedrooms. "It's a good thing that the flight won't be arriving for a couple of hours, Terry. The girls are going to need almost that much time just to get ready. I'm sure they'll want to look their very best for our guest of honor."

"I'm sure they will too, Al, and so will I, so I'd better start getting ready myself. We wouldn't want to keep Elvis waiting."

* * * * * *

Memphis: Early May 1977

CHAPTER NINE
Memphis: Early May 1977

"**I** didn't know you were coming to last night's contest, Larry. Why didn't you warn me first?"

"I thought I'd be working the graveyard shift, Ed, but we had a schedule change, so I thought I'd drop in. As usual, your voice was terrific, certainly the best Elvis-sounding voice in the contest. But I think I know what's preventing you from being more competitive."

"You do? Clue me in, Larry," replied Eduardo with a perplexed look on his face.

"One reason you're not finishing higher in the voting is because of your facial features. You just don't have that Elvis look like most of the other contestants. Also, you're entirely too passive . . too laid back. To be competitive down here, you have to be very outgoing in your presentation . . . very assertive. I'm told that in the major contests in Nashville and Las Vegas, and particularly here in the Memphis area, the judges place a lot less emphasis on the contestant's voice, you know . . one that sounds like Elvis'. But the winners always seem to look *somewhat* like Elvis, which means at the very least, you'll have to restyle your hair and wear longer sideburns . . and maybe get some minor cosmetic surgery. It also helps to have the basic Elvis moves and more of a sense of showmanship. And you'll *have* to get your front teeth fixed! Elvis always prided himself in his smile. Also when you compete, spend some time out in the audience. Go to some of the older ladies and sing them a love song. The crowd will love it."

"I guess I was relying too much on my voice and the Elvis outfits. That was usually enough for me to win most of the contests in Philadelphia. There's not much I can do about my face now, other than plastic surgery, and I could get my teeth capped. Of course, I could always go to Italy like you suggested before and enter the Elvis contests there."

"And you can still go to Italy, even if you get plastic surgery. The fact is, most of the serious competitors *here,* have had plastic surgery. But none of the ones I've seen and heard in the Memphis area has your voice, which is merely *spot on!* You can always work on the Elvis moves, and you can certainly hire a professional choreographer. You're just about Elvis' height and you both have similar skin tones, but unfortunately you have his excess poundage, too."

"Are you suggesting . . that I'm too fat, Larry?"

"Look Ed, just because *Elvis* is obese, and that's the medical term, you've got to lose some of that weight. Not only is it a health risk, but obese Elvis impersonators rarely win these contests, no matter how good their voices are, what they look like, or how theatrical their presentations are. I've been telling Elvis for months that he should go on a diet, but he doesn't think he has a weight problem. About all I can do is tell him to simply get on a scale. But in your case, Ed, I bet going on a diet is one of the first things Dr. Franklin tells you to do after he reviews your blood and urine test results."

"Okay, I'll concede I'm carrying a few extra pounds, Larry, and I'll try to get rid of some of them, but to be honest, plastic surgery is an option I'd never even considered until tonight. Do you think it would help? I mean, if it enabled me to win just *one* contest, I'd do it in a heartbeat, but I don't know any plastic surgeons."

"If you've made up your mind that you want plastic surgery, Ed, I know an excellent reconstructive surgeon. His name is Alan Kesre and he practices in Austin, Texas. I've known Al since childhood. In grammar school and junior high, we were almost always in the same classes together. Dr. Kesre has a first-class surgical clinic at his home, away

Memphis: Early May 1977

from prying eyes and curiosity seekers."

"How can he operate that way, Larry? Doesn't he need an operating room . . surgical assistants . . someone to administer the anesthesia?"

"Of course, Ed. But I'm not talking about some back room or basement operation. I'm talking about a state-of-the-art surgical facility that would rival most hospital ORs. Moreover, Dr. Kesre is assisted by his wife, Terry, who is also a nurse anesthetist, and three trusted colleagues, including two board-certified reconstructive surgeons and an anesthesiologist. Nobody else need be present and of course, nobody else will be, thus assuring total confidentiality. In addition, Terry is also a very accomplished musician, so you two should have a lot in common. About ten years ago, she decided to embark on a new career, went back to college, obtained her Bachelor's degree in Nursing, and subsequently, her Master's in Anesthesiology. As a team, the Kesre's and their colleagues have worked on a number of high-profile celebrities and politicians . . people whose names you'd recognize in a heart beat."

"I'm impressed, Larry, truly impressed," replied Eduardo.

"Ed, Al Kesre is the best there is as far as I'm concerned. You wouldn't believe some of the incredible work he's done, especially with severely burned children. I've seen the results on someone who came into my E. R. before we sent her to the burn center . . a young woman who received third-degree burns over most of her face. Today, she looks like a movie star. Kesre not only gave her back her face, but he literally gave her back her life."

"Kesre is that good?" asked Eduardo.

"Yes he is, Ed. He's truly gifted. If Dr. Kesre were to accept you as a patient, and he only takes referrals, you'd probably end up looking very much like Elvis, at least to the judges when you're performing on stage, and that's where it counts."

"How soon can you get hold of him, Larry? I'm ready to go to Austin on tomorrow's first flight."

"I'll give him a call tonight," replied Dr. Kaye. "I'm sure he'll take you on my recommendation."

"Thanks for everything, Larry. I really do appreciate your help . . more than you can imagine."

"I'm glad I *could* be of help, Ed. Assuming Dr. Kesre agrees to do the surgery, I think you'll be quite pleased with the results. I'll let you know how soon arrangements can be made, hopefully by tomorrow night when I come over."

* * * * * * *

The next evening, Dr. Kaye arrived at *EDUARDO'S* shortly after 10 PM for his usual cup of coffee, a custom he observes whenever he goes on the evening shift. As Larry approached his usual table, Eduardo was waiting with a look of apprehension on his face.

"What did Dr. Kesre have to say, Larry? Will he do it?"

"Shhhhhh . . . . ," whispered Dr. Kaye, holding his forefinger up to his lips as he approached the table. After sitting down, he continued speaking, but in a much lower voice, almost in a whisper. "You don't want everyone in the restaurant knowing about your impending trip to Austin, do you."

"No, I guess not," replied Eduardo in a softer voice only Larry could hear. "Should I interpret your remark about my *impending trip to Austin* to mean that Kesre agreed to do the plastic surgery?"

Memphis: Early May 1977

"Everything's a go, Ed. Just let me know when you can leave, and I'll call him. By the way, I wouldn't tell anyone here at the restaurant about why you're really going to Austin. Just tell them that you're taking a well-deserved vacation. And from what I hear, Ed, you haven't had one since you opened the restaurant. I also suspect that some of your employees won't be too disappointed. It seems that you have quite a reputation for being a real task master, and somewhat of a perfectionist, too."

"I won't deny that, Larry. Why do you think the food and service are so good? By the way, how about this Monday? That should give me plenty of time to arrange things here at the restaurant."

"Monday sounds good, Ed. In fact, Dr. Kesre suggested Monday himself. Of course, you'll have to make your flight arrangements on short notice, but that shouldn't be a problem if you fly first class. I'll call Al as soon as you get all the details worked out here."

"I'll take care of everything tomorrow," replied Eduardo.

* * * * * * *

The Resurrection of The King

CHAPTER TEN
Austin: Mid May 1977

When Eduardo arrived inside the terminal at Mueller Municipal Airport in Austin, Dr. Kesre was dutifully waiting at Northwest Airline's incoming flights gate. Kesre, at 5 feet 10, weighed a trim 173 pounds, a fitting testimonial to his daily workout routine. Although appearing to be younger, he would nonetheless be celebrating his 39th birthday on June 19th. Wearing faded jeans, a buckskin vest, and a white ten-gallon hat with a large red feather in its band, it's doubtful that Al Kesre's outrageous outfit was selected for anything other than quick recognition. It's even more doubtful that anyone in the terminal would have guessed that Kesre was one of Austin's most prominent reconstructive surgeons.

"Dr. Kesre?" asked Eduardo as he walked down the ramp.

"Yes, and you must be Eduardo. Welcome to Austin. Here, let me help you with that luggage. Dr. Kaye tells me that you're from Philadelphia, too."

"Well not originally, Dr. Kesre. I was actually born in Naples . . in Italy. We moved to South Philadelphia when I was a young boy," replied Eduardo as they headed out the terminal towards the airport's VIP parking lot. "After my father opened an Italian restaurant near Broad and Passyunk, he bought a home in the Girard Estates near 21st and Shunk, just off Oregon Avenue."

By now, they had reached Dr. Kesre's silver Rolls Royce. "I think I know where that is, Eduardo. I grew up in a little town in Delaware County just west of Philadelphia . . in Aldan. It's between Collingdale and Clifton Heights, if you know the area. Most of the guys in my neighborhood would drive down to *Pat's Steak*s in South Philly as soon as they got their driver's licenses. By the way, is *Pat's* still there?" asked

Austin: Mid May 1977

Dr. Kesre as he pulled the Rolls out of the parking lot. "I haven't been down to that area since I graduated from medical school."

"Yeah, it's still there. I used to go to *Pat's* a couple of times each week, usually after I finished one of my gigs in the local singles bars. *Pat's* was always open for the after hours crowd . . you know . . after the bars had closed."

"Yeah, *Pat's* was definitely the *in-spot*," quipped Dr. Kesre. "Did Dr. Kaye ever tell you what we did when we were about twelve? Larry, who I've known since Kindergarten . . . well, we decided to ride our bicycles down to Philadelphia International Airport . . all the way from Aldan. It must have been more than seven miles each way, and we didn't get home until after eight o'clock that night, well after dinner time. We never told anyone where we were going, especially our parents. If we had, they wouldn't have let us go. Any way, when we didn't return by dinner time, they were worried sick . . thought we were in an accident or something worse. I could be a pretty wild kid in those days, and Larry's mother thought I was a bad influence on her son. 'Some day, you'll get into *real* trouble if you keep hanging around that Al Kesre,' Larry told me she said the next day. Of course . . we still kept hanging around together."

"But did he?" asked Eduardo.

"Did he what?" replied Dr. Kesre.

"Did Larry get into trouble?" inquired Eduardo.

"No, he was a pretty straight arrow in spite of my influence. For some strange reason though, I got along pretty well with his father, and I know he liked me . . in spite of how Mrs. Kaye felt. Our paths would sometimes cross while I was on my way to school in the morning and he was walking to the Clifton-Aldan train station. Mr. Kaye always had something nice to say to me." added Dr. Kesre.

"Well, I guess it just goes to show that you can't be disliked by everyone, even when it comes to *both* of someone else's parents."

"Yeah, isn't that the truth? Incidentally, Dr. Kaye mentioned something about you wanting to be an Elvis impersonator."

"Actually, I've been doing Elvis impersonations for over twenty years. I won a number of contests, including the Greater Philadelphia finals twice, even before I came to Memphis. One reason I moved to Tennessee was because of its reputation for attracting some of the best Elvis impersonators in the country. It's always been a dream of mine to compete in the big contest held in Nashville each year. Besides, I wanted to combine an Italian restaurant with a night club, and Memphis seemed like a good location to try it, especially since Elvis lived there. I could also do my Elvis act in my own place whenever I wanted to. I've already entered several contests in the Memphis area, but I just can't seem to win over the judges. Dr. Kaye thinks it might have something to do with my not looking enough like Elvis. When I mentioned plastic surgery, he recommended you, Dr. Kesre. He said you're the best there is."

"Well, I certainly appreciate Larry's vote of confidence. I think we can do something about that nose of yours, and with a few minor changes to your cheekbones and lips, you'll look enough like Elvis that you'll be making it to the finals before you know it. Of course, there's something else you'll have to do, too."

"What's that, Dr. Kesre?"

"You'll have to let your hair and sideburns grow *much* longer. In that respect, you look more like Elvis did when he was in Army basic training." replied Dr. Kesre with a chuckle.

"That should be easy enough," replied Eduardo. "I just won't cut my hair for awhile, and as for the longer sideburns, I won't shave as high."

"That will help a lot, Eduardo. Dr. Kaye also tells me you have a terrific

Austin: Mid May 1977

Elvis voice . . that you sound so much like him that a blind man would have trouble telling the difference."

"Thank Dr. Kaye for the kind words, Dr. Kesre. I need all of the encouragement I can get. The competition in the Memphis area is incredible. Just about everyone sounds like Elvis, and most of the serious competitors even look like him, too. I'm finding that just sounding like Elvis doesn't really cut it, at least in Memphis. I can only imagine what it must be like in Nashville."

"And you can add Texas and Louisiana to that list too," added Dr. Kesre. "Elvis was very popular down here, even before he went into the Army. He used to perform with Johnny Cash and Buddy Holly on the *Louisiana Hayride*. On one occasion, he sold out the Astrodome for a solid week, and that's no small feat since it holds more than 50,000 people. Changing the subject for a moment, Eduardo, there is something Larry forgot to mention."

"What's that, Dr. Kesre?"

"In addition to the reconstructive surgery, you should probably have your teeth capped so you'll have more of an Elvis-looking smile. When Elvis had some crown work done last year, Larry asked me if I knew anyone. I recommended Dr. Antonio Paganini, perhaps the premier cosmetic dental surgeon in the world. Paganini moved to Austin from Brazil about three years ago, and we've collaborated on a number of patients. Believe it or not, working just from x-rays and impressions, Paganini can literally duplicate someone else's teeth . . but in another person's mouth. He pioneered the procedure to accommodate some wealthy Brazilians who wanted to have the same teeth and smile as their favorite celebrities."

"Are you putting me on, Dr. Kesre?"

"No, I'm serious, Eduardo. Anyway, after Paganini completed Elvis' dental work, he made impressions of his new *permanent* bridges. From those same impressions, he could actually duplicate Elvis' teeth . . in *your* mouth. I've taken the liberty to make an appointment for you to see Paganini tomorrow for an evaluation. If he were to do the procedure on *you,* Eduardo, no one would be able to tell the difference between your teeth and smile . . and Elvis'. Incidentally, I've made reservations for you at a local hotel where all of my out-of-town patients stay. I'm sure you'll find the accommodations quite comfortable."

A few days later, while the Kesre's two daughters were in school, Al, Terry, and Eduardo gathered in the family room. "How about performing one of your Elvis numbers for us, Eduardo. Terry and I would love to hear you sing."

"But I didn't bring my guitar, Dr. Kesre."

"Terry plays the guitar," replied Al, glancing over towards his wife.

"I'll get the guitar, honey. It's up in the attic."

Terry Kesre, a trim, blue-eyed blonde of medium height, appeared to look much younger than her 38 years. After more than fifteen years of marriage, she could almost read Al's mind, and before he could even ask her to get the guitar, she was on her way to the attic. Several minutes later, she returned and handed the guitar to Eduardo. It was a Martin, one of the world's finest, and it was in remarkably good condition.

"Where did you get this Terry? I haven't seen one like this in years."

"It was a gift from my parents when I graduated from high school," replied Terry. "I was really into folk music then, long before it became mainstream. In West Virginia where I grew up, it was almost a tradition to sing folk music. It must be in our genes."

Eduardo started strumming on the strings. For a 20-year old guitar, it was still in remarkably good condition, but understandably, badly out of tune.

Austin: Mid May 1977

After readjusting the tension in the guitar's strings, Eduardo started playing some basic chords.

"I think this will do just fine, Terry," he remarked. "What would you folks like to hear?"

"I'm kind of a spiritual person," replied Terry. "I never did care much for Elvis' early music, except for his ballads. I was more partial to his gospel music, but I also enjoyed his country recordings, too."

"How about *Bridge Over Troubled Waters,*" asked Eduardo. "I've been working on it for my next contest."

"That's one of my favorites," replied Terry. "I remember when Simon and Garfunkle first recorded it. Actually, I like Elvis' version better."

"Me too," replied Eduardo. "When Elvis sang it at Madison Square Garden, Simon and Garfunkle were in the audience. They loved it and they told Elvis so at the party he had afterwards. What could be a better compliment? Any way, here goes:"

"When you're weary . . . feelin' small . . . when tears are red . . . your eyes . . ."

"Eduardo . . . that's beautiful. I'd swear I was listening to Elvis himself," remarked Terry. "You'll definitely have to perform that one in your next contest. I think the audience will love it, and it should certainly get the attention of those judges."

"I sure hope you're right, Terry. Now it's your turn," as Eduardo handed her the guitar.

* * * * * * *

"Eduardo, you'll have to be a little more patient," remarked Dr. Kesre

The Resurrection of The King

over the telephone. "It's only been ten days since the surgery. I don't want to remove the bandages for another few days. I know how anxious you are to see the results, and so am I. We reconstructive surgeons are just as interested in the outcome of our work as our patients are, maybe even more so.

Finally, the big day arrived. Eduardo reached the Kesre residence shortly after 9 AM, and you could sense his nervousness. As soon as Dr. Kesre finished his cup of coffee, he got up from the kitchen table. "Let's go back to my office where we can see what you look like."

Back in the well-lit surroundings of his clinic, Dr. Kesre methodically began snipping away at Eduardo's bandages. Finally, he removed the last layer, staring intently at his latest creation. His face was nearly expressionless.

"Is everything okay?" inquired Eduardo with a hint of concern in his voice.

Dr. Kesre leaned down and began inspecting Eduardo as if he were appraising a rare document for authenticity. "I think everything will turn out just fine, but we still have to remove the sutures and allow for the swelling to go down before we'll know for sure. That could take another week, maybe ten days. Here's a mirror, Ed. Take a look for yourself."

"My God! Look how swollen my face is, Dr. Kesre . . . and look at all of those stitches. I sure don't look like I did before, but I can't say that I look much like Elvis, either."

"It's a little too early for *you* to tell, Eduardo, but I think you'll certainly at least *resemble* Elvis. Your lips and cheekbones turned out pretty good, and your nose looks just like Elvis' nose in the pictures Dr. Kaye sent me. Let's not form any judgments too soon. There's still a little more healing to take place and the swelling has to come down considerably

Austin: Mid May 1977

more. At least I can remove some of the sutures now. I really do think you'll be pleased with the way things turn out," continued Dr. Kesre, "but we won't know for sure for at least another week or ten days. At that time, we can decide if we need to do another procedure."

* * * * * * *

Ten days later, Dr. Kesre, Terry, and Eduardo gathered in the clinic. After removing the gauze, Al inspected his patient again, but this time, a broad smile lit up his face, as Terry moved around to get a better look.

"Oh . . my . . God!" exclaimed Terry with astonishment. "Al, you've outdone yourself. I can't believe who I'm looking at. If I didn't know better, I'd swear that Elvis Presley was sitting right here in our clinic. Here Eduardo, see for yourself." as Terry handed him the mirror.

Eduardo stared at his face for what seemed like an eternity. "It's unbelievable." replied Eduardo with equal astonishment. "I really do look like Elvis. Dr. Kesre, you're simply incredible!"

The operation was a stunning success. Al Kesre, usually restrained by self-imposed modesty at times like these, was truly pleased with his work. "Elvis, I'm inclined to agree with you. You certainly do look like yourself."

Everybody laughed, probably as much out of a sense of relief as from Dr. Kesre's pun.

* * * * * * *

Several weeks had passed since Dr. Paganini had completed his dental reconstruction, duplicating Elvis' teeth. At Al's request, Eduardo returned to the Kesre residence for one final inspection.

"Eduardo, when you get back to Memphis, you may have to rethink your original plan for going back to work. You look entirely too much like Elvis, especially after the dental work. In the meantime, we'll have to come up with a disguise for your return flight. The way you look now, you'd never get past the ticket counter. Incidentally, I was talking to Dr. Kaye last night, and he thinks it would be a good idea if you stayed at *his* house when you returned. He doesn't want anyone in Memphis to know that you're back in town, at least not yet."

* * * * * * *

Graceland: Early July 1977

CHAPTER ELEVEN
Graceland: Early July 1977

"Thanks for coming over for dinner tonight, Larry. I sure hope you have an appetite. We're having ribs, *Texas* style. I hear they use a very distinctive barbecue sauce down there, but between you and me, I think they just add some extra chili pepper. Not too hot, mind you, but certainly warm enough to get your attention."

"Ribs sound just fine, Elvis. I haven't had them in a long time. I've probably been spending too much time at *Eduardo's* eating his veal parmesan and spaghetti."

Approaching the dining room table, Elvis continued, "I don't think you ever met my Aunt Delta, Larry. She's my Daddy's sister, and she's been like a mother to me ever since Mama died. Aunt Delta, this is my good friend, Dr. Kaye. We've known each other since my Army days in Germany."

"I'm so pleased to meet you, Dr. Kaye," replied Aunt Delta.

"I'm happy to meet you, too . . can I call you Delta? And it's good to see you, Vernon," continued Dr. Kaye, nodding towards the elder Presley. "I don't get much of a chance to get up here now that Elvis and I spend so much time horseback riding in the back. And please . . call me Larry."

"It's hard for me to call a doctor by his first name, Dr. Kaye," replied Aunt Delta . . "I mean Larry. There, I already did it. And please call me Delta. I've heard so much about you from Elvis. At times like these, it's nice that he has such a good friend like you . . a friend he can trust," she replied emphatically, looking directly towards Elvis.

"I have to agree with Delta, Elvis," replied the elder Presley.

The Resurrection of the King

Immediately after dinner, Elvis and Larry went downstairs to the TV room and resumed their conversation from this morning.

"Elvis, as I was saying when we were horseback riding earlier today, from what I've been reading in the medical literature, you're displaying, at least to me, some of the classic symptoms of manic-depression."

"Yes, you mentioned that, Larry. What the hell is manic-depression?"

"It's like being on an emotional roller coaster, Elvis. When you're in the depressed state where you are now, there's a tendency to magnify everything negative out of all proportion. Sometimes you'll ruminate, that is, you'll keep thinking about things that happened in the past . . especially things that you think you should have done differently . . or not at all. When you're manic, it's just the opposite. At times you feel invincible. No one can tell you what to do, and you don't take constructive criticism very well. What you're thinking and feeling now and under the present circumstances, well it could be quite normal for someone who has gone through what *you* have in the past year . . Priscilla, who you're still in love with, turning you down when you tried to reconcile, plus the realization sinking in about the loss of that costarring role Barbra Streisand offered you in *A Star is Born*, the role that The *Colonel* said wouldn't be good for you. Few people can handle *big* setbacks like those at the same time."

"But Larry, it's not just 'Cilla or The Colonel or even the loss of that part in Barbra's movie that's depressing me now. I've been gettin' a lot of death threats recently and to be quite honest, they're scarin' the hell out of me. I'm really worried about Lisa Marie, too."

"You never told me about any of the death threats, Elvis. And it wasn't just that one role in *A Star is Born* that The Colonel turned down. I did a little investigating and discovered that there were several other movie roles offered you that The Colonel turned down. . . damn fine dramatic roles . . . in movies that turned out to be big hits at the box office . . . the

Graceland: Early July 1977

kind of scripts you always wanted, Elvis. You didn't tell me about those *other* movie roles that were offered you."

"I guess I just forgot to, Larry. Or maybe I just didn't want to admit it . . even to myself. But you know full well that The Colonel always handled the business arrangements. When he found out what type of parts I'd be playing in those movies, well, he didn't think they would be very good for my image . . . or my career."

"That may have been true in the late sixties for the *Joe Buck* role in *Midnight Cowboy,* Elvis, but it certainly wasn't true for *West Side Story* with Natalie Wood. I often wondered if John Voight would have had the successful movie career he had if The Colonel hadn't turned down the *Joe Buck* part when it was first offered to you. He may never have gotten the starring role in the remake of *The Champ."*

"Come on, Larry, John Voight is one hell of an actor. He would have been a big star without those two roles" replied Elvis with genuine conviction.

"Perhaps," continued Dr. Kaye, "but when I heard that Colonel Parker also turned down roles offered you in *Splendor in the Grass,* another movie costarring Natalie Wood; *Thunder Road,* with a part written specifically for you by Robert Mitchum; and the part that Steve McQueen played in *Baby The Rain Must Fall,* I had to wonder if The Colonel had taken leave of his senses. But after some additional checking, Elvis, it became quite apparent why he turned down those roles."

"And why was that, Larry? inquired Elvis with a noticeable hint of annoyance in his voice."

"For the most part Elvis, they were dramatic roles. Other than *A Star is Born* and *West Side Story,* there would have been little or no singing on your part. Without Elvis Presley singing, there would be no soundtrack

The Resurrection of the King

albums for The Colonel. And without those soundtrack albums, The Colonel couldn't keep ripping you off."

"What do you mean, *keep ripping me off?* The Colonel would *never* do . . he'd never do that . . not to me," stammered Elvis, by now visibly upset.

"Elvis, it was common knowledge in the record industry. I thought you and The Colonel had worked out the terms together."

"Worked out the terms? What terms are you talking about, Larry?" continued a very annoyed Elvis. "When The Colonel said that something wouldn't be good for my career, I always believed him. I'm sure The Colonel knew what he was doing, Larry, and I'm sure he knew what was best for my career. I mean, after all, he made me what I am. We were . . . *partners!"*

"Partners? I thought he was your *manager!* Managers only get 10 to 15 percent of their client's earnings . . not 50 percent! You certainly weren't partners in the usual sense, either. The Colonel was getting *more* than half of your record business, and almost 80 percent of your tour merchandise, you know, all those Elvis trinkets sold at your concerts. That amounted to millions of dollars over the years, Elvis . . millions of dollars that you may not have seen one dime of. But do you want to know the *real* reason why Colonel Parker didn't want you to have the costarring role in *A Star is Born*, the role that went to Kris Kristofferson?"

"Just like The Colonel said, Larry, it wouldn't have been good for my career."

"But it would have been perfect for your *movie* career, Elvis. Look what it did for Kris Kristofferson. And Elvis, if the truth be known, it wasn't The Colonel who nixed the deal. It was Barbra, and she had good reason to. Not only did The Colonel insist that you get top billing in the movie, but he wanted half the gross, too. And he most certainly would have

Graceland: Early July 1977

wanted to control the music. Remember, Barbra Streisand had won an *Academy Award* and a couple of *Grammys*. Your movie career, at least in 1976 when Barbra offered you the part, wasn't exactly setting the world on fire. You hadn't had a Number One hit in years. Just reverse the situation, Elvis. What if it was *you* who was producing the movie, and it was *your* money paying for it? What if it was *you* who won an *Oscar?* Would *you* have given Barbra Streisand top billing and half the gross? I seriously doubt it. And The Colonel certainly wouldn't have, either. Knowing him, he probably would've told Barbra to take a hike back to Brooklyn if *she* had demanded what he had."

"That bastard! And to think that Barbra was going to pay me two and a half million bucks. She actually came up to my hotel suite in Las Vegas and personally offered me the part. But that's the first time I heard *your* reason why The Colonel didn't want me to be in Barbra's movie. And Larry, I honestly don't know if I received any money for those concert souvenirs. Did you check this out with Daddy?" asked Elvis, who by now was trying very hard to control his anger.

"Yes, I did, Elvis. Vernon wasn't sure if he ever received any money *just* for the sale of the concert items. In fact, he wasn't even aware that you *had* such an agreement with The Colonel. Remember, Vernon was not a trained accountant. I suspect that there may have been a *number* of sideline deals with Parker that only you and he knew about. But that raises another question. What do you *really* know about *The Colonel?* I mean, do you even know where he's from, who he's managed, what his customary agent fees were . . *before* you met him?"

"What the hell does it matter where he's from, Larry? He used to manage Eddy Arnold, and I think he's from West Virginia. But I've also heard he's a foreigner. So what?"

"Elvis, Colonel Parker is not from West Virginia. And there was some real bad blood between him and Arnold when they parted ways. West

The Resurrection of the King

Virginia? Why . . the Colonel isn't even an American citizen! His name isn't really Tom Parker, nor is he a retired *military* Colonel. He's just an *honorary* Colonel . . a title he gave himself just to impress people. And another thing, Elvis. Parker's real name is Andreas Cornelius van Kuijk. He was born in Holland on June 26, 1909. I've even been told that he's an illegal alien. If that's true, and I have every reason to believe that it is, why do you think he didn't want you to tour outside of the United States? I'll tell you why, Elvis. He was afraid he might be deported when he went through customs. That's why he didn't want you to go to England where you are extremely popular. I also heard that Prince Charles wanted you to perform in his annual charity benefit concert in London. Knowing you, Elvis, you probably would have jumped at the opportunity . . if The Colonel had only told you about the invitation."

"How could The Colonel do this to me, Larry? How could he deceive me for all these years? Why didn't I just listen to my mama? She never trusted The Colonel. The more I think it about it, I'd just like to crawl into a hole and die. I don't care so much about the money, Larry, or even if The Colonel *is* a foreigner. What the hell, I've always had plenty of money. But I find his deception about all those movie roles so unbearable that I'd like to kill the son of a bitch. He knew damn well how I felt about those pictures I did in the sixties. And he sure as hell knew that I wanted better dramatic parts. Christ, the whole world knew that."

"You'd really like to *kill* The Colonel, Elvis?"

"Oh, you know I wouldn't do that Larry, but I might like to hang him by his balls. Christ, after hearing what you just told me, I don't much care whether I live or die. To think that for all these years, The Colonel has been deceivin' me. I'll never get those movie offers again," replied Elvis. "Larry . . I swear that if I could just disappear, I'd do it in a heartbeat. That's how bad I feel."

"You don't really mean that, do you?" inquired Dr. Kaye in a much sterner tone. "I mean . . the part where you don't care if you live or die.

Graceland: Early July 1977

That could be a problem, Elvis. Tell me . . . have you ever wanted to . . . take your own life?"

"Do you mean . . have I ever wanted to commit suicide, Larry? Well yes, to be perfectly honest . . once or twice."

"Are you taking any medications other than those uppers and downers that your Las Vegas doctor has been giving you?"

"Pain killers, sleeping pills, and I have to take them Larry. I couldn't make it through any of my performances without them. And how did you find out about my Las Vegas doctor?"

"I have my sources," replied Dr. Kaye. "Listen Elvis. You've got to stop taking those drugs. They're contributing to your depression, and sooner or later, they're going to kill you. But there is one drug I *do* want you to take. I don't think you can risk another OD, and you know what I'm talking about. You've overdosed a couple of times since I've been at Baptist Memorial. What the hell do you think I do there? I'm in the Emergency Room, for Christ's sake! I knew all about John Burroughs long before your daddy called me in the E. R. that time and asked me to go see you. Surely you remember that. It was the time you had food poisoning."

"Yeah, I remember. But the Las Vegas doctor? Christ, can't anybody keep their word? He told me that nobody would find out, and after all those precautions he was supposed to take. So what's this drug you want me to take, Larry?"

"It's called lithium carbonate, Elvis, and it's very effective in treating manic-depression. I have a colleague who is a psychiatrist, one of my classmates at Vanderbilt, Dr. Buck Lane. He practices complementary medicine as well as Jungian psychiatry. He also studied ancient Chinese medicine, and he said it really opened his mind to the possibilities of curing people's ills without totally depending on narcotics, the ones that we're so quick to use in this country, and the ones that you're *abusing*."

The Resurrection of the King

"Abusing narcotics, Larry? I'm not abusing nothin'! I only take what the doctors prescribe for me."

"I'll get back to that one later, Elvis. Let me tell you something about lithium carbonate. Think of it as having a similar structure, at least chemically, as bicarbonate of soda. Instead of the *metallic* part of the compound being sodium, it's lithium. Yes, sodium and lithium are metals. Administered in therapeutic doses, doses that have to be monitored very closely, it's had miraculous effects on people suffering from manic-depression. I truly believe it can help you, Elvis. Let's face it, if you *need* all of those prescription drugs you're taking, you have a drug problem."

"I don't understand all this chemistry stuff, Larry, but since you feel so strongly about this lithium, I'll give it a try. What do I have to lose, especially if it helps me get out of this depression?"

"I'm glad you feel that way, Elvis. But it's not an overnight cure. It may take several weeks before you even begin to feel better. Dr. Lane has been very successful in treating people with a drug dependency, and I think he can help you, too. I want you to see him as soon as possible about this lithium. I'll give him a call first thing in the morning. I'm sure he'll be able to see you at Graceland, perhaps tomorrow evening."

"Okay Larry, what you're saying makes a lot of sense. I'm certainly willing to at least *talk* to Dr. Lane . . as long as he can come to Graceland."

"You won't regret it, Elvis. You've got to give this lithium carbonate some serious thought. It seems to work for most people who take it, and there's a good likelihood that it will work for you too."

"You're making me feel better already, Larry. I'll see Dr. Lane tomorrow night. Besides, I'm gettin' kind of low on options."

"Elvis, the lithium carbonate . . it will only provide *part* of the solution.

Graceland: Early July 1977

Clearing up your depression and reducing your dependency on prescription drugs is bound to improve your health and make you feel much better, but it won't eliminate *all* of your problems, and it certainly won't do anything about those death threats."

"Well, after what you told me about The Colonel, Larry, he's one of my problems, too . . . maybe my biggest problem. I could never trust him again."

"Why don't you just buy out The Colonel's contract?"

"Larry . . even with The Colonel's immigration problems, he's still mercenary enough to want to fight me in court, and I just don't have the stomach to go through all of that nonsense. But the death threats are getting to be my biggest concern, because quite frankly . . they're making me paranoid. And who knows, they may even go after Lisa Marie out in California where I can't protect her."

"I can truly understand why you might want to put this all behind you, Elvis, and in your situation, maybe disappearing is not such a bad idea. You haven't lived anything resembling a normal life in over twenty years. But actually disappearing is a giant step to take. Are you absolutely certain you want to . . . to start a new life . . even if it means having a new identity . . and putting your career behind you?"

"Yes." replied Elvis emphatically. "I really want to."

"Well then, I have an idea that I'd like to run by you, so hear me out," continued Dr. Kaye. "With these death threats you've been receiving and your intense feelings of anger towards The Colonel, it makes even more sense that you back away from things. But I must warn you, Elvis. What I have in mind is pretty far out."

"What exactly did you have in mind, Larry?"

The Resurrection of the King

"Elvis, I have a friend I want you to meet. He owns a restaurant . . right here in Memphis. His name is Eduardo Pirelli, and get this, Elvis. He does an impersonation of you . . in his own restaurant. When I tell you he sounds just like you Elvis, I mean he sounds . . . just . . . like . . . you!"

"Am I missing something, Larry? I mean . . why would I want to meet this Pirelli fella?"

"Elvis, during World War II, there was a British General by the name of Montgomery. To confuse the Germans, the British high command hired an actor who looked remarkably like Montgomery. This actor would travel around England to create the impression that Montgomery was anywhere but in North Africa planning and leading his war effort against the Nazi's Afrika Corps. Wherever this actor went, you can bet there were film crews recording his every move . . and showing those films in every movie theater in England . . . a country where German spies had been firmly entrenched for years."

"I remember seeing a movie about that on the troop ship when I went over to Germany. But what does General Montgomery have to do with Eduardo Pirelli, Larry?"

"Eduardo Pirelli just underwent plastic surgery so he'd have more of an edge in those Elvis impersonation contests he enters. He thought he'd have a much better chance of winning if he looked more like you, Elvis. Any way, I just spoke with his reconstructive surgeon down in Austin, a Dr. Alan Kesre. I've known Al since we were kids, and he tells me that the surgery was a stunning success, well beyond even *his* expectations. According to Dr. Kesre, Eduardo is now a virtual dead ringer for you, Elvis. Were it not for his shorter hair and sideburns, and they'll grow longer, your daddy would have trouble telling you two apart."

"Okay, so Pirelli looks like me and he sounds like me . . . wait a minute, Larry. Are you thinking what I think you're thinking?"

"I don't know what *you* think I'm thinking, Elvis, but *I* was thinking that

Graceland: Early July 1977

maybe we could pull off a Montgomery, so to speak."

"You mean this Pirelli guy would be my double?" inquired Elvis incredulously. "What does *he* think about the idea?"

"I've already discussed it with him, Elvis, and he's all for it, but he's still down in Austin doing R & R. Besides, what performer wouldn't give his eye teeth to play the most famous entertainer in the world? Remember, he's already been doing impersonations of you several nights a week at his own restaurant, and that was *before* the plastic surgery. Of course, you'd have to brief him on what it's *really* like to be Elvis Presley, and he'd have to know, by sight, virtually everyone *you* know. He's already mastered your Memphis accent for his nightly act, and when he sings, he sounds just like you. In short, Eduardo Pirelli would have to pull off what Monty's double did during World War II, but with one big difference."

"And what's that, Larry?"

"The British military hierarchy knew all about Monty's double. It was their idea. Remember, he only had to fool a relatively few people when he was appearing in public . . . the German spies in England, Hitler, and members of the Third Reich's high command. But the Germans didn't have to meet him face to face, and they didn't have to live with him. Eduardo, on the other hand, will have to fool his fans *plus* everyone at Graceland, especially Ginger."

"And don't forget Lisa Marie, 'Cilla, and Dr. Nick," replied Elvis. "They certainly come to Graceland, too."

"I know it won't be easy, Elvis, but knowing how quick a study Eduardo is, I think after he has a sufficient number of rehearsals with you, Vernon, and me for several weeks, he can pull this off. Remember, your daddy is going to be with Eduardo whenever he's at Graceland and on tour,

The Resurrection of the King

except, of course, when he's alone with Ginger. He'll be like Eduardo's life line . . able to bail him out of situations that are bound to arise . . simple things like forgetting someone's name, what they do, or where he knows them from."

"When can I meet this Eduardo fella, Larry? You're gettin' my hopes so high that I'm beginning to believe that you're really on to something."

"Next week . . . at my home in Germantown. Fortunately, my wife and kids are visiting her sister in Louisville for several weeks, so we'll have the house to ourselves. Eduardo will be staying with me when he returns from Austin in a couple of days, so no one will even know he's back in Memphis, and certainly no one will know about the plastic surgery. He isn't scheduled to return to work for several weeks, and that's if he *does* return to work at all. Dr. Kesre made a powerful argument against Eduardo *ever* returning to his restaurant in Memphis, since he's a virtual dead ringer for you, Elvis. That gives us some additional time to review films and photos of everyone who lives, works or visits Graceland, as well as members of your band."

"But what happens after that, Larry? Surely they'll be expecting him back at the restaurant at some point in time, won't they?"

"That's going to be taken care of, Elvis. After Eduardo has switched places with you, Dr. Kesre is going to send a fax from Austin, under the name of Eduardo, to Joe Genuardi, his assistant manager, saying that he found a restaurant for sale in Austin, and he's going to buy it. Since he won't be coming back to Memphis for several months, Genuardi will be offered the opportunity to *manage* the Memphis restaurant until the new one in Austin is up and running. According to the rest of the cover story, that may not be for six months to a year. A month or so after that, Eduardo will have allegedly met his former girl friend from Philadelphia. They decided to get married and remain in Austin, since she's a tenured professor at the University of Texas. Joe will then be offered the opportunity to *buy* Eduardo's Memphis restaurant."

Graceland: Early July 1977

"Okay Larry, but I have another question. Shouldn't someone else besides Dr. Kesre, Daddy and you know about the switch? I mean, surely Joe Esposito and Larry Geller should be told. They're the two people I trust most around here."

"Not at this time, Elvis, but maybe sometime in the future. The whole world will have to believe that Eduardo Pirelli is Elvis Presley. And that includes Esposito and Geller, too."

"What about Dr. Nick and The Colonel, Larry? And how about Lisa Marie? Surely my own daughter should know."

"Perhaps when she gets older, you can start sending her presents. You don't have to identify yourself at first, but you can gradually lead into that when you feel she's mature enough to keep a secret. But Dr. Nick and The Colonel positively shouldn't be told. The fewer people who know about this, the better chance you'll have of pulling it off. There are just too many people who depend upon you for their living. They might try to talk you out of it, or let something slip out later on. Perhaps one of them would fall on hard times. They might go to the newspapers or even *Sixty Minutes*. Worse yet, they could even write one of those tell-all books."

"That never occurred to me, Larry, but you're probably right." And you're certainly right about The Colonel. But why can't I tell Joe? I've known him since the Army, and I trust him completely."

"Look, Elvis, I know how close you are to Joe and Larry, but you have to have faith that Vernon and Joe can handle any problems that come up, especially any financial decisions that have to be made. They already do some of that. Besides, some things should be kept in the immediate family. You can always tell Joe and Larry about the switch, even 'Cilla, at some time in the future."

"Well, now . . just suppose . . and I'm not saying I'm going along with your idea, Larry . . but just suppose I agree to go through with this. What's the next step?"

"First of all, we have to thoroughly prepare Eduardo. He has to learn as much about you and the people around you as he possibly can, and he has to know those people by sight. Fortunately, he knows your music, so doing your concerts won't be too much of a problem. We'll have him studying video tapes and films of your past concerts until he knows your various acts inside out and backwards. He'll have to practice your mannerisms and speech patterns until he can do them flawlessly. He'll have to learn how *you* behave when you're around Ginger, Dr. Nick, Joe, Larry, your step brothers, Aunt Delta, Lisa Marie . . everyone at Graceland. And don't forget your band, your background singers . . particularly the *Sweet Inspirations* and Kathy Westmoreland. As soon as we've all reached a confidence level that Eduardo can pull this off, you can pick a convenient time to make the switch. The decision about *when* to make the switch is one that only you can make, Elvis."

"Okay, I agree with you as far as *when* I decide the switch will be made, Larry. And Daddy can always tell the band that Eduardo's on this new medication if he forgets something or someone. But I still don't understand *how* we're going to make the switch."

"Elvis, I've been here at Graceland often enough to see what goes on around here, at least outside. One thing I've noticed when we're horseback riding is that from time to time, a laundry truck comes into Graceland, and it's always in the morning when I see it. I thought all of the laundry was done here at Graceland, Elvis?"

"Not our outfits, Larry. Every time we return from a tour, and sometimes before we go out on another one . . me, the band, the singers, we all have to have our outfits dry cleaned. And we always try them on just before we leave . . to make sure they fit properly."

"When's your next tour?"

Graceland: Early July 1977

"Well, Lisa Marie will be coming to Graceland in a few weeks, and we'll be going out on a short tour to the midwest in early August. Then there's Portland, Maine on . . let me think . . on August 16th or 17th. And I think we have something scheduled for September. The dry cleaner will be making a number of deliveries between now and September."

"Where does the driver park the truck when he's making the delivery, and what does he do with *your* clean outfits, Elvis?"

"He parks in the driveway, in front of the main entrance, and he gives the outfits to Aunt Delta. She then carries my outfits upstairs to my dressing room so I can try them on when I wake up. Al then packs them away for the next tour. The driver puts everyone else's outfits on the living room sofa. If there are too many of *my* outfits for Aunt Delta to carry up by herself, the driver takes some of them up, too. Normally, only certain folks are allowed on the second floor, but as long as the driver is with Aunt Delta, he can go up to my dressing room."

"On the day you decide to make the switch, Elvis, why don't *you* meet Eduardo, who'll be disguised as the driver . . at the front door . . by yourself? If possible, he should try to arrive at Graceland before the normal delivery time, preferably early in the morning. It might also be best if you keep your Aunt Delta out of this, especially since you'll be switching clothes with Eduardo. It also means that we'll have to get a laundry truck that looks just like the ones that come to Graceland. A former army buddy of mine, Walt Haley, earns his living as a sign painter in Nashville. Haley and I get together for Vanderbilt's home-coming game every year. If we take some color photos of the actual trucks that come to Graceland, I'm sure Walt could easily duplicate the lettering. Of course, we'll have to buy a truck that's the same make, model, and color as the ones that come here, but that shouldn't be much of a problem."

"What if Walt wants to know why you're doing this, Larry? Duplicating the lettering of a Memphis laundry truck in *Nashville* could arouse his curiosity. He might wonder why you wouldn't have it done in Memphis."

The Resurrection of the King

"I'll tell him it's going to be a surprise birthday gift you're giving to the owner of the laundry. What the hell Elvis, you're always giving cars away. Surely you can give a hard working businessman a *van* for his birthday. And here's another advantage for doing the lettering in Nashville. Haley has a big garage where he can personally do the work without anyone being the wiser. When he's finished, I'll go back to Nashville, drive the van to my home in Germantown, and store it in one of my garages. When you decide to make the switch with Eduardo, all that *he'll* have to do is gather up your outfits, which we'll keep at my place, and put them into the van. One other thing, Elvis. Have your daddy call the owner of the dry cleaners and ask him for a driver's uniform, one that fits *you*. It should also fit Eduardo, since you two are about the same size. Vernon can tell him it's for a Halloween party you're having this fall."

"God, Larry, you've thought of everything!" exclaimed Elvis.

"I certainly hope so. And Elvis, we'd better bring Vernon up to speed on the plan, and quickly. He has to be told about the timing of the switch as soon as you make that decision. Remember, Eduardo will need all of the support he can get to pull this off convincingly, and only Vernon will be able to provide that support after the switch is made."

"I agree, Larry. I'm sure Daddy will help Eduardo in any way he can. Remember, he's not one of The Colonel's biggest fans, either."

"I suspected as much, Elvis, but I don't know how Vernon's going to react to the whole idea of you making the switch, and we'll need his cooperation. We still have to work out the details about how to let him know *when* you're going to make the switch. We'll also need a contingency plan in the event he isn't here when you make that decision."

"I can always leave a message with one of the switchboard operators."

"Sure Elvis, and what are you going to tell them? Today's the day I'm making the switch? And aren't the phones still being tapped by the police ever since you started receiving those death threats?"

Graceland: Early July 1977

"You're right, Larry. But I have private, unlisted lines in my upstairs office, bedroom, and bathroom, lines that don't go through the main switchboard, and Daddy has unlisted lines in his bedroom and office. None of those lines are tapped. It's just the main incoming lines to the switchboard. If Daddy isn't in his bedroom to answer the phone, the call just trips over to his office. If he's not in his office, the call goes back to the switchboard, just like it's any other incoming call, and he'll be paged."

"But Elvis! If the call trips back to an incoming line on the switchboard, either the Graceland operators or the police might be listening in. We should have some kind of a coded phrase that means the switch is going to take place. It's not even a good idea for *you* to be the one making the call, now that I think about it. How about if you call *me* first, and then I'll call your daddy? I'll use the phrase, *we switched gears* to mean either the switch is *going* to take place, and I'll tell him at what time . . or it just *did*. We'll need a code name for Vernon, too. How about *Big Daddy?*"

"Okay, *we switched gears* is the signal. That should be easy for Daddy to remember. And his code name will be *Big Daddy*. He'll get a kick out of that name, Larry. *Cat on a Hot Tin Roof* was one of his favorite movies."

"While we're at it, Elvis, we'll need code names for you and Lisa Marie. How about *PJ* for Lisa and *Fast Eddy* for you? And Elvis. We can pull this off. We really can. I think we'd better get together with Vernon and talk about this as soon as possible . . like tomorrow at the latest."

"Okay, Larry. I'll tell him as soon as you leave. It might be better if *you* give Daddy the details of the plan. He might try to talk *me* out of it."

"In that case, let's go over the plan with him right now, Elvis . . while it's still early. When he hears *why* and *how* you arrived at your decision, I think he'll be much more inclined to accept it."

"I'll call him now, Larry. He's probably in the Jungle Room reading or watching television."

* * * * * * *

The Resurrection of The King

CHAPTER TWELVE
Memphis: August 16, 1977, 6:15 AM CDT

"Larry, it's Elvis. Boy am I glad you haven't left the hospital yet. Today's the day!"

"Today's the day? What do you mean, *today's the day,* Elvis?"

"I want to do the switch with Eduardo today . . this morning. I'm just not up to doing this tour, Larry. To be honest, I don't even feel like going to Portland. I had to go to the dentist late last night . . no, it was really early this morning . . and I still have this toothache. To make matters worse, Ginger and I have some major differences about marriage. She seems to be having second thoughts, and I guess I'm just getting tired of her indecisiveness."

"Where are you now, Elvis? Are you calling from a secure line?"

"Yeah, I'm on the phone in my bathroom. Ginger and I just finished playing racquetball with Billy and his wife. We were sweatin' so much that Billy came back up with Ginger and me to towel off. He just left a few minutes ago. Ginger finished her shower, and she's gone to bed. Call Eduardo and let him know it's time to get this show on the road. Let me know when he can be ready. I'm going to take a quick shower now, and I'll be waiting right here for your call."

"Okay, I'll call him right away, but I don't think it's a good idea for me to call *you* back, Elvis. The ringing phone might wake up Ginger. Call me back as soon as you take your shower. And while you're at it, see if Ginger's asleep yet."

"I'll check right now, Larry. Just hang on a minute while I'll take a look into the bedroom."

Memphis: August 16, 1977, 6:15 AM CDT

Less than a minute later, Elvis was back on the phone. "She's in bed Larry, and she seems to be asleep."

"Good. We certainly wouldn't want her to be awake while the switch is taking place. What's the best time to do this, Elvis? When do you want Eduardo to arrive at Graceland?"

"In about an hour . . sometime between 7:15 and 7:30 would be perfect. If we wait too much longer, people might be coming in for breakfast. Ricky is supposed to come back up around 8:30, but after I hang up with you, I'm going to call him and tell him not to bother. I'll just tell him I don't want to get up until about 4:30. The same goes for his brother David, so I'll remind Ricky to tell David about the new wake up time. Both of them take turns keeping an eye on me to make sure I'm sleeping okay."

"What time does Ginger usually wake up, Elvis?"

"When she goes to bed this late, she doesn't usually get up until three or four in the afternoon. I'll call you back in about ten minutes, after I take my shower. If everything's okay with Eduardo, I'll get things started here at Graceland. One thing I should probably do is tell Al that I'm expecting some of my outfits to come back from the cleaners early this morning, and I want to try them on first *before* I go to bed."

"That certainly sounds like a believable reason for the laundry truck coming over this early, Elvis. Nobody should be the least bit suspicious. What about the guards at the entrance gate?"

"Oh, they're used to the laundry truck coming, Larry, although it usually doesn't get here until a little later in the morning. As soon we verify that everything's a GO with Eduardo, I'll tell the guards that I asked the laundry to make their delivery a little earlier today, probably sometime between 7:15 and 7:30. I'll tell them that the owner will be driving the

The Resurrection of The King

laundry van and they should call me on the intercom when he arrives. As soon as I hear from them, I'll go down and meet Eduardo in the driveway and help him carry the outfits back up to my dressing room. When we go upstairs, we can't talk until we get to my dressing room, or we might wake up Lisa Marie in the adjoining bedroom. Once we get to my dressing room, Eduardo can change into my pajamas, and I'll put on his driver's uniform, including the wig, mustache, and glasses. It should all take less than five minutes. I'll then carry the outfits back downstair and drop them off on the living room sofa. I'll leave a note telling Al that I don't want to be awakened until dinner time, and that he should pack the outfits away with the rest of my clothes. By the way Larry, where are *my* clothes, the stuff I'll be wearing in Austin after I get there?"

"Everything's in your suitcase, Elvis, and it's sitting in my kitchen, right next to the door that goes out to the driveway. You'll be wearing the same suit to Austin that Eduardo wore when he flew back."

"Good. After I leave Graceland, Eduardo can go to bed, hopefully without waking up Ginger. One other thing, Larry. Remind Eduardo to drive all the way up the driveway to the main entrance. I'll be waiting for him at the front door. Also be sure to tell him about my toothache and the lithium I'm taking . . and that I went to the dentist early this morning and my tooth is still bothering me. He needs to know this so he can act like *he* has a toothache. Now that I think about it, forget the part about the lithium. I'd better take it with me."

"Right. I'll tell him as soon as I call him, and yes, you'd better bring the lithium with you. I'll tell Dr. Kesre about it. You know Elvis, when we met on Sunday, I think Eduardo sensed that you wanted to make this switch pretty soon. I never dreamed that you'd want to do it *this* soon."

"Well . . it just felt like today was the best time to do it, Larry, especially with the tour. Sometimes you have to go with your gut feelings. Eduardo is very perceptive, too. That's one of the reasons why I'm so confident he can pull this off. Any way, I'd better hang up now so you can call him

Memphis: August 16, 1977, 6:15 AM CDT

back. I'd hate to see this window of opportunity close on us, Larry."

"I have to agree with you, Elvis. Call me back after you take your shower. That should give me plenty of time to brief Eduardo. And Elvis . . it sounds to me like you have things pretty much under control at your end."

"For the most part, I do Larry. But I'm still a little concerned about how Eduardo is going to deal with Lisa Marie, as well as Ginger. I was planning on tellin' him what's really goin' on between us when he arrives. Frankly, I've been having second thoughts about our relationship. The way Ginger feels now, she might not even *want* to go to Portland. But that's a bridge Eduardo will have to cross when he comes to it."

* * * * * * *

"Ed? It's Larry. I just heard from Elvis. He wants to make the switch this morning. How soon can you be ready?"

"I'm just finishing breakfast. I guess I can be ready in about 15 minutes."

Do you have the driver's uniform ready?"

"Yes. It's right here Larry. And I have the hat, too."

"And how about the glasses, wig, and mustache?"

"Yeah, they're all here, too. What time does he want me to get there?"

"Sometime between 7:15 and 7:30 . . before everyone starts coming into the kitchen for breakfast."

"That should give me plenty of time. Tell Elvis I'll there before 7:30, as long as there aren't *too* many traffic problems."

"I'll tell him, Ed. By the way, the keys to the truck are in my bedroom,

The Resurrection of The King

on top of the dresser. The outfits, the ones that were dry cleaned after Elvis returned from his last tour, I put them in the closet next to the dresser. When you arrive at Graceland's front gate, tell the guards, who'll be expecting you, to call Elvis and let him know you've arrived. Just drive up to the front door. Elvis will be waiting for you by the time you get there. Once you've parked the truck, you can both carry the outfits up to his bedroom suite."

"That sounds easy enough, Larry."

"I think it will be, unless his Aunt Delta happens to be near the front door when you arrive. But Elvis told me she should be in the kitchen getting breakfast ready, so *he* should be the only one near the front door. I'll call him back and tell him that you'll be leaving soon. Before I forget, Ed, Elvis still has a slight toothache. He went to the dentist late last night, and he thought you should know about it so you can act accordingly. If anybody asks you about it, just tell them that it's hardly bothering you at all. As for Ginger, Elvis has been having some problems with her recently about setting a wedding date, so try to be diplomatic. Don't pressure her into doing *anything,* and don't even *talk* about marriage. Try to be agreeable and give her whatever she wants, at least until after you've gotten to know her better."

"That's the way I *always* treat women, Larry. Why do you think I'm still single?"

"Because none of your girl friends ever proposed to you? Just kidding, Ed. One other thing. Those outfits that you're taking back to Graceland, were you able to try them on, because you'll be the one wearing them in Portland?"

"Yes, just yesterday, and they fit like a glove, Larry."

"How about the driver's uniform?"

"That fits, too, and the pants are just the right length."

Memphis: August 16, 1977, 6:15 AM CDT

"Good. If Elvis' *outfits* fit you like a glove, then surely the driver's uniform should fit Elvis, too. And Eduardo. Either Tish or Aunt Delta might want to give you a pain killer for the toothache along with some sleeping pills. Of course, you don't have to really take them, but you might want to go through the motions."

"Thanks for telling me, Larry. But I suspect my biggest challenges will be Ginger and Lisa Marie. I'd be less than honest if I didn't tell you I'm a little nervous about having to deal with them, especially Lisa Marie."

"You wouldn't be human if you weren't nervous under these circumstances, Ed. But I think you'll do fine. Just be yourself. We've rehearsed this dozens of times, and you were always as sharp as a tack, especially when we gave you the video test to identify everyone who comes in contact with Elvis. At least you certainly convinced Elvis that you're ready. You appeared to know just about everything there is to know about the people at Graceland. You've also been briefed about Lisa Marie's friends, Priscilla, The Colonel, Dr. Nick, most of Elvis' former girl friends, as well as the boys in the band and the background singers. Elvis thinks you remembered their faces better than he did, especially his former girl friends. And Vernon will be there to back you up in case you have a temporary lapse of memory. Remember, since you're supposed to have a tooth ache, you might not be feeling your normal self. That should help cut you a little slack . . at least in the beginning. And one last thing, Ed, did you call Joe Genuardi and tell him you wanted to open another restaurant in Austin and you'd be away for a couple of months?"

"Yes, but I forgot to tell you, Larry. I called him yesterday. He was very grateful for the opportunity to run *EDUARDO'S*. He also appreciated the big raise I gave him, too. Oh . . and I told him I probably wouldn't be coming back for a couple of months, maybe longer, until I got things up and running in Austin. Joe's very dependable, Larry. He'll do a fine job."

"Good. That gives us some more breathing room. I think that just about covers everything, Ed. Is there anything we've forgotten?"

"Yes, I have to call Genuardi to let him know I'm leaving for Austin *today*. When you talk to Elvis, tell him I'll be on my way to Graceland in a few minutes, and I should be arriving by 7:15 . . 7:30 at the latest."

"I'll tell him, Ed. And Ed. Don't forget to give Elvis your wallet. He's going to need your driver's license and credit cards when he gets to Austin. I'll give him enough cash for the airline ticket and some spending money."

"I'll remember, Larry. Wish me luck."

* * * * * * *

It was shortly after 8 AM when Eduardo woke up. He already had more than five hours' sleep when Larry first called him, and he was having trouble staying asleep. He was also feeling anxious about the prospects of dealing with Ginger and Lisa Marie. Just as Eduardo was getting out of bed, Ginger woke up. "Are you feeling all right, Elvis?" she asked.

Using the Elvis accent he'd been practicing for weeks, Eduardo replied, "I can't seem to fall asleep, darlin'. I'm going into the bathroom to do a little reading. I'll be back before you know it."

"Okay, honey. I'll be here."

* * * * * * *

Memphis: August 16, 1977, 7:30 AM CDT

CHAPTER THIRTEEN
Memphis: August 16, 1977, 7:30 AM CDT

At approximately 7:35 AM, the laundry truck left Graceland with its new driver. Turning right onto *Elvis Presley Boulevard,* Elvis leisurely headed towards the expressway. "God, I still can't believe how smoothly things went." he thought. "Aunt Delta didn't even recognize me when I came back down to the foyer. I sure hope Eduardo didn't wake up Ginger when he climbed into bed. She's such a light sleeper. Fortunately, those new pills she got for her cramps should keep her sleeping until at least two or three this afternoon."

* * * * * * *

Twenty minutes later, Elvis pulled up in front of Dr. Kaye's home in Germantown. After stopping, he looked up and down the street to see if any cars were coming. None were. He then made a hard left and drove up the long, rambling driveway, pulling to a stop behind Larry's Porsche. Fortunately, the yard was surrounded by a stand of tall southern pines, so it was virtually impossible for the neighbors to see either the van or the garages at the end of the driveway. Of equal importance, virtually everyone in the neighborhood had left for work by now, a thought that would never have occurred to Elvis since he was rarely awake, let alone driving on the streets of Memphis, at this time of the morning.

Just then, Dr. Kaye opened the kitchen door and walked down to the van. Rotating his wrist in a circular motion, he signaled Elvis to roll down the window. "That was pretty good timing. I just got back from the hospital. I'll put the van in the garage. Wait for me inside."

"Okay Larry," replied Elvis.

A few minutes later, Dr. Kaye arrived back in the kitchen and immediately headed for the wall phone located above the sink.

"Who are you calling, Larry?"

"The airport . . . operator, could you give me the listing for Memphis International Airport? Thank you." Larry quickly jotted the number down, and dialed the airport's phone number. After what seemed like an eternity, the operator finally answered.

"Memphis International Airport. How can I help you?"

"Could you tell me when the next nonstop flight to Austin, Texas departs?" inquired Dr. Kaye.

"There's a Northwest Airlines flight leaving at 11:45 this morning, Flight 889," replied the operator. "Would you like me to transfer you to Northwest?"

"Yes, please," replied Larry.

"Northwest Airlines." replied the reservations clerk.

"Are there any seats remaining on this morning's Flight 889 to Austin?" asked Dr. Kaye.

"Could you please hold for a minute?" Less than a minute later, she had her answer. "Yes sir, there are."

"How many first class seats are available?" asked Dr. Kaye.

"We have three remaining, sir. Would you like to make a reservation?" inquired the clerk.

"No, not just now. I'll have to get back to you later."

"What's going on, Larry? Why did you call the airport?" asked Elvis

Memphis: August 16, 1977, 7:30 AM CDT

with a puzzled look on his face.

"Things happened so fast that I didn't have a chance to call Dr. Kesre to let him know we made the switch and to see if he could meet you at the airport in Austin today. But I had to call the airport first to find out if there were any available seats. There are, and they have a non-stop flight. Now I have to call Al to see if he can meet that flight at the airport later this afternoon."

"God, Larry, it never occurred to me, either. We never did tell Dr. Kesre *when* I'd be making the switch, and frankly, until early this morning, I wasn't exactly sure when I would be making it, either."

"I guess today was as good a day as any as it turned out, and everything seemed to go pretty smoothly. If Dr. Kesre can't meet you at the airport today, we'll just have to try for tomorrow or the next day. After all, you can stay here for awhile if you have to. My wife and kids are still in Kentucky, and they'll be gone for at least another week. Any way, let's not get too worked up over this . . at least until I reach Dr. Kesre. I'm going to call him right now," replied Dr. Kaye as he began dialing Al's phone number."

After two rings, Dr. Kesre picked up the phone. "Dr. Kesre."

"Al, it's Larry. Christ, am I glad I was able to reach you. I have some news for you! Elvis made the switch with Eduardo about a half hour ago, and he's here with me now . . . at my home."

"Wow, that was quick! What are they going to do at the restaurant when Eduardo doesn't show up for work today? Who is going to run things?"

"That's not going to be a problem, Al. Last week, Eduardo talked to his assistant manager, Joe Genuardi, and he told him that he was opening another restaurant in Austin. He asked Joe if he would like to run *ED-*

The Resurrection of The King

UARDO'S in Memphis, and he jumped at the opportunity. Eduardo told him he might might have to stay in Austin for at least two or three months . . maybe longer, at least until he got things up and running at his new restaurant. That's going to give us a hell of a lot of breathing room, Al. Eduardo called Joe this morning before the switch, to tell him he had to leave for Austin today. Of course, he doesn't really have to leave today, but he should fly down to Austin as soon as possible. We certainly don't want two Elvis Presleys in Memphis at the same time. I just called the airport, and there's an 11:45 AM flight to Mueller Municipal. Would it be much of an inconvenience for you if Elvis came to Austin today? I really apologize for the short notice, Al."

"You really lucked out, Larry. Tuesday's my golf day, it's pouring rain, and we had to cancel our tee times. And yes, Elvis can come today. I'm sure we'll be able to meet him at the airport."

"We?" asked Dr. Kaye.

"Terry will be coming with me."

"That's great, Al. As soon as I get a confirmation on the reservation, I'll get back to you with the flight number and arrival time. By the way, where in the hell did you get that God-awful brown suit Eduardo wore back from Austin?"

"Terry bought it at one of those hospital thrift shops so I could wear it to a Halloween party. I had to stuff a few pillows in it to make me look like I was 50 pounds heavier. And Larry, with the glasses and mustache, nobody guessed it was me . . . at least not for the first ten minutes."

"What took them so long..just kidding, Al. What finally gave you away?"

"My shoes. I was wearing those funny looking white shoes that I usually wear when I operate. They're really quite comfortable, but they stick out

Memphis: August 16, 1977, 7:30 AM CDT

like a corn stalk in a cabbage patch. Somebody at the party from my surgical team recognized them, or they probably wouldn't have guessed who I was in a month of Sundays."

"I understand, Al. Listen, I have another challenge for you. Do you think you could work your surgical magic on Elvis and make him look like Eduardo Pirelli did *before* his surgery?"

"You mean look like Eduardo *used* to look?" asked Dr. Kesre. "Surely you jest, Larry."

"But Al, you transformed Eduardo into a virtual Elvis look alike, and now he's a dead ringer for Elvis. Can't you make Elvis look like Eduardo? Isn't it simply a matter of reversing the procedure with Elvis?"

"It's not quite that easy, Larry. With Elvis, we have a much more difficult problem in attempting to make him look like Eduardo. To begin with, Pirelli had thicker lips, a wider nose, and larger cheek bones. As far as reducing the size of his lips, that was the easy part. With his nose, it was only a matter of cutting away some of the bone and cartilage to make it narrower like Elvis' nose. With Eduardo's cheek bones, we only had to make them smaller, and we did that by simply *removing* some of the bone matter. It's kind of like whittling. You can carve a piece of wood into a desired shape, but you can't reverse the procedure by turning that carving back into the piece of wood you started with."

"That certainly makes sense, Al. I never thought of it quite that way," replied Dr. Kaye. "I guess we can just forget the whole idea."

"I was talking about a carving, Larry, not reconstructive surgery. It may be impossible to reverse a carving, but it's not impossible to make lips thicker, or a nose and cheekbones larger. It's a little more difficult, but not impossible. We've come a long way in the past twenty years. Today, we can use bone grafts and other inert materials to change facial features.

And we can certainly make cheek bones larger as well as higher or lower."

"Well that's encouraging," replied Dr. Kaye.

"Don't get your hopes too high, Larry. It would still require incredibly good luck for Elvis to end up looking like Eduardo. But I have to wonder why it's so important for him to look like Pirelli. I would think he'd be more than happy if he just didn't look like . . . well . . like he did *before* the surgery."

"Under normal circumstances you'd be right, Al, but everybody is expecting Eduardo to come back to the restaurant."

"I thought you said Joe Genuardi would be running things in Memphis since Eduardo was opening a new restaurant in Austin."

"I did, Al, but sooner or later Eduardo . . or Elvis . . is going to have to come back to the Memphis restaurant. If he looked like Eduardo, that is, the *old* Eduardo, well, Elvis could at least *fake* it for a day or two, especif he acted like he had a bad cold."

"Okay Larry, you make a persuasive argument." replied Dr. Kesre.

"I'm trying to Al. A lot of planning went into this."

"What about Eduardo's apartment lease? He still has to pay his rent each month. And Larry, there are other factors involved with *Elvis'* surgery. This isn't going to be a simple nip and tuck procedure. It will probably require a minimum of two, perhaps even three, separate surgical procedures. At the very least, it would take a month. And how would it change things if Elvis *didn't* end up looking like Eduardo?"

"As far as the apartment goes, Joe can pay the rent until the lease expires in September. He can also fill out a change of address form for Eduar-

Memphis: August 16, 1977, 7:30 AM CDT

do's mail using a P. O. box that can be opened for him in Austin. All of the restaurant bills will still be sent to EDUARDO'S, and Joe can continue paying them just like before. If the surgery didn't turn out such that Elvis looked just like Eduardo, we have a contingency plan. Elvis simply wouldn't come back to Memphis. In that case, we'd try to sell the restaurant to Joe, and if he didn't want it, we'd put it on the market. That could be handled by realtors and lawyers without Elvis having to come back to Memphis. Let's just pray that the surgery turns out for the best and that Elvis *does* look like Eduardo Pirelli."

"Well I'll be praying too, Larry, but there's a much greater probability that Elvis will end up looking only *somewhat* like Eduardo. Just don't be too disappointed if he doesn't look like Eduardo's identical twin brother," replied Dr. Kesre.

"I won't be, Al, but we have to be damn sure that Elvis understands all that's involved with the surgery, including the various outcomes. We certainly don't want to give him any unrealistic expectations. Colonel Parker has been doing *just* that, and for too many years."

"I have to agree with you, Larry."

"Al, I better make that reservation for Elvis before the remaining first class seats are sold, so let me hang up now. I'll call you back with the flight information in a few minutes."

"I'll be here. And Larry, be sure to give Elvis some sort of a password so we'll be sure that it's him when he arrives at the airport. Also, you might want to give him a cane. That should make it easier for us to spot him when he comes into the terminal. I'll make arrangements to get a wheelchair. What the hell, people are moved around airports all the time in wheelchairs. Besides, it can be a pretty long walk back to the parking area, especially for an elderly man walking with a cane. And Elvis *will* be looking like an elderly man, won't he Larry?"

The Resurrection of The King

"I don't know about an *elderly* man. But he'll certainly look old enough to pass for *Terry's* father. He's much too tall to be *your* father, Al."

* * * * * * *

After Dr. Kaye hung up the phone, he immediately called back Northwest Airlines. "This is Ed Pirelli. I'd like to book a one-way, first class reservation for this morning's 11:45 flight . . . Flight 889 . . . from Memphis to Austin. I'll be staying in Texas for several weeks, so I won't be able to arrange a return flight until my plans firm up. I would prefer to pay for the ticket in cash. Will that be a problem?"

"Cash is fine Mr. Pirelli," replied the reservations clerk.

As soon as he hung up, Larry called Dr. Kesre again. "Al, before I forget, do you think Terry could make some sort of a sign that would identify you to Elvis when he arrives at the terminal?"

"Sure, Larry, and we'll keep it simple . . two words . . *ELVIS PRESLEY* printed in large red letters. Just kidding, Larry. We'll have a sign with the word TERRY written on it. What time does his flight arrive?"

"About 1:30 this afternoon. It's Northwest Airline's Flight 889. And how about the password that Elvis can use when he meets Terry?"

"Just tell him to say . . . *Hello, Darlin'.*"

"*Hello Darlin'* it is. And Terry's reply should simply be, *Daddy.* I'll be sure to tell Elvis," replied Larry.

After Larry hung up, he quickly briefed Elvis about Terry's sign and the passwords they would use. Elvis then went upstairs and took a leisurely shower. After toweling off, he then put on one of his dress shirts and a pair of slacks he had packed away in his suit case. Next, he struggled to put on his tie, the same tie that Eduardo wore back from Memphis. "I

Memphis: August 16, 1977, 7:30 AM CDT

wonder if Eduardo had as much trouble putting this tie on before he flew back from Austin . . as I'm having now?"

A few minutes later, Elvis arrived back in the kitchen as Larry was preparing for the makeover process.

"Elvis, I hate to tell you this, partner, but you're going to have to take your shirt and tie off. Here, just put on this robe."

"Damn, Larry." replied Elvis half jokingly as he loosened the tie. "Do you have any idea how long it took me to put this on? Nearly ten minutes!"

"No kidding . . ten whole minutes! Well . . when you put it back on for your trip to the airport, you ought to be able to do it in five. At least that's a little progress, isn't it?"

Elvis just shook his head and sat down in the kitchen chair that Larry had moved up to the sink. As soon as he was settled, Dr. Kaye put some shaving cream on Elvis' sideburns. He then picked up the straight razor that was sitting next to the sink.

"What are you planning to do with that razor, Larry? I hope you're not shaving off my sideburns. It took me a long time to grow 'em this long?"

"Yeah, Elvis . . and just about everyone in the world would recognize you with those sideburns, even with gray hair. Besides, most *mature* gentlemen aren't buying into these modern fashion trends. The goal here is *not* to make you look like an old Elvis, but to make you unrecognizable."

"Okay, Larry," replied Elvis with an air of resignation. "I just hate to part with 'em. Other than while I was in army basic training, I've been wearing long sideburns for more than twenty-five years . . . ever since I was in high school. They're like . . well . . part of me."

"Well, you'll remember your haircuts from the army after *I* get through with you. Besides, you wouldn't want your wig to fall off."

"But I wore this wig back from Graceland with my hair longer, and it didn't fall off. Even the guards at the gate didn't recognize me."

"I know, Elvis, but you were wearing the laundry driver's hat, and that kept your wig in place. Just imagine if that wig fell off while you were at the airport ticket counter, or worse yet, on the plane. I'll just trim it a little . . just enough for the wig to stay in place."

"Well, then why don't I just wear a hat?" asked Elvis. "That would certainly solve the problem, wouldn't it?"

"I guess so. Let me see if I have one," replied Dr. Kaye.

"You do, Larry. You always wear a cowboy hat when we go horseback riding at Graceland."

"You're right. It should be in the foyer closet," replied Dr. Kaye as he started walking out of the kitchen.

Although Elvis offered only token resistance over losing any more of his hair, he begrudgingly accepted the fact that this was something that had to be done, After finishing with the hair cut, Larry put the wig back on Elvis and had him try on the cowboy hat. It fit perfectly.

"How do I look, Larry?"

Patience, Elvis. Give me another minute. I still have to touch up your sideburns with this gray coloring so they match your wig. Besides, you'll look more distinguished. Remember, it's only temporary. You can wash it out after you arrive at the Kesre's."

"So I'll look distinguished?" asked Elvis. "Now you're really trying to

Memphis: August 16, 1977, 7:30 AM CDT

destroy my image."

"You're absolutely right, Elvis. That's exactly what I'm trying to do. I don't want *anybody* to recognize you. But it's only going to be for several hours. Once you leave the Austin airport, you can take the hat and wig off in Dr. Kesre's car."

"Okay Larry. I guess I can put up with it for a few hours."

Dr. Kaye completed the disguise with the same glasses and mustache that Elvis wore back from Graceland. He certainly looked like he could be somebody's grandfather for his upcoming flight to Austin. More importantly, he looked like someone who could pass for Terry's father.

"Give me that damn mirror, Larry." demanded Elvis jokingly. "Let's see if you ought to change professions."

"Well . . what do you think?" asked Dr. Kaye.

"Not bad, Larry, even if I say so myself. If I hadn't put on so much weight, I'd look a lot like my Daddy."

"I take it that your last remark was a compliment, but I'm not so sure Vernon would agree with your assessment. He'd probably say he's much better looking. By the way, Elvis, before you put on your shirt and tie, let me brush off those hair clippings from the back of your neck. If I don't, you'll be itching and scratching all the way to Austin."

After putting his shirt back on, Elvis completed the arduous task, at least arduous for him, of retying his tie, but in only half the time it took upstairs. Dr. Kaye then handed him the suit Eduardo wore back from Austin, having pressed it while Elvis was taking a shower. After buttoning the coat, Elvis inspected himself in the mirror. "What do you think now, Larry? How do I look?"

The Resurrection of The King

"You look great, Elvis . . like a TV star."

"Really . . . that good?" replied Elvis.

"Yeah . . . like a cross between Walter Brennan from *The Real McCoys* and a somewhat heavier *Captain Kangaroo*. Here, take this cane I found in the basement and practice walking with a limp. Just imagine you have Grandpa McCoy's arthritis. Keep practicing until it seems like second nature to you."

"*Somewhat* heavier, Larry? Very funny. Actually, I once hurt my knee playing touch football at Graceland, and I really did need a cane for a couple of days. Just give me a few minutes, and I'll get it down just right."

After limping around the kitchen for a few minutes, Dr. Kaye nodded his approval. "Well, you'd certainly fool me, Elvis. I'd never suspect in a month of Sundays that you were *The King of Rock and Roll*. Keep that memory of your bad knee in your mind when you arrive at the airport."

Larry then gathered up Elvis' slacks, and put them into the suitcase containing the rest of his clothing. "Here Elvis, try walking with that cane while you're carrying your luggage. Incidentally, when I came back from the hospital, traffic in the other direction on the expressway was moving pretty slowly. It looked like it was backed up for at least a mile ."

"Yeah . . I saw the same thing, Larry. It looked like they were resurfacing the left lane, beginning just past the Poplar Avenue interchange, on the way to the airport. Traffic was just starting to back up to where we'd have to get on. We better leave a little sooner in case it gets any worse."

After a little more practice walking with the cane, they both headed out to the Porsche, with Larry carrying Elvis' luggage. It was just a few minutes before 10:00 AM when they climbed into his car. Once inside, Larry inserted the key in the ignition, twisted it to the right, and the 911 Turbo

Memphis: August 16, 1977, 7:30 AM CDT

roared to life. After allowing the engine to warm up for a minute, he shifted into reverse and slowly backed down the driveway out into the street. He immediately headed for the Poplar Avenue entrance to the I-240 Expressway.

"It's normally only a 20-minute drive from here to the airport, Elvis, but with that construction project going on, it could take twice as long. Leaving a little early was probably the wise thing to do. Remember, you still have to buy your ticket."

The Tennessee Highway Department had indeed closed off the left lane for resurfacing, and traffic had slowed to a crawl for the first mile. Fortunately, they left with plenty of time to spare, for it took nearly an hour to get to the airport.

At shortly after 11:00 AM, Dr. Kaye pulled his Porsche up to the Northwest Airlines Terminal. Before he left Graceland, Eduardo had given his wallet to Elvis, the wallet containing his credit cards and driver's license. Just before they left for the airport, Larry had given Elvis enough cash to pay for his ticket. Without knowing how many surgical procedures Dr. Kesre would have to perform, there would be no way of determining how long he'd have to remain in Austin. If he had to rent a hotel room and especially a car, a credit card would be a necessity. In fact, it's virtually impossible to rent a car *without* a credit card.

After Dr. Kaye brought the 911 to a stop, Elvis slowly climbed out of the passenger side. No one even gave *him* a second glance, but several men were giving Larry's 911 a few envious stares. Suddenly, a young woman about twenty, seeing Elvis with his luggage and walking with a cane, graciously opened the door into the terminal. Elvis instinctively replied with his familiar, *Thank you very much.* Fortunately, the young lady only responded with *you're welcome sir,* but Elvis made a mental note never to speak in his normal voice again, for it was just entirely too recognizable.

The Resurrection of The King

Once inside the terminal, he slowly made his way back to the Northwest check-in counter. After purchasing his ticket, he walked with his well-rehearsed limp towards the gate where his flight was departing. Once he arrived near the gate, he sat down in one of the many rows of chairs overlooking the tarmac. "So far, so good," thought Elvis, "I hope the flight goes just as smoothly."

Just then, one of Northwest Airline's flight attendants, having seen Elvis walking with a cane, approached him from behind. "Pardon me sir, but would you like to board before the other passengers?"

Responding in what he felt was an older, deeper, more *mature* voice, Elvis replied, "That won't be necessary, ma'am. I'm in first class, and I should probably board last, but thank you for asking."

At 11:48 AM, the McDonnell-Douglas DC-9 was towed back from the jet way. After taxiing out to the main runway and getting clearance from the control tower, the pilot throttled up the engines and began accelerating down the runway. In less than a minute, Flight 889 was airborne.

* * * * * * *

Austin: August 16, 1977, 1:05 PM CDT

CHAPTER FOURTEEN
Austin: August 16, 1977, 1:05 PM CDT

The Kesres arrived at the airport shortly before 1 PM. After parking their *Rolls,* they made their way back to the far end of the Northwest Airlines terminal where the flight from Memphis was due to arrive. At precisely 1:45 PM, Flight 889 touched down and began its long taxi down the runway. Just prior to coming to a stop, the pilot made a left turn and headed towards the tarmac in front of Northwest Airlines' terminal.

Terry, normally somewhat reserved, was on this particular day positively exuberant, for she was about to meet the most famous entertainer on the planet. Even Dr. Kesre, usually unflappable and not a particular fan of Presley's, was excited about the prospects of meeting the *King of Rock and Roll.*

Since Elvis was sitting in the First Class section and the exit door in a DC-9 was located just behind the cockpit, he would be one of the first passengers to depart the aircraft. To assure that their meeting went as planned, Terry was holding her sign prominently, standing about ten feet in front of the door at the end of the jet way. Dr. Kesre had moved into position next to Terry, still maintaining a firm grip on the wheelchair.

After what seemed like an eternity, at least to the Kesres, Flight 889 finally arrived at the terminal. As soon as it was secured to the jet way, the doors leading into the waiting area were finally opened by one of the departing flight attendants. The Kesres inched closer, with Terry holding her sign high above her head.

The next person coming off the jet way seemed to fit Larry's description, but he didn't have a cane. Nevertheless, he *was* wearing a familiar-looking brown suit and a tan cowboy hat. After spotting her sign, a gray-haired portly gentleman appearing to be in his mid sixties, headed directly towards Terry. The first words out of his mouth were . . *Hello, darlin'.*

The Resurrection of The King

"Daddy," shouted Terry, as she ran up and gave Elvis a big hug.

"After kissing Terry on the cheek, Elvis continued, "it's so good to see you two again. And son, it sure looks like you've been taking good care of my little girl," as he gave Terry an additional hug. "You can't imagine how happy I am to be visiting you folks."

Terry was totally in awe. "Here I am," she thought, "in the arms of Elvis Presley . . . *the* Elvis Presley . . star of more than 30 movies and more hit records than anyone in the history of entertainment . . the same Elvis Presley who costarred with Ann Margaret in *Viva Las Vegas*. And to think, while I was majoring in music at Morris-Harvey, this Icon was singing *Love Me Tender* to Debra Paget. I must be dreaming. Can this really be happening . . to *me?"*

Just then, Al interrupted. "What happened to your cane . . . Dad? And when did you start wearing that cowboy hat? I thought you hated hats*."*

Elvis, speaking in a hushed voice so as not be be overheard, quickly replied, "I left the cane on my seat. I didn't realize I forgot it until after I got off the plane, so I just faked a limp. Frankly, I forgot which leg it was that was supposed to be botherin' me. As for the hat, Larry was concerned about my wig fallin' off, so he made me wear this hat to hold it down. I kept it on during the entire flight."

"Well, you did one heck of a job with the limp, even without the cane. I think Terry knew it was you when you first came through the doors, in spite of the cowboy hat. Woman's intuition, you know," whispered Dr. Kesre.

"I heard that, Al Kesre. Not woman's intuition this time," replied Terry in a hushed voice. "The bottom button was still missing . . just like it was on Eduardo's suit coat when he left for Memphis."

After hugging Terry again, Elvis sat down in the wheelchair, and the

Austin: August 16, 1977, 1:05 PM CDT

three of them headed back towards the parking area where Dr. Kesre's Rolls Royce was waiting.

Terry was still up on Cloud Nine. "The girls will never believe this," she thought; "Why . . I can hardly believe it myself."

After a five-minute walk back to the parking area . . a ride for Elvis . . they arrived at Dr. Kesre's gray *Silver Cloud*. With a press of the button on the key fob, the trunk door popped open, and Al placed Elvis' suit case into the cavernous storage area. After helping Elvis out of the wheel-chair, Terry opened the rear door, still overwhelmed, and helped guide him into the back seat. Before shutting the door, Terry, with the demean-or of a British chauffeur, graciously asked Elvis, "Will there be anything else, Sir?"

Elvis chuckled, recognizing Terry's affected gesture, and immediately put her at ease by replying in kind. "No thank you, Ma'am. Your obvious concern for my comfort and well-being is considerably more than any reasonable gentleman should expect."

Terry cracked up with laughter as she thought to herself, "I think I'm going to like this Elvis Presley. He's truly one charming man."

While Terry and Elvis continued exchanging pleasantries, Dr. Kesre folded up the wheelchair and placed it into the trunk next to Elvis' suit-case. "There's certainly no lack of storage space in the trunk of a Rolls Royce," he thought. "I think I still have room for several more suit cases, plus a couple of sets of golf clubs."

Dr. Kesre then climbed into the driver's seat, and after starting the en-gine, he shifted into reverse, and slowly eased the big Rolls out of its two parking spaces. Within minutes, they were out of the airport and back on I-35. Elvis was the first to speak. "Now that we're out of the terminal, we can speak a little more freely. I think I'm going to enjoy my visit with you folks. I've seen your work, Dr. Kesre. What you did for Eduardo was truly amazing. When my daddy first saw us together, he almost did a double take . . he couldn't even tell us apart."

"Well, I accept your compliment, Elvis" replied Dr. Kesre. "Let's hope things are going well for Eduardo, too. Being thrust into the role of Elvis Presley, especially on such short notice, is no small undertaking."

"I'm sure he'll handle things just fine, Dr. Kesre. He's a very quick study, and besides, whenever he's around any people for the first time, Daddy will be close by if he has any lapses in memory."

"Larry told me much the same thing, Elvis. Frankly, when Eduardo was here back in May, I had the same feeling you have. He's a very bright, resourceful guy. If *anyone* can play you convincingly, I think Eduardo Pirelli would be at the top of a very short list. One thing that surprised me though, was how poorly Eduardo did in those impersonation contests he entered in Memphis. Apparently, those judges weren't too impressed with his voice."

"That was *before* the plastic surgery, Dr. Kesre, and it wasn't because of his voice. But I'm not particularly surprised that he did so poorly. About 10 years ago, I entered one of those contests under another name and finished third. Do you believe that?"

"You've got to be kidding, Elvis. Did that really happen? And by the way, call me Al, and Mrs. Kesre likes to be called Terry. Since we're going to be spending quite a bit of time together, I think we should spare the formalities. You'll have to pardon Terry and I if we still seem a little star struck, but we really are. You're probably more famous than Jesus, if you don't mind me saying so."

"I'm not anywhere near that famous, Al, but I think I know how you feel. I remember when I first met Milton Berle. I used to watch him on TV

Austin: August 16, 1977, 1:05 PM CDT

when I was a teenager, and he was the biggest star there was. When I finally went on his show and met him for the first time in person, I was in awe of him. After awhile, that wore off. Mr. Bearle was a real down-to-earth guy. But I feel comfortable with you folks, and after you get to know *me* a little better, you'll feel like you've known me for years. You know, I still find it hard to accept all of this stardom stuff. Every once in awhile, I think I'm going to wake up one day, and it will all be a distant dream."

"I wouldn't count on *that* happening, Elvis," replied Terry confidently. "Look at all of those fans who keep coming back to your concerts after twenty years. That should be enough to convince even you that you're more than just a passing fad. Besides, there are literally millions of people in this country who really love you, and to your credit, you've never taken them for granted."

"Terry, that's one of the nicest things anyone ever said to me. I don't think most people have any idea how the entertainment business can distort your outlook on life. Now that Eduardo is fillin' in for me, I can relax for the first time in memory. It's like a tremendous burden has been removed. But let's talk about you folks. Dr. Kaye tells me that you have two daughters."

"Yes, we do Elvis, Becky who is ten and Lori who is twelve, but they're visiting their grandparents in Pennsylvania. They're such big fans of yours, too, and I'm sure they would have loved to have met you. Maybe sometime in the future we can tell them about your visit. Actually, things worked out for the best, what with them on vacation, for the fewer people who know about you being here, the better it is. And Elvis. I can only *imagine* how difficult it was for you to have made this decision."

"Yes ma'am, it certainly was," replied Elvis. "And by the way, I sure hope to meet your daughters some day and tell them in person, but that won't be for awhile, I'm afraid."

The Resurrection of The King

"I hope you don't mind if I turn on the radio, Elvis," interrupted Dr. Kesre. "I'd like to check the traffic reports. We drove by an accident on the way to the airport, and the outbound lanes were tied up for a few miles. If it's still that way, we can use some back roads."

"Go right ahead," replied Elvis, who by now was feeling even more relaxed. "It must be one of those days. We ran into a traffic jam on the way to the Memphis airport. By the way, Al, what time is it getting to be? I didn't wear my watch."

"It's a little after after 2:30." replied Dr. Kesre.

Terry reached over and turned on the radio just as the traffic reports were coming on.

The accident that occurred earlier this afternoon on I-35 near the airport has finally been cleared away, and all lanes have been reopened. Traffic is once again moving at it's normal snail's pace, replied the helicopter reporter in a manner that sounded remarkably like a *Saturday Night Live* skit with Bill Murray. Suddenly, a new voice broke into the programming, but with a tone of urgency:

We have to interrupt this broadcast for a special news bulletin. We're now switching to our local affiliate in Memphis.

An ambulance was seen leaving Graceland and heading north on Elvis Presley Boulevard. Our sources tell us that Elvis was taken to Baptist Memorial Hospital for observation. We contacted a spokesman at Graceland, but he had little to add, other than Elvis would remain in the hospital for a couple of hours until some routine tests were completed. The spokesman went on to say that there would be a news conference held later this afternoon, at which time a more detailed assessment would be made of Elvis' test results. Now back to our normal programming.

"What happened to Eduardo? I don't remember this being part of the

Austin: August 16, 1977, 1:05 PM CDT

plan." exclaimed Elvis.

"Now Elvis," replied Dr. Kesre reassuringly, "don't jump to any conclusions. Maybe Eduardo was feeling a little nervous . . you know . . having an anxiety attack, and they just wanted to check him out before he left for Portland. I read somewhere that *you* still get stage fright before your concert appearances, and you've been performing for years. Think how Eduardo must feel. This is his very first *acting* performance, and he's playing *you,* Elvis!"

"I see where you're coming from, Al, and I sure hope your right. Oh my God!" exclaimed Elvis, almost in a panic. "I wonder if Larry ever called Daddy to tell him we were making the switch today. I don't remember seeing him make the call before we left for the airport, and he never said anything to me about it before we left. I sure hope he called him when he got back from the airport. Al, could you call Dr. Kaye when we get back to your place? It's real important!"

"Of course, Elvis, as soon as we get there. It should only take a few minutes from here."

* * * * * * *

The Resurrection of The King

CHAPTER FIFTEEN
Graceland: August 16, 1977, 1:35 PM CDT

It was shortly after 1:30 in the afternoon when Ginger finally awakened. Noticing that Elvis wasn't in bed, she called her mother at work.

"How is Elvis feeling, Ginger?" asked her mother. "Does he still have his toothache?"

"Elvis went to the dentist early this morning, Mom, but he wasn't in bed when I woke up. He must have gotten up earlier."

After hanging up the phone, Ginger climbed out of bed, put on her make-up, and quickly dressed. She then walked over to Elvis' bathroom and knocked on the door. There was no answer. "Elvis. It's Ginger." Still no answer. Slowly opening the door, Ginger was startled by the sight of a body clad in gold pajamas lying motionless on the floor. "Elvis." she screamed. There was no response. Ginger immediately grabbed the intercom and shouted, "Is anyone there?"

Al Strada, Elvis' wardrobe manager, was in the kitchen and recognized Ginger's voice. He immediately went over to the intercom and answered, "This is Al, Ginger."

"Al, something's wrong with Elvis. He's lying on the bathroom floor, and he isn't answering me."

"I'll be right up, Ginger." Sprinting up the back stairs from the kitchen, Al arrived in the bathroom within seconds. When he spotted Elvis lying on the floor, he immediately called Joe Esposito. "Joe, come up to Elvis' bathroom .. now! Elvis is lying on the floor and he's not moving."

As soon as Joe arrived, he immediately bent down to feel for a pulse.

Graceland: August 16, 1977, 1:35 PM CDT

There was none. "Call the paramedics, Ginger, and then call Dr. Nick." ordered Joe. After he and Al turned the body over, Joe's worst fears were confirmed. Elvis' skin felt cold to the touch and his face had turned blue. It appeared that rigor mortis had already begun to set in. Suddenly, Joe began experiencing an uneasy feeling in the pit of his stomach.

Just then, Vernon and Patsey Presley, Elvis' cousin, arrived at the entrance to the bathroom. When Vernon saw the body lying motionless on the floor, he cried out, "Please don't die, son!"

Minutes later, Lisa Marie tried to enter the bathroom, "What's wrong with my Daddy?" she asked. No one answered.

Ginger immediately pushed her out of the bathroom and locked both doors, thus preventing the 9-year old from coming back in. Forced to wait outside, Lisa Marie was all alone and probably in tears, left to ponder the fate of her father. Meanwhile, inside the bathroom, there was a state of total chaos.

After what seemed like an eternity, the EMTs finally arrived and immediately begin applying CPR. Nearly ten minutes later after having failed to restore any vital signs, they placed the lifeless body onto a stretcher. Joe, Charlie Hodge, Al, and one of the EMTs carried the body downstairs, out the front entrance, and into the awaiting ambulance. The four of them then climbed inside, and one of the EMTs resumed applying CPR, as the driver sped down the driveway.

As the ambulance neared the front gate, Dr. Nick pulled up in his green Mercedes, sideswiping one of the gate posts. He quickly abandoned his car and climbed into the back of the ambulance, taking over CPR duties from the EMT. He continued applying CPR throughout the seven-minute trip to Baptist Memorial Hospital. His efforts were in vain.

* * * * * * *

CHAPTER SIXTEEN
Austin: August 16, 1977, 2:45 PM CDT

As soon as Dr. Kesre arrived in front of his home, he immediately activated his garage door opener. Slowing down just enough to make the sharp left turn, he sped up the long, rambling driveway, directly through the open garage door. After screeching to a stop, he jumped out of the Rolls and literally sprinted through the connecting mud room, into the kitchen. Grabbing the wall phone, he dialed Larry Kaye's home phone number, which by now he had committed to memory. There was no answer. "Christ, I hope he's at the hospital," thought Al as he grabbed the *Rolodex* off the kitchen counter and flipped through the cards until he came to the letter 'K'. After dialing Larry's extension, the phone began ringing, continuing for what seemed like an eternity.

Finally, someone picked up the call. "Emergency Room, Miss Hardy speaking".

"Miss Hardy, this is Dr. Alan Kesre. Is Dr. Kaye there?"

"Yes he is, Dr. Kesre. He was called in for emergency backup, and he just arrived about fifteen minutes ago. I think he's with another patient. Let me page him for you."

Almost a minute passed before Larry finally answered. "Dr. Kaye."

"Larry, it's Al. Boy, am I glad I was able to reach you. Terry and I just picked up Fast Eddy at the airport. On our way back, we heard something on the radio about Elvis being taken to Baptist Memorial Hospital. We're all very concerned about Big Daddy. Fast Eddy said that you were supposed to tell him that we *switched gears*. Did you get a chance to call Big Daddy?"

"Oh my God Al, no I didn't!" replied Dr. Kaye. I'd better call him now.

Austin: August 16, 1977, 2:45 PM CST

But Al, did you hear the latest? When they brought Elvis in, he was already dead. The Harvey team tried to resuscitate him, but it was too late. I was told that he must have been dead for several hours. They just moved the body over to Pathology for the autopsy. Dr. Nick, who was applying CPR in the ambulance, is still with the body. From what I hear, he's pretty broken up. By the way Al, that must have been great work. No one seems to have a clue."

* * * * * * *

"I think you'll be comfortable here, Elvis," remarked Terry in a soft, reassuring voice as she escorted him into one of the guest bedrooms. "It has a nice view, a king-size bed, and a private bath. Why don't you get out of that suit and change into something a little more comfortable?"

"Thank you, Terry. I'll do just that," replied Elvis. "But first, I'm going to take a quick shower and see if I can wash some of this coloring out of my sideburns."

Ten minutes later, Elvis arrived back in the kitchen wearing dark slacks and a white silk sport shirt. Without the gray wig, mustache, and glasses, he now looked far different from the performer his fans saw at his last concert in Indianapolis. Not only was his hair much shorter, but so were his sideburns, still slightly gray from the coloring Dr. Kaye had applied only hours earlier, and trimmed to a length not seen for nearly twenty years when he was in the Army.

Just as Elvis was about to sit down at the kitchen table, Dr. Kesre hung up the phone. "Elvis . . that . . that was Larry." stammered a visibly shaken Dr. Kesre. He's at the hospital. I have some terrible news, so maybe you'd better sit down.

"What happened, Al?"

"Eduardo is dead," replied Dr. Kesre.

"Eduardo is dead? Eduardo Pirelli is dead?" repeated Elvis as if he didn't hear Dr. Kesre the first time. "That's terrible, Al. I just saw him this morning. We were joking in my dressing room about who looked more convincing as a laundry driver. I mean . . . he's supposed to be me. Did Larry tell you how he died?"

"No, other than he was apparently dead by the time he arrived in the emergency room. They just took the body to Pathology. They won't know what the cause of death was until they complete the autopsy. And Elvis, Larry told me that apparently everybody believed it was you, including Dr. Nick, who is still at the hospital."

"Would you like a drink, Elvis?" interrupted Terry voicing genuine concern, and now taking charge once she was back in her kitchen.

"No . . no thank you ma'am. I still can't believe it. Poor Eduardo. Oh my God! Lisa Marie is at Graceland. My little girl. What's she going to do without her daddy? I've got to call her and tell her I'm still alive."

"Elvis . . you can't do that . . at least not now," replied Al. "To begin with, we don't even know if she's been told about your death. If she has, hearing from you might be a little too traumatic. We should at least wait until we get some additional information."

"I guess you're right, Al. I never thought for an instant that something like this could happen to Eduardo."

"None of us did, Elvis. We'll just have to wait until we hear from Larry again. He'll be calling back . . just as soon as he talks to Vernon and tells him you're still alive."

"He never called my daddy? Poor Daddy. He thinks I'm dead."

Just then, Terry interrupted, attempting to change the subject. "I'll bet you must be hungry, Elvis. We called Northwest just before we left for the airport, and they told us that your flight didn't serve any lunch. Those honey peanuts can only go so far when you haven't eaten all day. How

Austin: August 16, 1977, 2:45 PM CST

about some soup and a sandwich to tide you over until dinner time?"

"Thank you, Terry. Soup and a sandwich sounds just fine."

"Okay . . . do you want a BLT on rye, or would you rather have peanut butter with fried bananas on whole wheat toast?"

"Terry, you must be a mind reader!" exclaimed Elvis with astonishment. "How could you possibly know that BLTs and peanut butter with fried bananas are my all-time favorites? Have you been talking to Aunt Delta?"

"I'm not revealing any of my sources, Elvis." replied Terry with a noticeable twinkle in her eye.

Just then the phone rang, and Al, standing near the kitchen counter, immediately picked it up. "Dr. Kesre!"

"It's Larry, Al. I just got hold of Big Daddy and told him the good news. I'm going over to see him to help calm him down. He's still pretty agitated, and I hear his ticker isn't in the best of shape."

"Thank God you were able to reach him, Larry. I'll tell Fast Eddy. He's pretty upset about Eduardo's death, and he's concerned about PJ . . *very* concerned! He wants to call her."

"Tell him absolutely not . . at least not now. I'm going over to see Big Daddy as soon as the excitement dies down here at the hospital and I can leave. I'll call you back as soon as I get there."

"Thanks, Larry. I'll tell Fast Eddy what you said about not calling PJ."

After hanging up the phone, Al turned towards Elvis. "Larry just talked to your daddy and told him that you're okay and that you're here with us in Austin. He's going over to see him at Graceland. As soon as he gets there and they can get to a secure phone, he's going to call back. I'm sure

The Resurrection of The King

Vernon will want to talk to you."

"Thanks, Al. That's a big relief, but since Eduardo is dead, that changes everything. What am I going to do about Lisa Marie?"

"Elvis, when you first agreed to this plan, we weren't going to tell anyone, including Priscilla and Lisa Marie . . . at least initially. We left the timetable open so we could play it by ear. Perhaps at some point in time we'll tell Priscilla . . not now, not necessarily even next week or next month, but when the time is right. And events will dictate that. Let's see how things play out. As for Lisa Marie, that's something we'll have to discuss. Besides, the staff at Graceland is going to have their hands full arranging the viewing and funeral. Before making any final decisions about who will or won't be told, maybe we should wait until things settle down a little.

"I guess you're right, Al, but I feel terrible for Lisa Marie. When she finds out that her daddy died, she'll be devastated. That's my biggest concern."

Just then, Terry weighed into the conversation. "Elvis, Al is right. Children deal with death better than we give them credit for. Besides, and I've got to tell you this Elvis . . when a child first learns that her parents are getting divorced, that can be even more traumatic than telling them about a parent's death. I'm sure Priscilla will use the right words when she breaks the news to Lisa. Believe me, Elvis, Mothers always do."

"I hope you're right Terry. I just hope you're right . . . ."

"And *you* shouldn't tell Priscilla that you're alive . . . at least by yourself, Elvis," interrupted Dr. Kesre. "Larry or I should be there with you. That way, there won't be as much emotional baggage interfering with what, at the very least, will be a very difficult conversation. The last thing you want to do is rehash all of your reasons for doing the switch in the first place. Try not to worry, Elvis. Larry will think of some way to handle

Austin: August 16, 1977, 2:45 PM CST

this situation."

"I guess I'll just have to wait a little longer, Al." replied Elvis with resignation. "I'm just feeling a little low now because I can't do much of anything but sit and wait. Maybe I'll feel a little better when I hear from Daddy. I guess the only other thing that's remaining is the reconstructive surgery. And frankly, I'm beginning to have second thoughts about that, especially since Eduardo died. That changes everything."

"Does it really?" asked Dr. Kesre. "What does it change?"

Elvis paused for a moment. "Well . . ah . . I'll have to think about that one, Al."

"Take your time, Elvis. You certainly don't have to get the surgery now, but I'm not sure that Eduardo's death really changes anything. If it does, it changes things for the better. I don't want to sound too draconian, but the fact is, by tonight everybody in the world will believe that it was you who died. At least you won't have to worry about how Eduardo will get along with Ginger."

"But Al, I just wanted to disappear for . . maybe a year or two. Then we'd switch places again. I didn't mean it to be permanent."

"Okay, let's assume Eduardo hadn't died and he was successful in fooling everybody. Let's assume just that . . . at least for the time being. If you didn't get the reconstructive surgery, Elvis, there would now be *two* Elvis Presleys out there. Just imagine all of the rumors that would be making the rounds in the news media. Elvis was seen in Austin. Elvis was seen at Graceland . . on the same day, no less. Elvis was seen here. Elvis was seen there, and it would go on and on. You still wouldn't get a moment's peace, and that was one of the reasons why you wanted to change your identity. As they say in boxing, you can run but you can't hide. And you of all people, Elvis . . . you . . can't . . hide! You're one of the most recognizable faces on the planet.

The Resurrection of The King

"I understand what you're saying, Al. But if Eduardo didn't die, at some point in time we could have switched places again. But until I did, I could have used *some* sort of a disguise. I could have dyed my hair, grew a mustache, cut my sideburns, wore glasses . . you know, like I did for my trip down here."

"Well that sounds plausible from a theoretical standpoint, Elvis, but let's carry that thought a couple of steps further. Let's assume you wanted to switch back with Eduardo within the next year or two. Would you two look the same? Would you two weigh the same? Would you both cut your hair the same way? Let's face it Elvis. You couldn't even win one of those Elvis singing contests . . impersonating *yourself* . . back in the late sixties. What if Eduardo pulled it off so well and enjoyed the attention and fame so much that he didn't *want* to switch back? What if Ginger and Eduardo fell in love and got married? And when you came back to Graceland to claim your throne, what if Eduardo and Ginger were to accuse *you* of being the impostor? What would you do then, Elvis?"

"Now you're confusing me, Al." replied Elvis, "This is just getting too complicated for me to think about now."

"I'm sorry, Elvis," replied Dr. Kesre with genuine concern, "but that's not my intention. I'm just trying to bring you back into the world of reality. There were very sound reasons why you wanted to make this switch in the first place, and those reasons haven't changed. But now that Eduardo *is* dead, it's even more important that you go through with the reconstructive surgery. And one of the prime reasons is Colonel Tom Parker."

"The Colonel? What does The Colonel have to do with anything now that Eduardo's dead?"

"Elvis, I'll bet The Colonel is already thinking of ways to get his meat hooks into your estate. He'll probably be talking with your daddy to work out some kind of a deal within the next day or two, a deal that

Austin: August 16, 1977, 2:45 PM CST

would unquestionably favor Tom Parker. Remember Elvis, with the entire world believing that you're dead, every recording or movie you ever made will suddenly become in demand. It always happens whenever a famous entertainer dies prematurely. Look what it did for James Dean's movies. The same goes for the records of Janis Joplin and Jimmy Hendrix. They simply issued new albums where they merely reshuffled the songs around. Some of those albums actually sold more copies the second time around. I'll bet The Colonel is already talking to the record companies."

"Jesus, Al, that's the last thing in the world I want to happen. It's like he would be stealing money from Daddy and Lisa Marie . . . money that is rightfully theirs. But how can I stop The Colonel from doing that if I get the reconstructive surgery? How's that going to change *anything?*"

"Well, one way you *can't* stop him is to suddenly turn up alive . . especially since everyone *believes* you're dead. Even if you called The Colonel now, would he believe it's you . . or would he think it's some slick impressionist trying to con him? And knowing The Colonel, even if he really *did* believe it was you calling, it would still be to his advantage to accept *as fact* that you're dead."

"I think I understand where you're coming from, Al, and you're making one powerful argument for going through with the surgery."

"I'm certainly trying to, Elvis, because I truly believe it's the right thing for *you* to do. But it *has* to be your decision."

"Let me think about it, Al. This is really a big step for me to take."

"It would be for me too, Elvis. Take your time. If you decide to go through with the surgery, I want you to be absolutely convinced that it's the right thing to do . . that it's the right decision for you as well as for Lisa Marie."

* * * * * * *

The Resurrection of The King

CHAPTER SEVENTEEN
Graceland: August 16, 1977, 2:50 PM CDT

Just prior to speaking with Dr. Kesre, Larry had called Vernon at Graceland. The phone rang for well over a minute before the switchboard operator finally answered. "Graceland."

"Can I speak to Vernon?" asked Dr. Kaye.

"And who shall I say is calling?"

"Tell him it's Dr. Lawrence Kaye, and it's very important that I speak with him *now!*" replied Larry with a tone of urgency in his voice. "I'm a friend of Vernon's and he's expecting my call. And operator. Has there been any additional word about Elvis?"

"Oh . . Dr. Kaye. I didn't recognize your voice at first," replied the operator. "No, nothing new, but what we *have* heard hasn't sounded very encouraging. It's been like a zoo around here as you can well imagine. Could you please hold while I try to reach Mr. Presley? I think he may be in the dining room or kitchen." After what seemed like an eternity, the switchboard operator finally got back on the line. "I have Mr. Presley now, Dr. Kaye. I'll put your call through."

"Thank you, and I sure hope everything turns out okay," replied Larry.

Although Larry heard a detectable click, he wanted to make sure that the operator wasn't still on the line. Acting as if he had something else to ask her, he spoke into the phone again, "Operator?" There was no answer. Just then, a sobbing Vernon answered. One could immediately sense the despair in his voice. "This . . this is Vernon Presley."

"Vernon, it's Larry. *We switched gears* . . . early this morning. I'd like to come over to Graceland just as soon as I call Dr. Kesre and *Fast Eddy* to

Graceland: August 16, 1977, 2:50 PM CDT

let them know I was able to reach you."

Suddenly, Vernon perked up and became much calmer. For Dr. Kaye had used the words . . *we switched gears* . . words that confirmed that Eduardo Pirelli had indeed switched places with Elvis, and that Elvis had already left Graceland.

"Thank God, Larry." replied Vernon in a much lower, but calmer, voice. "Things are in total chaos here. People are running around like the world's coming to an end. Oh, oh! Here come three more guys. I don't think I've ever seen them around here before, Larry. I wonder how the hell they got past security?"

Just then, Shelby County medical investigator Dan Warlick, accompanied by police lieutenant Sam McCachern and Assistant District Attorney Jerry Stauffer, came into the dining room, holding up their their IDs as they approached Vernon in the kitchen.

"I've got to go now, Larry," replied Vernon, barely audibly. "Tell him I got your message and that I'm feeling much better now. Try to get over here as soon as possible."

Suddenly, Vernon's voice took on a dramatic reversal as he continued speaking into the phone. "And you want to know why I'm so upset? Because my baby is dead. They've taken him away from me. My baby is dead, do you hear me?" cried Vernon as he once again broke into uncontrollable despair.

* * * * * * *

As soon as he completed his call with Vernon, Larry immediately dialed Dr. Kesre's number. Al, who was standing near the kitchen counter, grabbed the wall phone. "Dr. Kesre!"

"It's Larry, Al. I just got hold of Big Daddy and told him the good news.

The Resurrection of The King

I'm going over to see him to help calm him down. He's still a little agitated, and I hear his ticker isn't in the best of shape."

"Thank God you were able to reach him, Larry. I'll tell Fast Eddy. He's pretty upset about Eduardo's death, and he's concerned about PJ . . *very* concerned! He wants to call her."

"Tell him absolutely not . . at least not now. I'm going over to see Big Daddy as soon as the excitement dies down here at the hospital and I can leave. I'll call you back as soon as I get there."

"Thanks, Larry. I'll tell Fast Eddy what you said about not calling PJ."

No sooner had Dr. Kaye hung up the phone, then it began ringing again. Larry grabbed the receiver before the first ring was completed. "This is Dr. Kaye."

"Larry, it's Harvey Franklin. I just heard about Elvis. What a tragedy. I feel so sorry for Lisa Marie and Vernon."

"Yeah, they called me in for backup as soon as they received word from the fire department that they were bringing Elvis in. They just took his body to Pathology."

"There's something else I forgot to tell you, Larry, and you're suspicians were right."

"Suspicions? What suspicions? What are you talking about, Harvey?"

"My patient and your friend, Eduardo Pirelli. You're not going to believe this, but Pirelli is a walking Class II pharmacy. I got the report back from the lab in Chicago a couple of months ago, and I apologize for not telling you this sooner. Wait 'til you hear what they found in his blood: Codeine, Morphine, Diazepam, Diazepam Metabolite, Ethinamate, Ethclorvynol,

Graceland: August 16, 1977, 2:50 PM CDT

Amobarbital, Phenobarbital, Pentobarbital, Methaqualone, Meperidine, and last but not least, Phenyltoloxamine. In spite of what they found, it's still probably not enough to kill him. It's the complications that can result from the combination of those drugs that I'm most concerned about, complications that can occur in the digestive track!"

"What complications are you concerned about, Harvey?"

"When you take the drugs he was taking . . in combination, they have the resultant effect of slowing down the digestive system. The bowels slow down, and sometimes stop functioning. Ultimately, they get packed with more and more food, and that causes the colon to stretch, which can also be a problem. The colon then becomes impacted with fecal matter, and frequent constipation results. Most people just take laxatives. Unfortunately, laxatives only provide a temporary, and sometimes *detrimental* fix, doing little to remove impacted fecal matter. You need to literally clean out the colon just like you have to clean out a clogged drain. If this isn't done, one might have such difficulty *trying* to have a bowel movement, that they could literally overstrain their heart in an attempt to *force* one. There have been cases reported where this resulted in a stroke or cardiac arrest, particularly among those who have high blood pressure."

"What *was* Eduardo's blood pressure? Did he have other risk factors?"

"His cholesterol and B. P. were much too high. His blood sugar was borderline . . prediabetic. But all of those drugs Eduardo is taking *could* lead to an impacted colon, and most certainly could also account for his rapid weight gain. With all of these things happening, if Eduardo ever attempted to *force* a bowel movement, the result could be cardiac arrest. As for the narcotics, you were right about those, too, Larry. They were prescribed by three doctors in Philadelphia, over a period of several years. I suspect Eduardo told those doctors, *individually,* that he couldn't handle the side effects of certain drugs, so each of them would prescribe alternative medications. He probably took the newly prescribed drugs in addi-

The Resurrection of The King

tion to the older ones, thinking that *more* was better."

Not wanting to reveal to Dr. Franklin that it was Eduardo who was brought into the E. R., not Elvis, Larry replied stoically. "I thought he might be on *something,* Harvey. He was displaying many of the symptoms you alluded to, including the rapid weight gain. Eduardo's not at his restaurant today, but when he returns, I'll have a serious talk with him. He's got to stop taking *all* of those drugs and get into a good exercise and nutrition program. It wouldn't hurt to get a colonoscopy, either."

"I agree, Larry. I hate to deal with patients who are in denial. I got the distinct feeling from Eduardo when I saw him in July for his physical, that he didn't think he even *had* a problem. How many times have you heard that one?"

"Too many, Harvey. Entirely too many."

* * * * * * *

Twenty minutes later, Dr. Kaye pulled up to Graceland's front entrance on Elvis Presley Boulevard. "I can't believe how many people are already here," he thought. "It looks like every newspaper and TV reporter in the country has staked out a claim." The guards, recognizing Larry and his Porsche, waved him on through.

Proceeding slowly up the now crowded driveway, Larry managed to find a parking space about a hundred feet from the front door. After parking his car, he walked briskly up the driveway, arriving at the open door where he was stopped by another guard. "Sir, I'll need to see some identification."

"Of course," replied Larry, trying to be cooperative. Pulling out his wallet, he showed the guard both his medical license and driver's license. "I'm a close friend of Vernon's. He asked me to come over."

"Yes, he told me you were coming. I believe he's in the dining room,"

Graceland: August 16, 1977, 2:50 PM CDT

replied the guard as he inspected Larry's ID photos.

"Why don't you go right in Dr. Kaye?"

"Thank you," he replied as he entered the foyer.

Upon walking into the dining room, Larry spotted Vernon in the kitchen, still talking on the phone. Larry approached him haltingly, just as he was hanging up.

"Larry, I didn't see you come in. Thank God you're finally here. That was The Colonel. Did you have any trouble finding a place to park?"

"No, I was lucky. There was a spot in the driveway, about a hundred feet from the front door," replied Dr. Kaye. Reverting to a hushed voice so no one else could hear, Larry continued. "Let's get the hell out of here. Is there some place we can go to where we'll be alone?"

"Yes. Upstairs in Elvis' office," whispered Vernon. "It's always locked, and nobody will bother us."

After walking up the back stairs from the kitchen, they quickly arrived at Elvis' office. Vernon looked around to see if anyone was still upstairs. Nobody was so he unlocked the door and ushered Dr. Kaye inside. After he shut the door, he locked it again. Larry was the first to speak.

"Vernon, the body you saw on the bathroom floor was Eduardo's. He and Elvis made the switch this morning at about 7:15. After Eduardo arrived at Graceland in the laundry van, they changed clothes in Elvis' dressing room while Ginger was asleep. Eduardo then put on Elvis' pajamas while Elvis was putting on Eduardo's laundry driver's uniform. Elvis then drove the laundry van back to my home in Germantown. He then changed out of the laundry driver's outfit, into a suit that Eduardo had worn when he flew back to Memphis from Austin, after he had gotten the

The Resurrection of The King

reconstructive surgery that turned him into an Elvis look alike. I then put a gray wig, mustache, and glasses on Elvis for his flight to Austin. He was met at the airport by Dr. Kesre and his wife, and . . ."

Before Dr. Kaye could finish, Vernon interrupted, "Yes, but you were supposed to call me when Elvis decided to make the switch, Larry, and you never did. I thought for sure it was him lying on the bathroom floor. Thank God he's still alive. Where is he now?"

"He's at Dr. Kesre's home . . just outside of Austin," replied Larry. "I just talked to him . . about a half hour ago. What with having to arrange his flight, getting him into his disguise, and driving him to the airport, I just plain forgot to call you Vernon. I'm so sorry I had to put you through all of that needless anguish. I should have called you before we left for the airport, and if not then, when I got back home."

"Oh . . there's no need for you to apologize now, Larry. I guess I was just angry because I wasn't told. You probably wouldn't have been able to reach me anyway since I was out in the garden most of the morning. After Ginger discovered the body, it was sheer pandemonium around here, even before the EMTs arrived. Shortly after they left for the hospital, all the phone lines became tied up from those reporters trying to call about the ambulance that was seen leaving here. But what matters most *now* is that Elvis is alive. Praise God Almighty! My boy is still alive! Before you called me, Larry, I never thought I'd be able to make it through the day."

"Vernon, I know it's asking a lot, but you have to continue acting like you believe Elvis is dead. Just try and recall how you felt when you first saw the body in the bathroom. Elvis wants to talk to you, too. Do you think it's safe to call from here, I mean, since the police are still tapping the lines? If not, we could call from *my* house."

"It should be okay, Larry. Remember, Elvis' office phone is unlisted, and his line doesn't go through the main switchboard," replied Vernon, by

Graceland: August 16, 1977, 2:50 PM CDT

now his spirits decidedly more upbeat. "Is my son all right?"

"Yes. I talked to him just before I left, and I told him we would call him as soon as I got here and told you what happened. He was really worried about you, Vernon."

"What's done is done, Larry. The important thing is that my boy is alive and well. Do you have Dr. Kesre's phone number?"

"Yes, but let me make the call. As an added precaution, Vernon, when you talk to Elvis, be sure to call him *Eduardo*. And above all, positively don't call him *son!* Try to keep your conversation as unemotional as possible. Act like you want to buy Eduardo's restaurant. I know it's going to be hard, especially under these circumstances, but give it a try."

"Yes, of course, Larry. I think I can do that." replied Vernon.

After reviewing the phone protocol again, Larry dialed Dr. Kesre's number. Al answered after the first ring. "Hello?"

"Al? It's Larry! I'm at Graceland with Vernon. I know it's a little soon, but did Eduardo show up yet? I might have a buyer for his restaurant."

"How in the hell could you possibly know that Eduardo was already here? He wasn't supposed to arrive for another hour or so, but he happened to be in the area scouting out restaurant sites and he just stopped in. Let me get him for you. Honestly, Larry, you must be a psychic."

Dr. Kesre called Elvis to the phone, placing his hand over the receiver. "It's your daddy, Elvis. He's calling from your office at Graceland. After you get on the phone, try to keep your conversation as low-keyed as possible. We're still not sure if *all* the lines at Graceland are being tapped, even though Vernon doesn't think your office line is. Try to make your voice sound a little bit deeper. Talk to Vernon just like he was a pro-

The Resurrection of The King

spective buyer for your restaurant. Remember, we might have to sell Eduardo's restaurant if Joe Genuardi doesn't want to buy it. And Elvis, Larry told your daddy to call you Eduardo. It might be best if you called your daddy by *his* first name, too."

"Okay, Al. I can sure give it a try." Taking the phone from Dr. Kesre, Elvis cleared his throat and went into his impromptu act. "Hello . . Vernon? Eduardo here. I'm sorry I didn't get back to you sooner, but I couldn't get to a phone. I understand you might still be interested in my restaurant."

* * * * * * *

Late that same afternoon, Terry walked into the family room. Elvis and Dr. Kesre were still discussing the day's events.

"Do you gentlemen mind if I turn on the TV to catch the news?"

"It's okay with me, Terry," replied Al. "How about you Elvis? Do you mind if we take a break and watch the news?"

"Not at all. Go right ahead, Terry."

Terry went over to the TV set and turned it on. *The NBC Evening News* was just about to begin. After the camera zoomed in on David Brinkley, he opened the program with a terse announcement that would shock the world:

Good Evening. Elvis Presley died today. He was 42. Apparently it was a heart attack. He was found in his home in Memphis, not breathing. His road manager tried to revive him. He failed. A hospital tried to revive him. It failed. His doctor pronounced him dead at three o'clock this afternoon.

* * * * * * *

Austin: August 18, 1977, 7:00 AM CDT

CHAPTER EIGHTEEN
Austin: August 18, 1977, 7:00 AM CDT

Life was still in turmoil at Graceland, as the staff was busily making last minute preparations for today's funeral. Yesterday's viewing had attracted an estimated 50,000 mourners. By mid morning, many of Elvis' celebrity friends had arrived for the funeral service, including Chet Atkins, Ann-Margret, her husband Roger Smith, and Tennessee's Governor Blanton. Throughout the rest of the world, tens of millions of Elvis' fans were still in a state of shock, as the reality of his reported death was just beginning to sink in.

* * * * * * *

Back in Austin, the morning had begun like most August days in Texas: sunny and hot, with just the hint of a breeze. The sky was cloudless for as far as the eyes could see, and by 9 AM, the temperature had already climbed into the low nineties. Forecasters were calling for another scorcher, with the high expected to reach 105.

Dr. Kesre, Terry, and Elvis were just getting ready to sit down for breakfast when the telephone rang. Al picked it up, and after a brief conversation, he came back to the kitchen table.

"That was Larry. He just talked with Vernon and he seems to be feeling a lot better today. His spirits were much more upbeat, in spite of his having to make some of the funeral arrangements. Priscilla had arrived, and she had a long talk with Lisa Marie."

"How was my little girl, Al? What did Daddy say about Lisa Marie?"

"She's still pretty upset, but Vernon said she seems to be dealing with it fairly well. Priscilla is doing a yeoman's job keeping Lisa Marie occupied

The Resurrection of The King

with little chores, but even that's a challenge with everything that's going on around Graceland."

"Cilla is a terrific Mom, Al. I suppose that if Lisa Marie were to have just one parent, I'd rather it be 'Cilla."

"I have to agree with you, Elvis," added Gerry. "It's better for little girls to have their mothers around when they go through adolescence."

"I never thought of it quite that way, Terry," replied Elvis. "Anyway Al, I've reached my decision. I want the surgery."

"Are you absolutely *certain* about this, Elvis?"

"No, of course not Al. I still have some doubts. But I'm 99% certain, and that's about as certain as anyone can be."

"I think you're making the right decision Elvis," stated Terry."

"I believe I am, too, Terry. Any way, let's get on with it. What do you think the chances are that I'll end up looking like Eduardo, Al?"

"Slim, Elvis, so don't get your hopes too high, As I told Larry when he first called about this, I can certainly change your features so you won't look like you do now, but I can't provide any assurance that you'll look like Eduardo, at least after the *first* operation. We'll still have to do at least one or two more procedures before you'll even *resemble* Eduardo. Even then the outcome is doubtful."

"I've got a feeling that things will turn out just fine, Al. You'll see."

"I appreciate your vote of confidence, Elvis, but as I said, don't get your hopes too high. Since you'll probably require some additional surgery after the first procedure, and our daughters will be coming back from their grandparents in Pennsylvania, we should probably rent you a hotel room

Austin: August 18, 1977, 7:00 AM CDT

in Austin *before* we operate. Fortunately, Eduardo's credit cards are registered under the name, E. A. Pirelli. Remember, no one here in Texas knows what E. A. Pirelli looks like. You can just wear the same disguise you flew in with when you check in. But first, we'll rent you a car. The hotel I picked has an underground garage accessible from your room by elevator, so you can come and go without having to walk through the lobby. After we pick up the rental car, we'll drive you over to the hotel so you can check in this evening, and then bring you back here."

"And don't forget your suitcase, Elvis. We also better make that reservation *now* before we get shut out. Lots of businessmen come to Austin and it's a very popular hotel," replied Terry.

"Right again, Terry, but we shouldn't have a problem. All of my out-of-town patients stay there, and we've never had any trouble renting their VIP suites before, even later in the day, but I'll call them now."

"Al, I can hardly wait to see my new face. Frankly, I can't remember the last time I could walk around in public without a mob descending upon me like a flock of vultures. That leaves only one remaining issue. When do we get started with the surgery?"

"I've already rescheduled my appointments for the next couple of days," replied Dr. Kesre, "so I guess we could begin with the first procedure tomorrow. Remember Elvis, you'll be wearing some gauze bandages on your face for a couple of weeks, so you probably shouldn't be leaving your hotel room. Room Service can bring you all of your meals, and Terry and I will come over to visit you every few days to check your progress and change the bandages. Of course, you can call *us* anytime."

"I really appreciate that Al . . and you too Terry," replied Elvis.

"Then we're all in agreement." replied Dr. Kesre, "We'll get started tomorrow. I'll call the rest of the team to let them know, and Elvis, their lips are sealed. As far as any of *them* knows, you're a retired Elvis impersonator who wants to look more like Robert Goulet. Since your sideburns have been shaved off and your hair cut shorter . . they won't even recognize you. Nevertheless, we should give you another name. How about if we use *John Burroughs?"*

"I think you've been talking to Larry again," replied Elvis.

* * * * * * *

The following morning, Elvis, Terry and Al met in the kitchen for an early breakfast. Dr. Kesre was the first to speak. "Today's the big day. As soon as we finish eating, we can get started with the initial preparations. Dr. Martin, Dr. Patrick, and the rest of the surgical team should be arriving shortly."

"I can hardly wait," replied Elvis with the ambivalence of anticipation and apprehension. "I'm beginning to feel like a huge burden is about to be lifted, and I can start a new life again. Boy, will I do things differently this time."

"Well . . maybe a *little* differently," replied Dr. Kesre.

* * * * * * *

Nearly two weeks had passed, and on Thursday, Dr. Kesre decided to remove Elvis' bandages. Terry was apprehensive, but she was even more excited about the prospects of seeing the new Elvis. Both Lori and Becky, who returned last week from their grandparents, had just left for school. As soon as Terry saw them board the school bus, she called Elvis at the hotel.

"Elvis? This is Terry. Al would like to remove the last of your bandages this morning. The girls just left for school, so as soon as you can get over here, we can remove them in a couple of minutes."

"I'm on my way, Terry."

Austin: August 18, 1977, 7:00 AM CDT

After hanging up, Elvis donned a hooded sweatshirt that partially covered his face. Prior to leaving, he slowly opened the door from his hotel room and looked up and down the corridor to make sure that no one was there. It was deserted. He quickly walked to the elevator and after pausing to look up and down the corridor again, he pushed the DOWN button. Just then, the elevator arrived. Standing off to one side, he glanced inside as soon as the doors opened. It was empty. He then walked into the elevator and pushed the 'G' button. It soon arrived at the garage level, and after the doors opened, he jogged the short distance to his parked car. Ten minutes later, he pulled into the Kesre's driveway.

* * * * * * *

After Elvis was comfortably settled underneath the clinic's bright, overhead lights, Dr. Kesre, began snipping away the gauze with utmost deliberation. Finally, he removed the last strip, staring at his latest creation.

"How do I look, Al," inquired Elvis with anticipation. "Terry, do I look like Eduardo?"

Terry just stared, hardly believing her eyes. "Elvis, I think when all the swelling goes down, you'll look like Eduardo did when he first arrived here." Turning towards her husband, "Al, you may have outdone yourself this time."

Dr. Kesre simply smiled. The proof of his skill and artistry was obvious. No one had to tell him that his first surgical procedure was a stunning success, exceeding even *his* expectations.

Elvis sensed Dr. Kesre's pride, just by the expression on his face. "Let me have the mirror, Al. I want to see what I look like."

Terry picked up the mirror and handed it to Elvis. He stared at his new image for what seemed like an eternity. "Well I sure don't look like I did before the operation, but I don't know if I look like Eduardo, either. I've only seen him when he looked like me . . I mean . . how I used to look. How long do you think it will take for the swelling to go down, Al?"

"About a week . . ten days at most. We won't know until then whether we'll have to do any additional surgery. Let me remove the last of the sutures, and then I'll clean you up. Since you're still in the process of growing new skin, as a precaution, I'm going to put some medication on your face to prevent any infection. I'll have to put a light covering of gauze back on, too, but you're used to that by now."

"You're going to put that gauze on *again?*" asked Elvis half joking. "Well, I guess you'll just have to call me . . . *The King of Tut,*" and they all broke into laughter.

* * * * * * *

Ten days had passed since the removal of the sutures. Dr. Kesre decided it was time to take another look at his famous patient. Once again, as soon as the girls left for school, Terry called the hotel. Fifteen minutes later, Elvis was back inside the clinic, underneath the overhead lights.

"Here we go." remarked Dr. Kesre as he began removing the gauze.

After cutting away the last strip, Al inspected his work closely. Pausing, he backed up a few steps, and then his face literally lit up like a beacon.

"What's that look on your face supposed to mean, Al?" inquired Elvis with more than a hint of anticipation in his voice. "Do I look like Eduardo, or will you have to do some more surgery?"

"You look just fine, Elvis," replied Dr. Kesre, trying to downplay the results of his work while still basking in his pride. "I don't think we'll have to do another . . ."

Before Dr. Kesre could finish, Terry interrupted, "Al is being modest, Elvis. You look just like Eduardo *used* to look. If I had been away for the

Austin: August 18, 1977, 7:00 AM CDT

past several months, I would have sworn that Eduardo had come back to pay us his *first* visit. Take a look at this picture of him when he first arrived."

"Unbelievable!" replied Elvis as he stared in the mirror. "Terry, I look just like him."

Terry nodded in agreement.

"Elvis," added Dr. Kesre. "Here's something else that should put your mind at ease now that you have a new identity."

"What's that, Al?"

"Nobody but Terry and I know what you look like. Even my surgical team won't have the foggiest idea what you *really* look like!"

"Now that you mention it Al, I never thought of it that way. To think that I'll be able to go anywhere without being recognized. I haven't been able to do that for more than twenty years. After all that's happened, I think I'd like to get away from it all, at least for awhile," replied Elvis by now sounding a little tired. "Larry was telling me about this monastery in Italy . . Saint Antonio's in Siena . . wherever that is. He knows the choir director, and he thinks it would be the perfect spot for me to relax while thinking about what I want to do with my future. But I'm not really sure I want to leave the country *now,* since Lisa Marie doesn't have a daddy."

"I think Larry's right," replied Terry. "Al and I took a trip to Italy several years ago. We visited that same abbey in Siena, and they have this magnificent choir. It's very peaceful there and the surrounding gardens are absolutely beautiful. And something else, Elvis. There's a school right in Siena that teaches Italian to foreigners. You'll probably want to learn some basic Italian since you might be doing some traveling while you're there. At least it will give you something to do, and it never hurts to learn another language."

The Resurrection of The King

"I don't know about learning *another* language, Terry. Some people think I have enough trouble with *English,*" replied Elvis, while glancing directly at Al. "But the way you describe Siena and Saint Antonio's, I should probably leave on the next flight."

"Now just a minute, Elvis. It wasn't your *English* I was referring to," replied Al. "It was your too easily recognized *voice*. But as far as taking the *next* flight to Italy, I wouldn't be thinking about that quite yet. You'll have to remain in Austin for just a little while longer. There are still some other matters that have to be taken care of."

"You sure talked your way out of that one, Al. Just what *other matters* were you referring to?" asked Elvis, now with a puzzled look on his face.

"To begin with, there's Eduardo's restaurant. If you go to Italy now, we might have to sell it, hopefully to Joe Genuardi if he wants it. That can be handled by lawyers, and it won't require your presence in Memphis like we thought. Joe thinks Eduardo is still here in Austin starting up his new restaurant. We could always say he wants to stay *permanently.*"

"I forgot all about that Al. But since my presence won't be required in Memphis, why should I have to remain in Austin any longer?"

"You shouldn't, Elvis, but there are several other things you should address *before* you leave. First, there's your weight, and I have some serious concerns. Larry tells me you've put on quite a few pound in the past year, just like Eduardo did. But Eduardo died, and now we know why."

"What do you mean, *now we know why?*" replied Elvis.

"I'll try to simplify things for you, Elvis. Eduardo, like you, took a number of prescription drugs. Those drugs when acting in combination, and coupled with all that junk food you've been eating, don't bode too well with your digestive track. The result can be frequent constipation like *you* seem to be having and that's another warning sign. It can become a life-

Austin: August 18, 1977, 7:00 AM CDT

threatening situation if your colon becomes impacted, like Dr. Franklin, Eduardo's doctor, believes happened to *Eduardo!* Larry got a call from Franklin the other day, and he gave him the graphic details. Larry told *me* the same day. With your high blood pressure, Elvis, if *your* colon were to become impacted, it could result in a fatal heart attack."

"Jesus, Al. Are you serious?" replied Elvis.

"Yes I am, and that's why I want you to make a few changes in your diet, and get into an exercise program *before* you go to Italy. I belong to a gym in Austin and I want you to work out with me for a few weeks. You should also start substituting more nutritious foods for that junk stuff you're always eating . . snacks like high-fiber fresh fruits, nuts, and especially more salads and steamed vegetables at mealtime. Salads really fill you up, and they're high in fiber. They also contain very few calories.

"You mean you want me to stop eating just about everything that I really like, don't you Al?" remarked Elvis sarcastically.

"It's not that bad, Elvis. Just replace the cheeseburgers and french fries with turkey sandwiches and almonds. And use whole wheat or pumpernickel toast with mustard instead of traditional hamburger rolls with mayonnaise. With all that excess weight you're carrying around, you'll drop 20 pounds before you know it. It's also better to establish a regular exercise program to go along with your change in dietary habits. You'll lose weight faster, your blood pressure will drop, and it will improve your muscle tone, including your *heart's* muscle tone. Listen Elvis, if you were to know the *real* causes of Eduardo's death, it would scare the shit out of you, pardon the language, and I'm damn tempted to tell you. I suspect that terrifying fear is the only thing that will make *you* change!"

"Well, you're doing a damn good job of scaring me, Al. Does that mean I won't be able to eat any peanut butter and fried banana sandwiches?"

"Nor BLTs, especially with mayo, at least until you reach your desired weight, which for your height and age, should be about 180 pounds. At

The Resurrection of The King

that point, you can begin eating some of your favorite foods, as long as you don't overdo it and you continue with your exercise program. As soon you gain another five pounds, you'll have to go back on the diet."

"Okay, Al, you're the doctor. I'll give it a try, but I'm going to need your support. I'm appointing you to be my personal trainer."

"You're on, Elvis! Remember, we'll be working out together. They call it the buddy system, and it's a big help for maintaining motivation. Before I forget, Elvis, there's still one other matter."

"And what's that, Al?"

"Your drug dependency!"

"My drug dependency? What drug dependency? The only pills I take are prescribed by my doctors. I'm not a drug addict, if that's what you're thinking. Now I know you been talking to Larry!"

"Yes I have, Elvis. Prescribed or not, you still can't get through the day without them .. even here. That's what is meant by *dependency.*"

"By that definition, I guess I you're right. I just don't know if I can stop taking them."

"It won't be easy, Elvis, but I know you can do it. I just read about a drug rehab program involving gradual withdrawal. Each week, you reduce your medication by a small percentage. Within a couple of months, you could be off those drugs entirely. Larry gave me a list of everything you're taking. He also told me that Dr. Lane wants you to stay on the lithium. You'll probably have to take it for a month or two *after* you're weaned off the drugs, but at a gradually declining dosage. Combined with your exercise and nutrition program, I think by that time your depression will have eased up considerably, maybe even disappeared."

"Great! Just to change the subject, Al, how did Larry ever get the names

Austin: August 18, 1977, 7:00 AM CDT

of the prescription drugs I'm taking?"

"Larry has many friends and colleagues at Baptist Memorial, Elvis, including in Hematology where they do the blood work. Remember when you were admitted to the hospital and your Daddy called Larry in the E. R. to see if he could come up and visit *John Burroughs* in Room 725?"

"Yeah, I remember, Al, but ain't *nothin'* sacred?"

"Not among us doctors. When you came to the hospital *that* time, it was for food poisoning. But it wasn't the *only* time you were admitted to Baptist Memorial under the name, John Burroughs. You used it the last time you OD'd. Whenever someone OD's, Elvis, they *have* to do blood tests. They found everything you were taking, including what that doctor in Las Vegas gave you. Apparently he was overwhelmed by your celebrity status, and it diminished his medical judgment. Anyway, now you know why I told my surgical team that your name was John Burroughs. It was the first name I thought of. I certainly couldn't use Elvis Presley."

"I know, but they can tell the medicines I was taking from a blood test?"

"They certainly can, Elvis, and you're damn lucky it wasn't reported to the authorities. I just wanted to make sure that both of us were on the same page when it came to *your* drug problem, and it *is* a problem. One other thing, Elvis. I want you to get together with Larry and me before you leave for Italy. He can fly down here so we can give you a briefing."

"Briefing? replied Elvis. "You make it sound like I'm going on a spy mission."

"Elvis! Since you're going to *be* Eduardo Pirelli at Saint Antonio's, you should know everything about him, at least everything that Larry and I know. That's what I meant by a briefing. And you're going to have to work a little on your accent and speech patterns, too."

"My accent and speech patterns? What's wrong with my accent and speech patterns?" asked Elvis somewhat defensively."

The Resurrection of The King

"Everybody in the world recognizes your voice, Elvis, and you might come in contact with some of your fans at the monastery. But don't worry. Terry minored in speech at Morris-Harvey. More importantly, she's a director in a local theater group, and she has quite an ear for dialects. Didn't you have a speech coach when you made all those movies?"

"Yes, but they pretty much wanted me to talk the way I normally do. In my first movie, they were much more concerned with me remembering my lines, but that was never a problem for me."

"Good. I have every confidence then that Terry will have you sounding like a South Philadelphian in no time at all, Elvis. View it as just another acting role."

"But a South Philadelphia accent? You want me sounding like you, Al?"

"Well, not exactly like me. More like Fabian. You remember him, don't you Elvis? He's the young guy they found in South Philly who looked somewhat like you. He made some movies, too, but . . uh . . he had to struggle a little when it came to singing like you. Terry will have you talking like Fabian a lot sooner than you think. But you'll positively have to get rid of that Tupelo-Memphis accent, even though you probably don't think you have one."

"I guess you're right, Al. But a South Philadelphia accent? That could take me years to learn. And by the way, Fabian's a pretty good guy. He's just trying to make a buck like the rest of us. I once gave him a song to record. It did pretty good on the charts, too."

"I still think you underestimate Terry's dedication and resolve, Elvis. She'll have you sounding like a South Philadelphian, Fabian or otherwise, in just a few short weeks. Regarding that monastery in Italy, Larry tells me there's an exchange program run by the Catholic Church in Memphis. Here's the way it works: One of Saint Antonio's choir members comes to America to sing at that big cathedral in Memphis, while an

Austin: August 18, 1977, 7:00 AM CDT

American from Memphis goes to Saint Antonio's to sing in *their* choir. Larry arranged everything. *You,* or rather Eduardo, are the replacement from Memphis. Call Larry and have him get in touch with Father Collivera after you've made your flight arrangements to let him know when you're arriving."

"Father Collivera? Who is Father Collivera?" asked Elvis.

"He's the choirmaster at Saint Antonio's. Larry tells me he's a big fan of yours, too."

"I didn't realize Larry was so well-connected with the Catholic Church. Next thing you'll be telling me is that he's an adviser to the Pope."

"Not quite, Elvis. But Catholic priests are coming into the E. R. all the time to administer the Last Rights. Larry probably knows half the priests in Memphis. One of them was from Vanderbilt . . someone he met when he was in medical school. They've remained good friends ever since."

"Larry never ceases to amaze me, Al. And you're absolutely right about my accent. When I flew down here, I made the mistake of talking in my usual voice to a young lady who held the door open for me at the airport. For a moment, I thought for sure she recognized me, even with the disguise I was wearing. I've been thinking about changing my voice, but it didn't occur to me that I should talk like someone from South Philly."

"You never know who you're going to meet, Elvis. Remember, you look just like Eduardo. You could meet someone who knew him from his old neighborhood . . or one of his customers from his restaurant in Memphis. I really think Terry will be a big help."

"Getting back to something you said earlier, Al . . when you mentioned that I should learn Italian, I don't know if you knew this, but Daddy used to listen to Enrico Caruso records at home when I was a young 'un in Tupelo. After I grew up, I took quite a likin' to opera myself. Mario Lanza was one of my favorite tenors, and if memory serves me correctly, he was from South Philadelphia, too. I once met him out in Beverly Hills, and he showed me some special breathing exercises he used. I practiced them for a couple of months, and it really paid off . . probably increased my range by half an octave. Mario was much too young when he died. What a terrible loss! Whenever I get a chance to on Saturdays, I still listen to the Met on the radio. After I appeared in my concert at Madison Square Garden, I met Robert Merrill at a party, and we talked for quite awhile. I like all types of music, Al, but there's one thing that always bugged me about opera."

"What was that, Elvis?"

"I could never understand what they were singing. "

"Well there's a benefit I never thought of, Elvis," replied Terry. "When you *do* learn Italian, you'll enjoy opera even more. By the way, when you get to Italy, would you keep in touch with us? You can always call us here, collect. And if you can't call us, at least send us a post card from time to time."

"I'll keep in touch, Terry, don't you worry 'bout that. You folks have given me a new life, and I'll be forever grateful. I don't know exactly how long I'll be staying in Italy, but you'll be in my thoughts every day."

"Okay, enough of this sentimentality, you two," interrupted Al. "Elvis and I have some serious exercising to do." Turning towards Elvis, Al continued. "They just built this new air conditioned indoor driving range a few miles from here. What do you say we go out and hit a few?"

* * * * * * *

Austin: June 25, 1989, 2:00 AM CDT

CHAPTER NINETEEN
Austin: June 25, 1989, 2:00 AM CDT

The Kesres arrived at Robert Mueller Municipal Airport shortly after two in the morning. There was hardly a soul to be seen, other than the clean-up crews and the security patrols. After parking their car in the short-term lot, they walked into the terminal and headed towards the charter flights arrival gate. Terry and Al were still excited at the prospects of seeing Elvis again, but Becky and Lori were understandably quite nervous. Lori was the first to spot the snack bar, and it was open. "Anyone for a coffee and Danish?" she asked.

"How could you even *think* about eating at a time like this, Lori?" asked Becky. "This isn't just *anybody* that we're meeting."

Fortunately, nobody was in earshot, so everyone could speak quite freely. "How are you two holding up?" inquired Terry, attempting to change the subject. "It's a good thing that it's Friday . . I mean Saturday morning. You'd have a pretty tough time getting up for your classes if this were a week day."

"Mom, how are *you* holding up? School's out for the summer, but we still have to go to work this afternoon, and you know how much I need my sleep," remarked Becky.

"And that goes double for me too, Mom," chimed in Lori. "Who knows what time we'll end up going to bed? I don't know about you, Becky, but I can't even think about sleeping now. The prospect of meeting Elvis Presley, even if he doesn't look like the old Elvis, is about the most exciting thing I could ever imagine. Just thinking about it gives me goose bumps. I sure hope I don't turn into a blubbering idiot when I meet him. After all, I did have a gigantic crush on him when I was a teeny bopper."

"Yeah," replied Becky, "and as far as everybody else in the world knows,

The Resurrection of The King

he's been dead for twelve years. I mean, this is *really* a big deal, Lori."

"Mom," interrupted Lori, "you've met Elvis before. So have you, Dad. What's he really like?"

"He's a pretty down-to-earth guy and very personable." replied Dr. Kesre. "He doesn't come across like most celebrities. He's easy to talk to, and he doesn't take himself too seriously. Elvis has a terrific sense of humor, too, always poking fun at himself. After you get to know him, he seems like . . well . . like you've been lifelong friends. But remember, Elvis is 54 now. He's not the same Elvis Presley you remember, nor for that matter, the Elvis your mother and I remember when he came to Austin twelve years ago. He's lost quite a bit of weight since then, too. I made sure of that before he left for Italy . . made him work out at my health club for a couple of months after the surgery. You probably noticed that he was much slimmer when he appeared at the concert last month."

"Yeah, come to think of it he was. I would have never dreamed it was Elvis Presley," replied Lori, "at least not the Elvis I remember from back in the seventies."

"And girls," interjected Terry. "When Elvis stayed with us twelve years ago, he was very polite, very mannerly . . almost overly polite. And he had a certain innocence about him that's hard to put into words . . kind of a boyish charm, we used to call it. You might say that I kind of got caught up with his charm. Your father, being merely a man, simply wouldn't understand. He fails to grasp what it's like for a lady when she meets Elvis Presley for the first time."

"Was his boyish charm, as you call it Terry, anything like mine when you first met me at Morris-Harvey?" asked Dr. Kesre with a slight hint of jealously in his voice. "You used to think I was pretty charming, didn't you honey? At least you used to say I was. Of course, it's getting harder

Austin: June 25, 1989, 2:00 AM CDT

and harder to remember, it's been so long ago. It's more like a *distant memory*," chuckled Dr. Kesre.

Terry, while glancing at the girls with a smile on her face and a winking eye, replied sternly to Al: "Dr. Kesre, since I'm a Christian lady and now a Texan, I'll refrain from answering that question about how charming you were . . . that is . . if you don't mind, honey."

Glancing out the terminal window, Lori noticed a plane coming down the runway. "Mom! Dad! I think I see his plane."

As if on cue, the rest of the Kesre family jumped to their feet and headed towards the closest window overlooking the tarmac. "I think it *is* Elvis' plane," remarked Dr. Kesre. "He said he was on a Lear Jet, and it sure looks like one, even in the runway lights. It should be stopping in front of the terminal building in just a few minutes, so we better get going. Remember, we have to meet him out on the tarmac. The smaller charter planes don't taxi up to the terminal. And one last thing, girls. Don't forget to call him *Mr. Pirelli*. Not even the flight crew knows that their passenger is Elvis Presley."

At 2:45 AM CDT, the Lear Jet carrying Elvis taxied up to the tarmac. After coming to a complete stop, the pilot immediately cut both of the engines. A moment later, the passenger door opened, and the copilot lowered the stairs. Elvis soon appeared carrying a large suitcase. Holding his other hand over his eyes to shade the bright lights beaming down over the tarmac, he finally spotted Al and Terry and waved to them.

Lori gasped in a hushed voice, "Oh my God, Becky! It's Elvis . . I mean Eduardo. I hope I can keep it together. I'm already a nervous wreck."

"I know just how you feel, Lori. My legs are literally turning to jelly, and I think I'm beginning to blush. Please, God," as Becky uttered a silent prayer, "help me get over this nervousness. I'm beginning to feel like I did when I went out on my first date, only much worse."

Just then, Dr. Kesre spoke up. "Let's go, girls. We don't want to keep our guest waiting."

As Terry and Dr. Kesre walked the last few yards to the Lear Jet, the Kesre daughters followed in virtual lockstep, staying slightly behind their parents. Elvis placed his suitcase on the tarmac, reached out, and shook Al's hand. A few seconds later, he shifted his attention towards Terry and gave her a big hug.

Lori turned and whispered to Becky, "Do you believe what we're seeing? Elvis Presley is actually hugging Mom. Oh my God, he just kissed her!"

After releasing his embrace, Elvis turned his attention to Lori and Becky. Dr. Kesre then spoke up. "Eduardo, I'd like you to meet our daughters, Lori and Becky. They've been so anxious to meet you after they heard you were flying into Austin."

Elvis immediately replied in his halting Italian accent, looking directly at both of the girls. "I'm a so happy to meet a you two. Your mama and a papa have a been telling a me so much about a you. Becky, I hear you a study the opera? Have you a performed a yet?"

Becky, still in awe, at first mumbled something unintelligible. Quickly collecting her thoughts, she then replied tentatively. "Only . . in college productions, Mr. Pirelli. And we really enjoyed your concert last month. You have such a magnificent voice, too. Lori and I were so disappointed when we couldn't meet you."

"That's such a nice a thing for you to say, Becky." replied Elvis. "And I was a so disappointed, too. But better a late than a never, no?"

Becky thought to herself, "This man really *is* charming. I just wish when I saw him last month, I would have paid more attention to his voice, if

Austin: June 25, 1989, 2:00 AM CDT

only to hear if I could detect any of the old, more *familiar* Elvis."

"And a Lori," as Elvis redirected his attention. "Your mama tells a me you're a teacher . . . that a you work with a . . . how you say in English . . *Autistic* a children? I think that's a so nice."

Lori was literally melting inside as she thought to herself, "To think I'm here, face to face, with *The King of Rock and Roll.* I still can't believe it. And now he's an opera star. What puzzles me is his speaking voice. He doesn't sound at all like Elvis Presley. He sounds like many Italians I've met who have to struggle with English. And why did I think his hair would still be black instead of gray or that he'd be wearing long sideburns? I wonder if this is all a cruel joke? Careful, Lori, you're getting paranoid." Suddenly, she was back in the real world. "Mr. Pirelli . . ?"

Elvis suddenly interrupted Lori before she could complete her question. "Please a call me Eduardo. That a goes a for you too, Becky. Let's a go inside. I'm a sure we have a much to talk about."

Dr. Kesre reached down and picked up Elvis' suitcase. Heading towards the terminal building with Terry by his side, Lori, Elvis and Becky, walking hand in hand, were following close behind. A few minutes later, they were inside the terminal building and headed for the parking area.

Upon approaching Dr. Kesre's car, Elvis was the first to speak. "What a happened to your Rolls a Royce, Al? Why are you driving this . . this a Cadillac a? Just a kidding. Cadillacs are nice a cars. I've had a few myself . . and a Ferrari and a Rolls a, too. But that was a many years ago."

"I still have my Rolls, Eduardo, but this is one special Cadillac," replied Dr. Kesre as Elvis and the girls settled into the back seat of the oversized Sedan Deville. "I had this one customized, and as you can see, it's as roomy as a limo. It also has a reworked Corvette engine that I had bored and stroked, and they bolted on an Eaton supercharger to give it a little

The Resurrection of The King

more pep. It now puts out more than 500 horsepower. Believe me when I tell you Eduardo . . this Caddy can really scat."

Now that they were all in the car, Elvis was starting to lose some of his Italian accent. "I believe a you, Al. It sure doesn't sound a like no stock Caddy engine, either. By the way, you used to live in Philadelphia. Did I ever tell you about the time I came up there . . to buy a rare Cadillac station wagon?"

"No, you never told me *that* story, but I wonder if was the same place I went to?" continued Dr. Kesre. "They used to specialize in restoring classic cars, didn't they?"

"I believe so," continued Elvis, now speaking almost entirely in his more familiar voice. "They had one of only two Cadillac station wagons ever made, and I just had to have it for my collection. Shortly after arriving, the owner took me on a tour of his dealership. When we got back to the Service Department, I must have surprised some of those body and fender boys. I was only wearin' a pair of jeans, a silk shirt, and cowboy boots. Nothing fancy, mind ya."

By now, he sounded just like the old Elvis. "Anyway, this young fella in the Parts Department, I think his name was Dontee . . or some funny name *like* that. Well, he nearly choked on his soda pop when he first saw me come in. The owner was introducing me to everybody in sight like I was some kind of a celebrity, so when he finally introduced me to Dontee, we shook hands. Well, let me tell you, Al, that boy had one powerful grip . . *real* powerful. He squeezed my hand so hard, he liked to sprain one of my fingers. I had trouble playing my guitar for nearly a month after that."

"Really?" replied Dr. Kesre, almost nonchalantly. "Did they have to take you to the emergency room?"

"Real funny, Al. No, it wasn't nothin' like that." continued Elvis while

Austin: June 25, 1989, 2:00 AM CDT

cracking a big smile, "After I climbed into that wagon and started it, Dontee comes over to me and says, 'That's some *Academy Award* performance you've been putting on, nearly as good as Elvis' forgettable role in *Change of Habit.* You almost had me fooled, too, especially with that imitation silk shirt you're wearing. Where did you get it from . . the thrift shop around the corner?' "

"He really said that?" replied Dr. Kesre, by now trying very hard not to break up with laughter.

"I tell ya, Al, that kid had a real smart mouth. His mama should a put some chili pepper on his tongue when he was a young'un. Any way, as Dontee watched me start up that Caddy, I got the distinct feelin' that he thought the dealer hired me as one of those impersonators . . you know . . one of those . . *rent-a-celebrities.* I don't think he ever believed it was really me."

"You're probably right. By the way, did I hear you say you came to Philadelphia just to buy a Cadillac *station wagon?"* asked Dr. Kesre with a slight touch of skepticism in his voice. "Are you sure it was an *authentic* Cadillac station wagon?"

"Of course it was *authentic!* You don't think I'd come that far just to buy some *counterfeit* station wagon, do you Al?" replied an *appearing* to be annoyed Elvis.

"Well . . I didn't think you'd have done it knowingly." replied Dr. Kesre. "The reason I asked is because back in the sixties when I was going to medical school at Hahnamann, I had this jug band that played at fraternity parties in the area, mostly at Hahnamann, but also at Penn and Temple where they had medical schools, too. We used to carry the instruments around in an old Cadillac hearse. I kept that hearse until the early seventies before I finally sold it to a local dealer who specialized in rare car restorations."

The Resurrection of The King

"No kidding." replied Elvis, sensing that Dr. Kesre was about to make him the victim of a hoax.

"Yes, it's true." continued Dr. Kesre impassively. "I was later told by the dealer's body shop foreman that there were a lot of similarities between a Cadillac station wagon and a Cadillac hearse. They were both built on the same platform, and they used many of the same parts. The foreman went on to say that they bought every Cadillac hearse they could get their hands on so they could convert them into station wagons. All they had to do was remove those racks inside, you know, the ones where they put the coffins. Then they would install some rear seats and the side doors from an Olds station wagon. The whole process took less than two days to complete."

"That's amazing ingenuity for a body shop in Philadelphia, Al. Guys with that kind of skill usually move to California," mocked Elvis. "Sure must be a lot of old Cadillac hearses in Philadelphia. Funeral business must be pretty good, too."

"Well, I had every reason to believe the shop forman," continued Dr. Kesre. "Any way, he went on to tell me that during one stretch in the early 70's, they were cranking out as many as a dozen Cadillac station wagons every month. They always kept an ad running in one of those car collector magazines and they'd just sit back and wait for the calls to come in. I can remember seeing that ad myself, just as if it were yesterday: *FOR SALE: RARE CADILLAC STATION WAGON. One of Only Two Ever Made.* In the back pages of that same issue, they ran another ad, only this one was much bigger: *WANTED: CADILLAC HEARSES! Top Dollars Paid.* Of course, it was the second ad that really caught my attention. When I brought that old hearse of mine into the body shop, the foreman told me they hadn't seen one for nearly six months."

"Sounds like they needed a new ad agency, Al, but I think I know where this is leading to," replied Elvis with a smile spreading across his face.

Austin: June 25, 1989, 2:00 AM CDT

"Just think," continued Dr. Kesre. "That rare Cadillac station wagon you bought? It could have been my old hearse. By the way, was the one you bought, black?"

"As a matter of fact, it was white." replied Elvis. "Thought you got me on that one, didn't ya, Al?"

By now, Terry and the girls had begun to snicker, even though they had heard this story from their father at least a dozen times. What they hadn't known before, however, was that Elvis really did come up to Philadelphia from Memphis to buy a rare Cadillac station wagon, back in the early 70s, right around the time Dr. Kesre sold his hearse to the same dealer.

"Well, I just wanted to be sure." continued Dr. Kesre, still maintaining his deadpan manner. "Of course, they had to do a little body work first and then repaint those old hearses before they could sell them . . what with the different color doors they had to buy from all the local junk yards. Come to think of it, the foreman told me they had an order for a white one. Some guy from Memphis was coming in the following week to pick it up."

"Okay, Al. You sure got me good on that one." laughed Elvis. "I guess we can all relax a little bit, now that we've broken the ice. That's a real funny story about your hearse, but I sure hope it wasn't true. If I'd dwell on it for too long, I might even get to believin' it, you were so convincing. I paid good money for that Cadillac station wagon. I'd hate to think it was a *restored* hearse. And I'd dislike it even more if I allowed myself to believe that it was *your* old hearse, Al."

"I guess we'll never know," replied Dr. Kesre, still maintaining an expressionless look on his face.

Listening to all of the bantering between Elvis and her father, Lori began

The Resurrection of The King

feeling more at ease. "Dad was so right," she thought to herself. "Elvis does have a terrific sense of humor, and now his Italian accent has all but disappeared. Come to think of it, he does sound a *little* like Elvis used to. I guess he lost his southern accent after living in Italy for so long. And it *has* been twelve years. Eduardo Pirelli really *could* be Elvis Presley."

No sooner had the thought crossed Lori's mind, when Elvis spoke up. "By the way Al and Terry, now that we're in the car, I'd like to properly introduce myself to your daughters."

Elvis, sitting between Lori and Becky, turned to his right and looked directly at Lori. Pausing briefly, he searched for just the right words. Finally he spoke, but this time in his familiar Memphis draw. "How do you do, Lori? My name is *Elvis* . . Elvis Presley . . and I'm so pleased to meet you." He then turned to Becky and spoke the words she never thought she'd hear, from the one person in the world she never thought she'd meet. "Hello Becky. I'm Elvis Presley. I've been wantin' to meet you for a long, long time."

"There was no doubt about it," Becky thought to herself. "This man sitting right next to me really *is* Elvis Presley. Oh my God, I still can't believe it."

Suddenly, in a spontaneous display of affection, both Becky and Lori hugged Elvis together. Elvis was stunned. He didn't know quite how to react or even what to say. In fact, he was speechless.

Finally, Becky, with tears streaming down her face, could no longer contain herself. "Oh Elvis, we just knew you didn't die. We thought for sure that it had to be someone else. Don't you ever do that again . . do you hear? Don't you ever go disappearing on us again." ordered Becky.

"And that goes for me, too," echoed Lori. "Even if you have to have your looks changed again, at least let us know where you are. We don't have to know exactly where you live, or what you look like. We just want to

Austin: June 25, 1989, 2:00 AM CDT

know that you're alive and well."

"Yes, ma'ams," replied Elvis. "You have my word on it."

Elvis was stunned by the girls' spontaneous behavior, and in particular, by their heartfelt concern. Now he was beginning to understand why the audience in Las Vegas had acted the way they did.

"All of those people in the audience," continued Elvis with a flash of insight, "they were hoping . . . wishing . . . that it really *was* me. But I still don't understand why people feel that way about me, especially after all these years."

Just then, Terry interrupted. "Elvis, there are just some things in life that we'll never fully understand because they defy *any* rational explanation. *After all these years,* you ask? They've never forgotten you Elvis. And Al and I are so grateful just to have met you . . and to have gotten to know you, too. Most of your fans haven't, and I'm sure they would trade places with us in a heart beat."

"I am truly at a loss for words, Terry. I simply don't know what to say. But I do know one thing. For whatever the good Lord's intentions were, He must have had a good reason for bringing you folks into my life. You know, when I lost my Mama, I felt lonely and confused. And then I met Priscilla. Maybe God didn't want 'Cilla and me to *stay* married, but apparently he wanted us to have a daughter. Perhaps I'll go back to Italy, but first I want to spend some time with Lisa Marie before Al works his magic again. I really like Milan, and I have a standing offer just north of there to help train some race horses. It's something I've wanted to do for a long time, and it sure would be an interesting change of pace.

"That sounds wonderful, Elvis. I'm so happy for you." replied Terry.

"And one other thing, Terry and Al. You folks are becoming like a safe harbor for me. It seems like every time I'm in trouble, or I need some help, well . . . I feel like I can just come home to port. You are truly good friends, and I'm eternally grateful. And Al . . . you're really not such a bad guy after all . . . for a *yankee.*"

"And you're not such a bad guy either, Elvis . . for an Italian opera star. What do you say we continue this mutual admiration society after we get back home and have some breakfast? After that, we'll all need a good night's sleep. Or is that a good *morning's* sleep?" replied Dr. Kesre rhetorically, as he pulled the Caddy out of the airport and onto the virtually deserted freeway.

* * * * * * *

Off the Record

CHAPTER TWENTY
Off the Record

In CHAPTER ONE of *The Resurrection of The King,* a recess was called in the hearing when it became apparent that Glen Watson's testimony would continue well past the lunch hour. What was not revealed in open court, however, was what happened shortly after the lunch recess, and specifically, what occurred in Judge Blackwell's chambers. As the judge entered the court room, the bailiff repeated his familiar greeting: "Please rise. Would the courtroom please come to order? Thank you."

As soon as he reached the bench, Judge Blackwell turned towards Desmond Howard. "Mr. Howard, please continue where you left off before the lunch recess. Mr. Watson, you're still under oath."

"Thank you, your Honor," replied Howard. "Would the court's stenographer please read back the last portion of Mr. Watson's testimony, the part just prior to the lunch recess?"

"Yes, I'd be happy to Mr. Howard," she replied.

MR. HOWARD: Referring again to Baptist Memorial Hospital Mr. Watson, did you interview everyone who was present in the emergency room when Elvis' body was first brought in?

MR. WATSON: Not everyone, Mr. Howard. I only interviewed those in the ER who either knew Elvis or could make a positive ID, including the nurses and Cardiologists on the Harvey Team who tried to revive him.

MR. HOWARD: Among those you interviewed, had any of them ever met Elvis in person prior to August 16, 1977?

MR. WATSON: Yes, two. Dr. Nick who accompanied the body in the am-

bulance and Dr. Lawrence Kaye who was called in for backup after the EMTs had advised the ER that they were bringing a cardiac arrest patient in from Graceland. Dr. Kaye had arrived just a few minutes before Elvis' body was brought in.

MR. HOWARD: Was Dr. Kaye able to identify Elvis' body?

MR. WATSON: No, he never saw the body because he was examining another patient. Everyone else in the ER who saw Elvis' body and could make a positive ID, believed it was Elvis Presley.

MR. HOWARD: Mr. Watson, did you interview everyone in the Pathology Department who participated in the autopsy?

MR. WATSON: Yes I did Mr. Howard and that included the county coroner who was called in for the autopsy.

MR. HOWARD: Did anyone you interviewed at the hospital who saw the body, believe that it wasn't Elvis Presley's body?

DR. WATSON: No, not a single person Mr. Howard. Not one.

MR. HOWARD: You stated earlier that Dr. Kaye had met Elvis prior to August 16, 1977. Where and when did Dr. Kaye meet Elvis?

JUDGE BLACKWELL: Mr. Howard, I'm getting the distinct feeling that your examination of Mr. Watson is going to take us well past the lunch hour. Let's take a break now and we'll continue with his testimony at 1:30 this afternoon. Court's adjourned.

"Thank you," replied Howard to the stenographer. "Mr. Watson, you stated before the lunch break that Dr. Kaye had met Elvis Presley *before* August 16, 1977. What did Dr. Kaye tell you about his previous meeting or meetings with Elvis Presley?"

Off the Record

"Dr. Kaye had been an E. R. physician at Baptist Memorial Hospital since 1970. Presley had been admitted previously to the hospital, but under the name, John Burroughs so as not to cause a feeding frenzy among the press. On one of those occasions, Vernon Presley called Dr. Kaye in the E. R. to see if he could go up and see *Mr. Burroughs* in Room 725. Elvis and Dr. Kaye were good friends, having met in Germany while they were in the Army. Elvis had been admitted to a private room, apparently suffering from a drug overdose. As it turned out, it was food poisoning."

"Mr. Watson, when Elvis' body was brought into Baptist Memorial Hospital on the afternoon of August 16, 1977, you indicated that Dr. Kaye was was on duty in the E. R. but didn't see the body, is that correct?"

"Yes, that's correct, Mr. Howard."

"You also said that Dr. Kaye was treating another patient and wasn't able to see Elvis' body when it arrived in the E. R. How about *after* Elvis' body had arrived, Mr. Watson . . after the Harvey Team had attempted *unsuccessfully,* to resuscitate him? Was Dr. Kaye able to see him then?"

"No, Mr. Howard."

"Did Dr. Kaye go into Pathology during Elvis' autopsy, Mr. Watson?"

"No, he really didn't have time to, Mr. Howard. Keep in mind that Dr. Kaye was on emergency backup duty and had only arrived at the hospital shortly *before* Elvis was brought in. After Dr. Kaye arrived, he had to remain in the emergency room to cover for one of the staff physicians who already was on duty in the E. R. This allowed *that* E. R. doctor to attend to Elvis as soon as he arrived. As it turned out, another patient *was* admitted to the E. R. *after* Elvis had arrived, and Dr. Kaye examined and treated *that* patient."

"Was there anyone else you interviewed, other than the EMTs that arrived at Graceland, who had any concerns about the identity of the body of Elvis Presley?" continued Howard.

The Resurrection of The King

"I don't know if I would characterize this as a concern, but Donna Lewis, Elvis' diarist, said that when she saw Elvis' body at the viewing, he didn't looked like himself at all. *He looked awful* is the way she described him. In fact, she said that a number of his fans attending the viewing felt the same way, too. Of course, looking awful doesn't mean that the body they saw in the open casket *wasn't* the body of Elvis Presley. Perhaps Ms. Lewis will clarify this when she testifies, Mr. Howard."

"Mr. Watson, during your first investigation in 1977 . . did *anyone* you interviewed lead you to believe that the body found by Ginger Alden on the bathroom floor at Graceland on the afternoon of August 16, 1977 . . the body that was transported to Baptist Memorial Hospital that same afternoon . . did any of those you interviewed say or even *suggest* . . that it might *not* be or *wasn't* . . the body of Elvis Presley that they saw?"

"In my *1977* investigation? Other than the EMTs and perhaps Donna Lewis, no! Everyone else I interviewed in 1977 who was either at Graceland, in the ambulance, the E. R., or in the Pathology Department at Baptist Memorial Hospital on the afternoon of August 16th, and who actually saw or came in contact with the body, believed it was Elvis Presley's body. Nevertheless, some of those I interviewed admitted to not actually seeing the body's face."

"Mr. Watson, did you receive any information from anyone in your *1989* investigation . . that led you to believe that the body found by Ginger Alden on the bathroom floor at Graceland on the afternoon of August 16, 1977 . . the body that was subsequently transported to Baptist Memorial Hospital that same afternoon . . was *not* the body of Elvis Aaron Presley?"

"In 1989? No, at least not as a result of *my* investigation."

"Not as a result of *your* investigation, Mr. Watson? What did you mean, not as a result of *your* investigation?"

Off the Record

"From the time when Elvis Presley's death was first reported on August 16th, 1977," replied Watson, "and until a few months ago, I had every reason to believe, at least based on my investigation, that Elvis *was* dead, at least, that is, until this past June."

"This past June, Mr. Watson? What happened this past June?"

"Back in June of this year," continued Watson, "I got a call at my office from a neighbor and friend of mine, Steven Dunne, a former wedding photographer who was now in the video recording business in Las Vegas. Dunne told me during our phone conversation that he had recently videotaped an Elvis impersonator show. He went on to tell me this incredible story about one of the performers, and asked me if I knew anyone with expertise in voice printing. I told him one of my college fraternity brothers, David Abbott, worked for the FBI and was considered a leading authority on voice printing. I also told Steve that I'd be more than happy to give Dave a call. Dunne, who sounded very anxious, asked me to call Abbott immediately, *yesterday if possible* were the words he used."

"And did you call David Abbott, Mr. Watson?"

"Yes, as soon as I hung up the phone. Fortunately, I was able to reach him at his office in Washington, and he agreed to fly to Las Vegas the next day. I told Dave I would meet him at the airport and take him to see Dunne, but that I couldn't stay with him because I had a previous appointment. I would, however, come back to Dunne's studio and pick him up just as soon as I was finished with my appointment."

Just then, the bailiff handed Howard a note. After reading it and pausing briefly to digest its contents, a look of grave disappointment spread over his face. Howard then handed the note back to Judge Blackwell. Upon reading it, Blackwell handed the note to Hillary Caruthers, counsel for Elvis' estate. Hilliary quickly read the note and let out an almost inaudible sigh of relief. A smile appeared on her face, a smile so brief that

The Resurrection of The King

if you weren't looking directly at her, you would never have noticed it. Howard approached Judge Blackwell. Upon reaching the bench, he spoke in a near whisper so as not to be overheard in the court room. "Your Honor, the information in this note has a direct bearing on the foundation of our case. Could we have a brief recess to discuss this in private?"

"Of course, Dezi. Let's go back to my chambers."

* * * * * * *

Back in the judge's chambers, Howard spoke first. "Your Honor, the note I just received and which both you and Hillary read, was a fax from a very good friend of mine, a prosecutor for the Justice Department in Washington. David Abbott was just found dead in his apartment, and it appears to have been suicide. Abbott was the FBI's voice analyst who came out to Las Vegas to interview Steve Dunne, the videographer who recorded Eduardo Pirelli's Elvis tribute show this past June. While here, Abbott picked up Dunne's video tapes of that show, along with some previous video recordings of Elvis when he appeared in concert in Las Vegas back in the mid seventies, video tapes of the same songs that Eduardo Pirelli, the touring opera star from Italy, sang in his Elvis tribute show this past June. Yesterday morning, before the start of the trial, Abbott called Watson and Dunne to tell them both that he was finally able to make voice prints from both Eduardo's and Elvis' tapes. Abbott went on to tell them that he was now convinced that Eduardo Pirelli and Elvis Presley were one and the same person, and that he would be coming to San Francisco tomorrow, meaning today, to testify about his finding in open court. For all we know, those video tapes and voice prints may still be back at his office, or even in his apartment. Without those video tapes, voice prints, and Abbott's testimony, we don't have much of a case."

"I'm inclined to agree with you, Dezi. Is there anything else I should know that could influence my ruling?" asked Judge Blackwell.

"Yes, Your Honor. Unfortunately, we couldn't take Abbott's deposition,

Off the Record

since he didn't perform the voice prints analysis until yesterday. Due to the suspicious nature of his death, and since Abbott's testimony was so crucial to our law suit, I'd like to move for a continuance, at least until we can come up with those video tapes and voice prints and bring them back to San Francisco. Without David Abbott's testimony, or the voice prints, we can only rely on Glen Watson's and Steve Dunne's testimony, testimony based on their telephone conversations with Abbott yesterday. Although Abbott *did* tell Watson and Dunne that he was convinced that Eduardo Pirelli and Elvis Presley were one and the same person, neither Watson nor Dunne had actually examined the voice prints themselves. Even if they had, neither of them had the credentials or expertise to be considered an expert witness."

"Dezi," replied Judge Blackwell, "you mentioned that Abbott called *both* Watson and Dunne. Did either of them record their phone conversations?"

"No, Your Honor. And I guess we can't be certain that it was really Abbott who called. Consequently, their testimony detailing their phone conversations with Abbott would be considered hearsay. Of course, if Glen were to come up with the Pirelli tapes, we could always make another set of voice prints and bring in another analyst from the FBI to testify. Hopefully, the new analyst would confirm the results of Abbott's initial tests. One last thing, Your Honor. The Justice Department wants to interview Watson tomorrow in Washington. That means he'll have to fly back on tonight's red eye. While he's there, he'll try to locate the missing tapes and voice prints, but until he does, we'll need that continuance. And Your Honor . . Glen will need a search warrant, too."

"Any search warrants will have to issued in D. C., Dezi. Is there anything *you* would like to add, Hillary?" asked Judge Blackwell.

"Yes, you're honor. To be fair about this, I think it reasonable for Glen to have to produce those tapes within . . let's say . . four weeks from today. That should be plenty of time to search Abbott's office and apartment. If he *doesn't* find them by then, he can petition the Court for an extension."

The Resurrection of The King

"That sounds *quite* reasonable, Hillary," replied Howard.

"I agree with both of you. Continuance granted," replied Judge Blackwell.

****

Several months passed and after an intensive investigation, the FBI concluded that David Abbott had been murdered. The events surrounding his death were never fully disclosed due to his involvement with an ongoing criminal investigation at the Justice Department. The video tapes and voice prints of Eduardo Pirelli's appearance at the June 1989 Elvis Tribute Show in Las Vegas were never recovered.

FYI: Inasmuch as Watson and Dunne hadn't yet testified in open court about their phone conversations with David Abbott, a conversation where Abbott revealed his findings from his voice print analysis, there was never any *open-court* testimony that even suggested that Pirelli and Presley were one and the same person. Nevertheless, Sierra Life had stated in their pretrial *discovery* hearing that they would introduce evidence that would prove that Eduardo Pirelli and Elvis Presley were one and the same person. Howard, during his opening statement at the onset of the trial, chose *not* to mention this. Neither did Caruthers in *her* opening remarks, since on the first day of the trial, the voice print analysis of Pirelli's and Presley's video tapes didn't exist yet. Since Abbott was also involved with another trial in D. C., he simply didn't have time to conduct the voice print analysis *until* the day the Sierra Life trial began. If the truth be known, Howard never mentioned this in *his* opening remarks at the Sierra Life trial because he wanted to put doubt in Hillary's mind as to what exactly the evidence was that *would* be introduced. Moreover, Abbott, an expert witness, could have merely testified to his findings without necessarily producing any tapes or analysis at the trial.

When Howard asked Watson if he turned up anything from his *1989* investigation that would lead him to believe that the body Ginger Aldan found in Elvis' bathroom in August 1977, was the body of someone *other* than Elvis Presley, Watson certainly left the door open to speculation.

Off the Record

MR. HOWARD: Mr. Watson, did you receive any information from anyone in your 1989 investigation that led you to believe that the body found by Ginger Alden on the bathroom floor at Graceland on the afternoon of August 16, 1977, the body that was subsequently transported to Baptist Memorial Hospital that same afternoon, was not the body of Elvis Aaron Presley?

MR. WATSON: In 1989? No, at least not as a result of my investigation.

MR. HOWARD: Not as a result of your investigation, Mr. Watson? What did you mean, not as a result of your investigation?

MR. WATSON: From the time when Elvis Presley's death was first reported on August 16th, 1977 and until a few months ago, I had every reason to believe, at least based on my investigation, that Elvis was dead, at least, that is, until this past June.

MR. HOWARD: This past June, Mr. Watson? What happened this past June?

MR. WATSON: Back in June of this year, I got a call at my office from a neighbor and friend of mine, Steven Dunne, a former wedding photographer who was now in the video recording business in Las Vegas. Dunne told me during our phone conversation that he had recently videotaped an Elvis impersonator show. He went on to tell me this incredible story about one of the performers, and asked me if I knew anyone with expertise in voice printing. I told him one of my college fraternity brothers, David Abbott, worked for the FBI and was considered a leading authority on voice printing. I also told Steve that I'd be more than happy to give Dave a call. Dunne, who was very anxious, wanted me to call Abbott immediately, yesterday if possible were the words he used.

* * * * * * *

Without any *empirical* evidence confirming that Eduardo Pirelli and Elvis Presley were one and the same person, the lawsuit to recover the

The Resurrection of The King

proceeds of the insurance policy from Elvis Presley's estate was subsequently dropped by Sierra Life. Howard, Caruthers, Watson, and Dunne were ordered by the Court to never divulge David Abbott's phone conversations with Dunne and Watson where he claimed that Elvis and Eduardo were one and the same person. Moreover, the results of Abbott's voice print analysis were communicated *telephonically* by Abbott (inadmissible hearsay evidence), the details of which were revealed only in Judge Blackwell's chambers. Thus, it was never a matter of public record.

Steve Dunne was so despondent over the loss of his tapes, as well as the Court's gag order restraining him from discussing his phone conversation with David Abbot, he moved to Canada in 1990. "If Eduardo Pirelli wasn't Elvis Presley," remarked Dunne in a subsequent interview on Canadian television, "he had to be the greatest Elvis impersonator of all time. Based on what Abbott told me about the voice prints before he was murdered, Pirelli would've had to have a voice that was identical to Elvis Presley's voice in every way, and that's like two people having the same finger prints. Keep in mind, I've videotaped dozens of Elvis' concerts in Las Vegas, and had seen, heard, and videotaped the best of the best Elvis impersonators to ever appear on the strip. As far as I'm concerned, Eduardo Pirelli *is* Elvis Presley. There's not a doubt in my mind!"

****

Two months after his 1989 reconstructive surgery, Elvis went back to Italy to train race horses for a wealthy Italian industrialist, something he wanted to do ever since Dr. Kaye took him to Brandywine Raceway and introduced him to Standardbreds. Several years later, a 57-year old horse trainer, Elio Perenzi, won the Northern Italy Elvis regionals in Milan. This qualified him for the Italian finals held in Rome, where Perenzi's stunning victory earned him a trip to Memphis in August during *Elvis Week.*

Instead of going to Memphis, however, Elio traveled to East Ruthersford, New Jersey, the home of The Meadowlands Racetrack. A trotter with Italian connections had been entered in The Hambletonian, harness racing's most prestigious event, and Elio was an assistant trainer. One of

Off the Record

his tasks was to warm up the trotter on the Meadowlands one-mile track before the start of the race. Little did any of those 25,000 fans know that the driver they were watching, Elio Perenzi, was none other than the *King of Rock and Roll*. Elvis had finally trumped Pat Boone's brief career as a harness horse driver, albeit one that occurred in the movies.

In August 1997, Elvis met Dr. Kesre and his wife Terry while they were attending a reconstructive surgeons convention at a Tunica County, Mississippi casino-hotel just south of Memphis. Elvis, who had kept in touch with the Kesres after receiving his 1989 makeover, was again performing, but this time in a Legends show held at the same hotel. His rendition of *Suspicious Minds* still ranks as one of the most convincing Elvis impersonations ever seen in the state of Mississippi.

* * * * * * *

FYI: In July 1977, after the plans to make the switch with Eduardo Pirelli had been finalized, Elvis purchased a $1,000,000 prepaid, whole-life insurance policy, making a one-time, up front payment of $200,000. The policy was obtained from Sierra Life Assurance's branch office in Beverly Hills while Elvis was out in California. The interest earned on that $200,000 would more than pay the policy's annual premium, as well as provide ample *cash value* for Elvis to borrow from, if and when he needed money. Also while in Los Angeles, Elvis opened a *trust* account at one of Switzerland's largest banks, in the name of Elvis A. Presley *and* Vernon E. Presley, his father. Vernon and Elvis were the only ones who knew the account number and could access that account.

When he originally purchased the policy, Elvis had no idea that Eduardo would die on the day they switched places, nor that he (Elvis) would be going to Italy. Fortunately, Vernon anticipated that Elvis would need money for living expenses, no matter *where* he was, and that if Vernon had to wire him the money, either frequently or in large amounts, it could easily raise red flags with the accountants or leave a traceable paper trail.

Under the provisions of the will, the $1,000,000 face value of the insur-

The Resurrection of The King

ance policy would be paid upon Elvis' death to Vernon, also executor of the will. After Eduardo (believed to be Elvis) died, Vernon took the proceeds of the policy and purchased $1,000,000 worth of U. S. Long-Term Treasury Bonds, at the time paying 7.8% annual interest. He then had the bonds placed in their Swiss bank's trust account that Elvis had previously opened. In December 1977 after Elvis (Eduardo) went to Italy, Vernon added Eduardo Pirelli's name to the account, as well as to *Vernon's* name appearing on the treasury bonds, in both cases as joint tenants with rights of survivorship. This meant that Eduardo Pirelli *(nee Elvis)* could now access the trust account, as well as withdraw interest from those bonds. Vernon, however, died in 1979, leaving Eduardo the only one who could now access the account. After Vernon's death, the bonds were then reissued to Eduardo Pirelli, *individually,* by the Swiss bank's trust administrator.

In a phone conversation with Dr. Lawrence Kaye in December 1997, Elvis, in an off-the-cuff remark, mentioned that when he was studying opera in Venice and Milan, he was living off the interest from those bonds. In that nine-year period, Elvis estimated that he had withdrawn approximately $200,000 from the Swiss bank account.

Larry was adamant. He had no idea that Elvis, was in effect, living off the proceeds of his *own* life insurance policy, or that the proceeds of the policy had been used to purchase $1,000,000 worth of treasury bonds. He told Elvis in no uncertain terms that he had to return the bonds, plus the money he had withdrawn, plus any *remaining* accrued interest on the bonds, or he would, in effect, be committing fraud. Elvis certainly didn't want to knowingly commit a criminal act, so he immediately began the process of making amends with the insurance company.

Prior to that phone conversation with Dr. Kaye in 1997, twenty years had elapsed since Elvis' reported death. During that period, the bonds had accrued $1,560,000 in interest. Moreover, those bonds were still in the Swiss bank's trust department in Zurich. Since the bonds wouldn't ma-

Off the Record

ture until 2007, they couldn't be *called* (repurchased by the U. S. Treasury) before 2007.

Following Larry's instructions, Eduardo wrote to the Swiss bank's trust administrator, requesting that the treasury bonds and any accumulated interest be forwarded to his bank in Milan. He then wrote to his bank in Milan, requesting that they cut a *treasurer's* check payable to Sierra Life Assurance, Ltd. for $200,000. This represented the interest he had withdrawn. The funds for this check would come from his personal account, no doubt enhanced by his North American concert tour earnings in 1989, and estimated to be in excess of $750,000. The remaining accrued interest, $1,360,000, was transferred from his Swiss bank's trust account, to his personal account in Milan. After allowing time for the check to clear, Eduardo again wrote to his bank in Milan, requesting they cut *another* treasurer's check, also payable to Sierra Life, for $1,360,000.

On Wednesday, December 24, 1997, Glen Watson, now President of Sierra Life, was about to receive the Christmas present of his life, the proof he'd been seeking ever since his company's 1989 lawsuit in San Francisco had to be dropped for lack of evidence. For waiting in Glen's outer office was a bonded courier by the name of Elio Antonio Perenzi. Perenzi had just flown in from Milan, Italy with a briefcase containing two large envelopes, envelopes that were to be personally delivered to Watson.

As soon as Elio entered Glen's office, he introduced himself "Signore Watson? My name a is Elio Antonio Perenzi. I think this is a something you might have a wanted Santa to bring a you for Christmas," as he handed Glen the two envelopes.

Glen opened the larger envelope first. It contained ten U. S. Treasury Bonds, each with a face value of $100,000, bonds that had been transferred over to Sierra Life Assurance, Ltd. Included with the bonds was Pirelli's letter of instruction to his bank in Milan, requesting they deliver the bonds to Sierra Life's corporate headquarters in Las Vegas, Nevada, USA. In the second envelope were two treasurer's checks for $200,000

The Resurrection of The King

and $1,360,000 respectively, each marked with the notation *PAID IN FULL*, along with a letter from Eduardo Pirelli directing his bank in Milan to make those checks payable to Sierra Life Assurance, Ltd. The letter also stated that a bonded courier, Elio Antonio Perenzi, would pick up the treasury bonds and both checks, and hand-deliver them to Glen Watson, President of Sierra Life, in Las Vegas. It also requested the bank to send a *telex* to Watson, advising him that Perenzi would be arriving with some important documents requiring Watson's signature, on Wednesday afternoon, December 24th, at his corporate headquarters in Las Vegas.

As soon as Glen saw the name *Eduardo Alberto Pirelli* imprinted on the face of the bonds, his eyeballs nearly popped out. Was this the same Eduardo Pirelli as the opera star and Elvis impressionist who appeared in Las Vegas in June 1989, a name that Glen would remember for as long as he lived? After verifying that the bonds and checks had matched the amounts in Eduardo Pirelli's instruction letters, as well as agreed with Glen's *own* calculations, Perenzi and Watson both signed a receipt that detailed the contents of the envelopes. Glen then placed his copy of the receipt, signed by Elio, on top of his desk, between one of Eduardo's signed instruction letters and Elvis' July 1977 insurance policy application. (On a hunch, Glen had removed the application from the corporate dead files after receiving the telex). Now, virtually staring him in the face, were three signed documents, each with different signatures: *Elvis Aaron Presley, Eduardo Alberto Pirelli,* and *Elio Antonio Perenzi.* Although the names were different, there was a remarkable similarity to their penmanship.

Just as Elio neared the door on his way out of the office, Watson called to him. "Mr. Presley?"

Startled, Elio stopped dead in his tracks and slowly, almost sheepishly, turned around to face Watson.

"Mr. Presley," continued Watson, "you have a very Merry Christmas and by the way . . that *was* the nicest Christmas present I've ever received.

Off the Record

Can I assume that you'd like to keep your policy in force?"

Elvis, having recovered from the shock of Watson's revelation, replied haltingly. "I would appreciate that very much, Mr. Watson, and you have a very Merry Christmas too," as he replied with a smile on his face and a twinkle in his eye, but this time speaking in his unmistakable Memphis draw.

As soon as Elvis left the office, Glen logged on to his desk top computer, typed in his 7-digit access code, and brought up Elvis' original policy. First, he changed the status code on the policy from *Inactive-Paid to Beneficiary (IPB)* to *Active-Prepaid (AP)*. He then changed the name of the beneficiary from Vernon Elvis Presley, to *Lisa Marie Presley.*

As of July 2006, Elvis Presley's $1,000,000 life insurance policy with Sierra Life Assurance, Ltd. was still in force.

* * * * * * *

AFTER THOUGHTS. Although there have been numerous alleged Elvis sightings since his reported death in 1977, no one has stepped forward to claim that he *is* Elvis Presley. Moreover, virtually all of those sightings involved someone who looked like or strongly resembled Elvis Presley.

If in fact Elvis *did* receive plastic surgery after his reported death as alluded to in my novel, and there indeed *was* someone like Eduardo Pirelli who looked enough like Elvis in death that he would have fooled most observers, doesn't it stand to reason that the real Elvis Presley *after* August 1977, wouldn't look the least bit like the King of Rock and Roll that we remembered? So much for the alleged Elvis sightings.

* * * * * * *

Regarding his ability to sing opera as suggested in my novel, remember that Elvis loved opera, as it was among some of the earliest music he heard as an infant. Vernon was an Enrico Caruso fan and used to play

The Resurrection of The King

Caruso's music in Tupelo when Elvis was very young. Elvis also recorded several numbers where some of the stanzas reached into operatic tenor range. *It's Now or Never, Unchained Melody,* and *Surrender* come to mind. Moreover, Elvis actually did record a song in German *(Wooden Heart)*. Is it really such a stretch to believe that with several years of operatic and voice training, Elvis could well have learned enough Italian and German to at least sing *some* opera arias? I'll leave that up to the reader.

* * * * * * *

For those who have doubts about whether anyone could perform plastic surgery that would virtually duplicate another person's face, consider this: Dr. Robert A. Ersek, a lifelong friend whom I've known since childhood, was the character model for Dr. Alan Kesre in *The Resurrection of the King*. Dr. Ersek is a prominent plastic surgeon still practicing in Austin, Texas. He has also been seen on television by millions of viewers from his appearances on *Good Morning America, Heartland, Geraldo at Large,* and as the plastic surgeon who transformed numerous volunteers into celebrity lookalikes on MTV's, *I Want a Famous Face*. Among Dr. Ersek's more noteworthy transformations include Keanu Reeves and John Travolta lookalikes.

Bruce Lawrence Kearns

REFERENCES

Publications

Careless Love: The Unmasking of Elvis Presley, Peter Guralnick, Little Brown, 1999.

The Colonel & The King, Alanna Nash, Reader's Digest, July 2003.

The Death of Elvis: What Really Happened, Charles C. Thompson II and James P. Cole, Delacorte Press, Bantam Doubleday-Dell Publishing Group, Inc., 1991.

Elvis and Me, Priscilla Beaulieu Presley with Sandra Harmon, Berkley Publishing Group, a Division of Penguin Putnam, Inc., 1986.

Elvis Presley, Bobbie Ann Mason, Viking Press-Penguin Group, Penguin Putnam, Inc., 2003.

Last Train to Memphis: The Rise of Elvis Presley, Peter Guralnick, Little Brown, 1994.

Private Presley, The Missing Years -- Elvis in Germany, Andreas Schroer, Harper Entertainment-Harper Collins, 2002.

VHS Tapes and DVDs

Almost Elvis; John Paget, Producer; Blue Suede Films, 2000.

Elvis: His Best Friend Remembers; Joe Esposito, Executive Producer; Universal Studios Home Video and Proletariat Filmworks, 2002.

Elvis on Tour; Pierre Adidge and Robert Abel, Producers; Metro-Goldwyn-Mayer, 1972.

The Resurrection of the King

Elvis '68 Comeback Special; Lightyear Entertainment and Elvis Presley Enterprises, 2000.

Elvis: That's The Way It Is, Special Edition; Rick Schmidlin, Producer; Metro-Goldwyn-Mayer, 1970.

Elvis: The Final Chapter; Passport Video, 2001

Finding Graceland; Priscilla Presley & Barr Potter, Executive Producers; Cary Brokaw, Producer; Largo Entertainment, 1998.

He Touched Me -- The Gospel Music of Elvis Presley, Vol. 1; Bill Carter and Barry Jenning, Executive Producers; Coming Home Music, 1999.

Miscellaneous

Urban Legends, Barbara and David P. Mikkelson, December 31, 2005; http//:urbanlegends.about.com/

Elvis & Friends with host Ron Cade; WOGL 98.1 FM, Philadelphia, PA. Sundays, 7 AM to 10 AM.

America on Line, World Wide Web, various internet web sites.

* * * * * * *

Made in the USA